Ruthie Deschutes O'Hara has Ulterior Motives

Books by Cathy Lamb

JULIA'S CHOCOLATES

THE LAST TIME I WAS ME

HENRY'S SISTERS

SUCH A PRETTY FACE

THE FIRST DAY OF THE REST OF MY LIFE

A DIFFERENT KIND OF NORMAL

IF YOU COULD SEE WHAT I SEE

WHAT I REMEMBER MOST

MY VERY BEST FRIEND

THE LANGUAGE OF SISTERS

NO PLACE I'D RATHER BE

THE MAN SHE MARRIED

ALL ABOUT EVIE

TEN KIDS, TWO LOVE BIRDS, AND A SINGING MERMAID

RUTHIE DESCHUTES O'HARA HAS ULTERIOR MOTIVES

Ruthie Deschutes O'Hara has Ulterior Motives

Cathy Lamb

Thornburgh Bennett Publishing

Ruthie Deschutes O'Hara has Ulterior Motives
Copyright © 2024 Cathy Lamb

ALL RIGHTS RESERVED

The unauthorized reproduction or distribution of this copyrighted work, in any form by any electronic, mechanical, or other means, is illegal and forbidden, without written permission of the author, except in the case of brief quotations embodied in critical articles and reviews.

This is a work of fiction. Characters, settings, names, and occurrences are products of the author's imagination or used fictitiously and bear no resemblance to any actual person, living or dead, places or settings and/or occurrences. Any incidences of resemblance are purely coincidental.

Cover Design by Elizabeth Mackey

For all my funny, splendiferous girlfriends...

This one's for you.

1

Ruthie Deschutes O'Hara was upset.

She sat in her familiar blue armchair in her old yellow farmhouse out in the country, stars blinking at her in the pitch-dark sky. The moon was tilted like a golden cradle, highlighting the white honeysuckle vine that wrapped around her home, and a slight wind meandered through as if checking out what was going on in people's lives.

It was past midnight, but Ruthie did not want to go to bed. She petted the four cats who shared the armchair with her. She was covered in cats, so to speak. Two dogs were at her feet, one small pig snuffled in the corner, and a white rabbit hopped nearby. The matching blue armchair next to hers was still empty. This was not a surprise to Ruthie as she did not believe in ghosts.

The TV—nothing fancy, a regular TV—flickered from across the room. *Marry Me* was on. She used to watch *Marry Me*, a reality dating show with a "groom" and "brides," or a "bride" and "grooms," with her daughter, Willow, but her daughter wasn't speaking to her. Neither was her granddaughter, Lucy. They were both "furious."

Ruthie sighed, and tears rolled from her bright blue eyes down her face. Two unfortunate stars cascaded through the galaxy and burned out at the same time over her house, but she couldn't see them, nor could she see the three deer prancing like ballet dancers through her backyard, searching for delicious flower snacks.

Ruthie lived about five miles away from where she was born seventy years ago in a trailer with a leaking roof. Her parents were twenty at the time. They had married at eighteen, right out of high school, madly, wildly in love. They were in love for over seventy years. In her family, they were "ridiculously late" to start breeding children and "pushing out the whippersnappers." No one could understand what the holdup was.

Giving birth in their own homes (trailers, odd log cabins, lean-tos, twice in a tent, three times out in the open air for "free breathing") was tradition for the family. Why give hard-earned money to a doctor if you didn't have to? Especially when there was a plethora of aunts, grandmothers, and two helpful uncles who could guide the woman through it, along with the numbing qualities of their family's tequila. One of the great-aunts, Rathburn, was reputed to have been a witch, but that was because she'd known exactly how to successfully use herbs to heal the mothers, and she cast spells, so she'd gotten a bit of a reputation.

Ruthie, born with a shock of blonde hair, which was now a mix of wavy white and blonde, exited her mother's womb with a scream during a thunderstorm. Water trickled through the trailer's roof at the same time lightning streaked across the sky. Aunt Rathburn raised her arms to the heavens and declared her birth a "magical moment" in between rolls of crackling thunder.

Ruthie's family, the Deschuteses, via her father, owned hundreds of rolling acres filled with forests, farmland, lakes, ponds, wetlands, a skinny river, and flower-studded meadows outside the town of Triple Mountain in Oregon. When Ruthie was growing up, almost everyone lived together around Rattlesnake Lake or up in the hills if they wanted more privacy or a view.

Things had changed since she was born. There were lots of houses now for cousins, uncles, aunts, grandparents, and great-grandchildren but not many trailers. Cousin Fordham still preferred his one-room—not one-bedroom, but one-*room*—house he'd built himself. It had two doors—just in case he had to make a quick exit. No one quite understood why he would need to make a "quick exit," though they nodded politely whenever it came up.

But that was neither here nor there, so let's get back to the pets for a moment.

Fitzwilliam, who was emotionally mature, reached up a paw and touched a tear on Ruthie's cheek. The cat tilted his head as if to say, "What's wrong?" Darcy, who was an old fighter, snuggled in as if to give Ruthie more comfort. He licked her hand to express his concern. Elizabeth Bennet, a black cat, stretched on her lap then put her forehead smack against Ruthie's, and Lydia Bennet held up a paw for Ruthie to shake.

The pig, Gatsby, snuffled and stared right up at Ruthie, while Scarlett O'Hara, the sometimes-screaming rabbit, hopped up close. Atticus, the old brown dog, knew his job was to keep Ruthie's feet warm. The new dog, Mr. Rochester, wanted to take Ruthie for a walk. Surely, she would feel much better then? Mr. Rochester liked walking Ruthie and pulling her along on her leash.

Ruthie had dozens of children and grandchildren and family members who were constantly in and out of her house, bringing pies and cakes and, from a teenage granddaughter, one joint. But she wanted to talk to Willow and Lucy. She wanted to restore their fun relationship. She loved them so. Yes, she had done wrong, but she had also "done right," in her mind, and had saved Lucy from heartache. Unfortunately, they didn't see it like that. Ruthie took a shot of her family's tequila and considered the joint.

She tried to refocus on *Marry Me* to distract herself and her aching heart.

"That man has to be the dumbest groom yet, and there has been stiff competition for that position," she said aloud to Russell. Her husband did not answer from his blue armchair, but she knew he would agree.

Gatsby, a happy troublemaker, snorted, which caused Atticus to wake from his nap, panic and bark twice, twirl around, make a huffing noise, and then lay back down on Ruthie's feet.

Atticus was elderly and easily confused. He was eighteen. He could hardly see or hear. It wasn't easy growing into his senior years. His knees hurt, but he had been with Ruthie a long time, and he owed it to her to keep her feet warm, that he knew. He grumbled again. Gatsby the pig snorted again to tease the dog, and the same routine of panicking and barking ensued again until Atticus grumpily settled down for good. Gatsby almost giggled.

"Don't marry this one, ladies," Ruthie said to the contestants on TV. "Unless you want your brain to turn to mayonnaise and then slide out your ears. He's not a real man. He simply has wiggly male plumbing. There's a difference."

Marry Me had been on for years. One man trying to choose from twenty-four women who wanted to be his bride. Or one woman trying to find her groom among twenty-four men. The couples rarely stayed together after all the glamor of the show and the exciting dates ended. How could they?

"This is not real life, ladies. We have a ridiculous premise and a dull, wet noodle for a groom, who is probably illiterate. Wouldn't even know who Louise Erdrich or Margaret Atwood is," Ruthie muttered. "How do you fall in love over a few dates anyhow? Real life is not about wearing skirts that barely cover your buttocks and flirting all day long in Norway. It's about work and stress and people getting sick and sometimes dying on you."

She turned her head to the empty armchair next to her. "And it's about falling in love and excellent sex and laughter and family and birthday parties and picking peaches off a tree and helping other people, especially the relatives who believe they've been branded by aliens or dance around bonfires."

She held her hand out, as she had done for decades, but no one reached back. He hadn't for five years. She told herself to look forward so she didn't get yanked back to the past and that pit of churning, all-consuming grief.

"What are you looking forward to, Ruthie?" She asked this question of herself out loud. Darcy meowed. Atticus snored.

One of her grandchildren, who had been seven years old at the time, had asked her that question years ago, and she'd tried to incorporate it into her life. She thought of different things she might look forward to now, and nothing held much interest, but then, by golly, she had it! She was looking forward to Rattlesnake Lake Jump Day!

Rattlesnake Lake Jump Day was a tradition in the Deschutes family. There were a few rattlesnakes rumored to be seen here in Central Oregon, but if you jumped in the lake in the middle of winter, family lore said, you wouldn't get bitten that year.

Everyone, young and old, all jumped in the lake on Rattlesnake Lake Jump Day. They gasped and dog-paddled in that freezing water, then they jumped out. Later, they had venison (from hunting season), chili (to produce their own "family methane"), steak (thanks to the cows!), and Deschutes Family Tequila ("may we live forevermore!").

Since Ruthie hadn't moved far from her childhood home, her relatives—quirky, loud, clannish, secretive, protective of their own, slightly crazy, kind, helpful, temperamental, rarely dangerous, loving, devoted—were all around. She straddled two lives by living in her yellow farmhouse ten minutes from town and ten minutes from the Deschutes family homestead.

She would look forward to Rattlesnake Lake Jump Day. She wiped the tears from her face. "Silly old woman."

Rochester, sweet dog, hmphed in disagreement.

She turned her attention back to the TV. "Do you even know how to speak, you clueless homo erectus?" Ruthie demanded of the groom. "It's like you're still prehistoric. Barely past the caveman stage. Try a grunt. There ya go. That sounded like a grunt." Ruthie knew the directors probably had to prod the dull groom along, telling him what to say while speaking slowly. Maybe writing sentences on flash cards so he wouldn't forget what was supposed to come from his unignited brain synapses. She took another swallow of tequila. Dang, their family tequila was good.

The women on this show were always smarter than the men, but even they seemed to lose their faculties when dating these dim-witted wildebeests.

"These women must be desperate to marry," she said to Darcy the cat, who agreed. "For God's sake. Can he even tie his shoes? Does he know what the word 'literature' means?"

Scarlett O'Hara hopped through the room. One of the cats on her lap made to follow—he liked to spy on the rabbit—but Ruthie foiled him. "Now, now, Fitzwilliam. Stay here. Watch this illiterate man attempt to communicate. He says the exact same thing to each woman. His vocabulary is limited. Any word with more than two syllables is a prickly challenge."

The cats would never try to eat the rabbit. Here was the proof: Ruthie was often gone for most of each day, and the rabbit was alive and well. She didn't know it, because until last June she'd been teaching high school English, but one day, very early on, a cat had gotten too close, and the rabbit had made a screaming sound. It had scared all the cats to pieces. Even the dogs had squealed in fear and tumbled over each other, trying to escape the hopping she-devil.

It was as if something out of a horror movie had split through the home. That rabbit's screams had sent shivers up all the animals' spines, and they'd cowered from the trauma. It had taken them days to recover their equilibrium and sense of peace.

The rabbit forevermore hopped around freely, never worried for her safety because of her impressive screaming capabilities.

Ruthie blinked at the TV. She thought she wasn't seeing or hearing things clearly. She was a bit buzzed from the tequila. But there it was. The overly cheerful voice of the show's host, Jackson Coleman, booming and fake, bounced into her family room.

"Do you know a senior bride who would like to be on *Marry Me*? We're looking for women to date our first senior groom and possibly become his wife. And guess what, ladies? We already have our man! That's right! We've already chosen our next *Marry Me* groom!"

A man's face appeared on the screen. Ruthie sat up a smidge. My, he was handsome. He had the weathered face of Robert Redford, the blue eyes of Paul Newman, the broad shoulders of Tom Selleck, the cool of Denzel Washington, and the smoldering sexiness of Jimmy Smits.

Ruthie did not see any of this, though. None. She slammed the shot glass down on the small table next to her. She didn't care about the groom or any sexiness he might share with Jimmy Smits.

What she saw was an *opportunity*!

She, Willow, and Lucy loved watching *Marry Me* together. They all laughed and talked and analyzed who would marry whom and why as they watched the show. They even placed early bets on which bride/groom would "win," and the winner received a box of chocolates from their favorite chocolate company, Julia's Chocolates. That wasn't happening anymore.

But she saw a *resolution*. A chance at *reconciliation*.

She, Ruthie Deschutes O'Hara, would go on *Marry Me*. She would be a contestant! If she went on *Marry Me*, then her daughter and granddaughter would be so excited, they would call her. They would come to dinner like they used to and invite her out to get her hair and nails done. They would go to bookstores and to coffee. They would go to the Deschutes family homestead for raucous parties and celebrations together.

It was a brilliant idea. She could hardly believe she'd thought of it.

Ruthie looked at the empty armchair next to her and said, "What do you think, Russell?"

She became a little teary-eyed again, but then remembered it had been five years. This was not a betrayal. She wasn't interested in the man who looked like Robert/Paul/Tom/Denzel/Jimmy. She was interested in repairing the relationship with her and Russell's daughter and granddaughter.

Ruthie grabbed the joint she'd received from one of her favorite rebellious granddaughters. She lit up one end of it. It was the wrong end. She realized her mistake and blew it out and lit the other end. Then she accidentally dropped it, and the joint landed on a lazy cat's back. Elizabeth Bennet wouldn't move for anything. She liked sleeping. Ruthie blew on the joint. It smelled like a skunk. The skunk under the house would not like the comparison, but she was an easygoing skunk, prone to thinking that she smelled like roses, so it would not have been a big deal.

"I'm going on *Marry Me!*" she announced loudly to the animals. Atticus, poor thing, barked again in alarm, stood up on creaking knees and made a teetering circle. The rabbit taunted the cats. The cats appeared frightened and curled in tight to Ruthie, and the pig snorted in approval.

"Cheers!" she said to the animals. "I have ulterior motives, but I shall date the next dumb bachelor."

2

Marry Me

Initial screening interview with Ruthie Deschutes O'Hara, Triple Mountain, Oregon.

Tyler Graham, an associate producer, who received the job not because he deserved it but because of his rich and powerful father who works for the studio and called in a favor. *Again.* Tyler thinks he got the job because he's impressive. He's not that bright.

Tyler: Hello, Ruthie. Thanks for talking to me. I'm glad you got the videoconferencing thing figured out on your computer so we can chat face-to-face.

Ruthie: Oh, that wasn't me. I had to have one of my kids come over to help.

Tyler: Well, that brings me to my next question. How many kids do you have?

Ruthie: Thirty-two.

Tyler: What?

Ruthie: I have thirty-two kids.

Tyler: You gave birth to thirty-two children?

Ruthie (sighing): Yes, I had eight sets of quadruplets.

Tyler: You did?

Ruthie (sighing again): You're very young, aren't you? Maybe it's me. I am seventy. Everyone seems young to me now. I have one biological daughter, but then thirty-one children who had difficult home lives stayed with my husband and me for various lengths of time. Some did go back to their parents. Most didn't. In my heart, they will always be the children of my late husband and me. We love them all very much.

Tyler: You adopted them?

Ruthie: Not formally.

Tyler: That was very kind of you.

Ruthie: I hate when people say that.

Tyler: That it was kind of you to take in kids who needed a home?

Ruthie: Yes. They all gave far more to us than we gave to them. They were gifts.

Tyler: How long were you married?

Ruthie: More than forty years. Russell was excellent in bed.

Tyler: Uh...

Ruthie: Did that embarrass you?

Tyler: Uh...

Ruthie: I see that it did. You're blushing. As an associate producer of a show for older men and women who are trying to find a spouse, you need to get over it. We have sex even at this age, even if you find it impossible to believe or nauseating. Dear me. You're blushing more, but you need to know that the anatomy is still there and so is the desire. We might need a little more time to wind up the engine, but we can still crush it. I learned that term— "crush it"—from a granddaughter. It was not in relation to sex, but I thought it was an adequate term to use here and one that you might understand.

Tyler: Uh…

Ruthie: Young man! I was an English teacher for forty-five years. You must start to articulate and enunciate. I hope you read books. You do read, don't you?

Tyler: Yes, uh, I do. Sometimes. Can you tell me more about yourself?

Ruthie: It's in the email I wrote. Didn't you read it?

Tyler: Yes, I did. It says you were born in a trailer. That your whole family—parents, four brothers, grandparents, aunts and uncles, and cousins—all lived together around, let me see here, Rattlesnake Lake in Triple Mountain, Oregon.

Ruthie: That's right. We hunted, fished, and made tequila. First, it was only for the family, then we decided to form a business and sell it. Deschutes Family Tequila—that's the name of our company. It's tequila that will make your insides feel like they're burning up as the tequila slides down. It'll take the hair off your chest. It'll set small fires in your brain. Everybody loves it.
Tyler: I've had Deschutes Family Tequila. It's the best. I did think that it momentarily affected my brain.

Ruthie: Felt liberating, didn't it?

Tyler: Yes, it did. I couldn't think about anything else because I thought I might die, but then I had this feeling of peace. Like a warm wave inside of me. I went to Stanford, but I drank it at my parents' country club. Now, your paperwork. You live in a yellow farmhouse in the country with many animals, including dogs, cats, a pig, and a rabbit. Your husband, the town doctor, died five years ago.

Ruthie: Yes. Don't mention him again.

Tyler: Okay, but can I ask why?

Ruthie: Because I still love him and miss him every minute. The grief is exactly as it was the day he died. Next question, young man.

Tyler: Uh. Okay. Lemme see. If you're chosen to be on *Marry Me,* what can you contribute to the show?

Ruthie: I can bring Deschutes Family Tequila.

Tyler: You'll contribute tequila?

Ruthie: Yes. For the crew and cast and the dumb bachelor.

Tyler: He, uh, he isn't dumb. Very smart. Successful businessman...Uh.

Ruthie: Dear God, please stop saying "uh." Did Jane Austen say "uh"? Did Charlotte Brontë? Did Virginia Woolf? No, they didn't.

Tyler: Who is Virginia Woolf? And Charlotte who?

Ruthie: Dear God, tell me you're kidding.

Tyler: Uh. No. Moving on. Why do you want to be on the show?

Ruthie: Because I want my daughter and granddaughter to talk to me again.

Tyler: Why won't they talk to you?

Ruthie: That's not your business, young man.

Tyler: Don't you want to fall in love with the groom?

Ruthie: Oh please. I'm not a fool. Do I look like a fool to you?

Tyler: No.

Ruthie: Why chase down another male? Besides, this guy is seventy. Men his age want a nurse and a servant and someone to listen to them whine about their ailments and afflictions. Aching knees and stiff back, etc. They look around for a woman to fulfill the servant and ego-boosting role and are absolutely baffled, caused by their unwavering mental denseness and impenetrable ego, about why no woman wants that role.

Tyler: You don't have a good view of men?

Ruthie: Babies, most of them. Put a diaper on them, slip them a pacifier and a bottle full of beer, turn on football, and they're happy. Except for the men in my family. Now those are genuine men. Smart. Strong. Sensitive. They all know that the woman runs the house, and their role is to do what they're told.

Tyler (laughing): Our groom is a great guy.

Ruthie: If I need a great guy, I pet my dog Atticus. He's a great old guy, even though he can hardly hear or see. Staying in a mansion, swimming, hot tubbing, making new friends with the other ladies, and having meals made for me with as much wine as I can drink, I could do that. Sounds like a fun time on someone else's dime.

Tyler: Do you get along with other women?

Ruthie: Usually. But not the last principal I worked for. She had the hips of an irritated buffalo, the face of a mean crane, and the temperament of a patronizing bat. And don't get me going on the twenty-four-year-old teacher-twit I had to work with who apparently knew way more than I did about education and teaching and English and treated me like an old, doddery, out-of-touch dementia patient. I hope she chokes on her condescension, and it gets stuck in her gut, causing constipation and rumbling gas.

Tyler: I like how you talk.

Ruthie: Flattering. But look here, young man, if you're asking me to be the woman everyone hates, I'm not doing that. I don't want to be the she-devil, psych-ward, narcissistic Barbie. I'm there to have a fine time, dance late at night, drink with new friends on top of bars, and wait until my daughter calls me, and then I'm outta there. So when and where do we start filming? And do not pause and use the word "uh" again. It is improper English.

To: Shonda Bankole; Pearla Patterson
From: Tyler Graham
Subject: Ruthie Deschutes O'Hara

I interviewed Ruthie Deschutes O'Hara from Oregon.

YES.

Tyler
Associate producer, *Marry Me*

To: Tyler Graham; Pearla Patterson
From: Shonda Bankole
Subject: Ruthie Deschutes O'Hara

We are a yes for her, too. We watched the video she sent and read her application.

Thanks, Tyler!

Shonda
Co-director, *Marry Me*

To: Shonda Bankole
From: Pearla Patterson
Subject: Ugh

I can't believe we've been stuck with Tyler Graham. I know who his daddy is at the studio, but he's the one who's going to do some of the interviews for *Marry Me*? Are they kidding us? My God. Nepotism at its finest.

He always talks about how he went to Stanford. He neglects to mention that he's a legacy and that his father and grandfathered have donated over $40 million to that school. Hello? That's how you got into Stanford, Tyler.

This is so annoying.

Pearla
Co-director, *Marry Me*

To: Pearla Patterson
From: Shonda Bankole
Subject: Ugh

I already complained to boss lady. Charlene said we don't have a choice. Daddy too powerful. She doesn't want him here either. Insecure and so braggy. He's going to need a lot of help in terms of what questions to ask the potential brides. I don't know if he even knows how to have a conversation. When I interviewed him and pretended that I didn't know he already had the job, he could hardly talk.

Uh. Uh. Uh. Then it's the Stanford line.

We'll have to give him a list of questions for each interview and hope in his perennial confusion that he doesn't veer off them much.

See ya for drinks tonight at 8 at Stanley's.

Shonda
Co-director, *Marry Me*

3

When you're a Deschutes, you don't simply disappear. If you did, the entire family, dozens of them, would be out looking for you in the backs of pickups, guns ready to blaze. Everyone knew where everyone else was all the time, even if was out of state or out of the country. It wasn't controlling. It was love. They all texted one another constantly to say hello and announce sightings of UFOs, possums, Big Foot, or how Cousin Chico won yet another high school state championship in math.

There was a family group chat for the entire clan to announce dates of weddings, fishing days, camping events, beer-can target practice, archery contests, poker, ghost-hunting hikes, witch bonfires, Big Foot exploration trips, etc., then smaller group chats with various family members to exchange recipes or jokes. The teenagers had their own group chat where they could cackle at their misdeeds and cause trouble and get their lies straight. The Deschuteses' lives and social lives revolved around family, their longtime family friends, and their family tequila business.

Ruthie knew this and knew she couldn't simply take off into the wild blue yonder without notice. Her Deschutes family would be up in (literally) arms if she disappeared. Her face would be plastered on the news, helicopters piloted by Deschutes family members would be dropping leaflets, and the Triple Mountain police would be pounding door to door to make sure she hadn't been kidnapped by an evil fiend and held for ransom.

She closed the light blue door of her peaceful yellow farmhouse with the white honeysuckle vine dripping along the porch and climbed into her truck. She drove by two rustling willow trees then the pink cherry trees lining her long driveway and drove farther into the back country to the Deschutes family homestead.

She passed a white-headed woodpecker, a black-backed woodpecker, and a hairy woodpecker, but she didn't know it—they were way up in the trees. She also passed a lost baby fox whose mother would find her soon. Ruthie respected nature and would have been disappointed to know that she had not seen all that.

It was her cousin Harley's seventieth birthday, and she had to be on time. They were born two months apart and grew up together. They were more like brother and sister. Ruthie's dad had five brothers, and they each had between four and six kids, a mix of boys and girls. They all had kids, too, and so did their kids.

Harley and Ruthie were tight. Harley knew what happened all those years ago. It was one of many family secrets that never, ever got out. If it did, that would be a problem. They were the Deschuteses, and they protected one another. There had never been a betrayal in their family because family was all they had. Loyalty was in their DNA.

Erroll Deschutes started their family. He was Ruthie's great-grandfather. His father was white, and his mother was Mexican. He got the burly build of his father and the dark eyes of his mother. His real last name wasn't Deschutes. He gave himself that name as, unfortunately, he couldn't continue with his original name because he had been in a fist-pumping, window-shattering brawl in a seedy bar in Missouri. It had also involved a small table crashing into a man's head after the man had unromantically attacked his own fiancée. Erroll had protected the fiancée. The raging husband-to-be had fought back and ended up dead.

Erroll was not troubled by the murder because the man got what was coming to him. He should not have attacked a woman. But that man's family did not see things the same as Erroll. They hunted far and wide for Erroll, but searching far and wide was not far and wide enough, as Erroll had tucked himself into the last car of a train heading west. He would put his past behind him and start anew.

The train rides were long and monotonous, and the fleeing twenty-three-year-old Erroll was kicked off twice and had to scramble up on other trains. He met a man named Duck, who looked like he'd been out of the water for years, lines grooved into his face like wings. He met another man named Wallace. Wallace talked to himself, but he always spoke nicely. And Erroll met a woman named Lavender. She was eighteen. A tough life had forced her to make tough choices she didn't want to make. But when you did not have parents, both taken by the fever years ago, you did what you could to survive, especially as a woman. When Erroll met her, she'd been beaten up in more ways than one and was scared and shaking, cowering in the corner of the train.

Erroll treated her with kindness and gentleness. At first, traumatized by what had come before, Lavender couldn't speak. She hid behind her long blonde hair. Erroll was patient, and he protected her on their journey, beating off two men on separate occasions who thought that Lavender needed "some fun." The second time Erroll got in a fight protecting her honor, Lavender picked up a piece of wood and slammed the head of the man who was pummeling her new friend, Erroll. That was the end of the fight, and they rolled the man off the moving train. Again, Erroll was not troubled by the death, because the man got what was coming to him, praise the Lord.

Afterward, Erroll and Lavender sat in the train car, in the dark, the countryside flying by, an appropriate and proper three feet apart, and continued their discussion about books. They finally arrived in Oregon, ending up in Central Oregon, and Erroll chose the new last name of Deschutes because they stood on the river's banks and were awed by its beauty, strength, and length.

Erroll and Lavender married within one month. Erroll told her, "All I know is hunting, farming, and making tequila, Lavender, and that I love you. I will provide for you and protect you for the rest of our lives. Will you do me the honor of becoming my wife?"

All Lavender knew was that she loved this tough young man because he was kind and gentle. "I will, Erroll," she said softly. "Thank you."

"Thank you, sweetheart."

They kissed, but they did not sleep together until their wedding night, because Erroll said, "I will not disrespect you, Lavender."

It was the first time that this particular act did not terrorize or hurt her. She hadn't known that she could enjoy sex. They would later describe their relationship as "lusty in the bedroom." They had eight children—five obedient boys and three rebellious girls—who grew up in a home filled with love.

The Deschutes family began. The Deschutes men and women in the family line did not always see fit to follow laws that they felt were unfit, so to speak. But they all followed the family laws:

Deschutes family first.
Love, protect, defend.
Drink our tequila only.

So when Ruthie went out to the homestead, packed with Deschutes family members, pet dogs, pet goats, pet horses, and cats, she was greeted warmly. She brought three homemade pies with her: Ass-Kicking Apple Pie, Ruthie's Great Pecan Pie, and Deschutes Family River Mud (chocolate).

They had dinner together on ten long picnic tables laid end to end on the grass and decorated with bell jars filled with flowers. The old people told stories, the children giggled and ran around as half-feral children do, and the babies and toddlers were handed off from one to another to hold and to love. Out on the homestead, the wind knew to blow lightly, the pine trees knew to release a little extra scent, and the curious deer watched from the corners, intrigued. These people, with their loud ways and their clanking tequila shot glasses and the songs they sang that were handed down from generation to generation, were immensely peculiar but entertaining.

At the end of the night, Ruthie stood, clicked her shot glass with her fork, and when things quieted on down said, "I have something to say, Deschuteses."

This was what they all said when they had something to say. They were proud of themselves and of their family.

"What is it, Ruthie?" they all shouted back. It was tradition.

"I'm going on *Marry Me*. The dating show for old people."

There was confused silence from some, gasps and then cheers from many of the women and teenage girls, and a lot of, "Now what's that, Ruthie?" and, "What do you mean marry me?" and, "Are you getting married, Ruthie? Good for you, honey."

Ruthie explained, "You all know that my Willow and Lucy are not speaking to me."

They nodded. No one liked a family rift. Not at all. The Deschutes family should stick together! This was rule-breaking, and it made them sad.

"Willow, Lucy, and I always watched *Marry Me* together." She stopped and tried to compose herself. "I'm doing this so maybe Willow and Lucy will see me on the show, and we can…" She paused; her sky-blue eyes sad where they had been happy moments ago. "And we can reconcile."

"You mean you're going to date a man who is dating a hundred other women?" Harley asked. "Then Willow and Lucy will come back to you?"

"It's twenty-three other women. Or maybe twenty. Could be more," Ruthie said. "I don't know. I don't care about dating him. I want Willow and Lucy to forgive me. My being on the show will give us something to talk about again."

Everyone nodded. Forgiveness was important. Talking things out. But that didn't always work with the Deschutes family, as with other families. During arguments, bottles had been thrown at one another. Knitting needles had been used as weapons. When Marley had accidentally tipped the drift boat over that one time in the river, Eleanor had had it with him because she had brought her knitting needles and the red blanket she'd been working on for their granddaughter. The blanket had gotten soaked, dang it! He'd needed only twelve stitches, though. Eleanor hadn't meant to poke him that hard with the knitting needle in the buttocks. Her temper had gotten the best of her.

There had been a few fistfights, wrestling matches that got way too heated, especially that time when Roger's girl had put Ella's boy in a headlock. Years ago, two cousins in the family had found out they were dating the same girl. That hadn't been pretty. There'd been no need for Chewy to use the tractor to smash Norman's truck, though. That was a bit much.

Another time, MaryLynn and Barbara Sue got into it. They were always competing, those girls, and MaryLynn had thrown cow poop at Barbara Sue, and Barbara Sue had not appreciated that at all. MaryLynn never saw what came straight at her face seconds later.

There was also that one attempted murder a long time ago, in the sixties, but the women had been drunk, and Gilda hadn't meant it. And...well, maybe there was that other time when a dull knife had been thrown, and it had landed in a shoulder. But they had gotten things cleaned out and disinfected the wound with some family tequila, and it had been all sewn up. The thrower of the dull knife had apologized, and the two had shared a beer. Gilda and Jilly were sisters, after all, and sisters shouldn't fight with each other.

"When are you leaving, Ruthie?" Uncle Sherman asked after she explained what *Marry Me* was.

"Tomorrow at eleven o'clock."

"What?" was the collective whine. "Tomorrow? No time for a party to send you off to *Marry Me*, then! You've ruined our fun, Ruthie."

"I'm sure I'll be back quickly," Ruthie said. "You see, the groom has to get rid of a few women every night. It'll probably be me the first night, but I intend to enjoy myself while I'm there. I'm going to eat the food they make and swim in the pool and get in the hot tub and make myself at home. We're all headed to a private lodge in Whitefish, Montana. I love Montana, so it'll be a pleasant vacation. I've even shipped off some of our tequila, and you know with Deschutes Family Tequila..."

She paused, and everyone yelled together, "Any time is tequila time!"

Everyone laughed because that was one of the family's favorite sayings. They'd created a successful business with that slogan. *Any time is tequila time!*

And, with that, the family raised their shot glasses and clinked them together. "To Ruthie!" everyone shouted.

Then Harley's wife, Patty, brought out the cake, and they all sang to Harley, Patty on one side, Ruthie on the other. Behind Harley's back, the two women held hands. They had been close friends forever, Ruthie and Patty.

The wind picked up a bit, as if to remind Ruthie of why she loved the land, and the pine trees bent and swayed, as if waving, as she drove down the road toward home hours later. Two owls hooted back and forth, and a family of deer looked up and followed Ruthie's car. A coyote stopped prancing. A beaver stopped patting more sticks into his dam until Ruthie had driven by, his nose in the air.

About two miles away, an old hermit stared into the flames of his river rock fireplace. He'd built it himself. The wind had already visited him. He had listened to the owls' conversation. He knew the deer family—they slept near him in a grove of trees surrounded by tall grass. The prancing coyotes hardly noticed him anymore, as if he were one of them.

He lived on his family's land in a ramshackle, but warm, cabin. He preferred animals over humans. His name was Harold, and he and Ruthie had gone to school together. They had been friends since kindergarten. He came from a snobby, wealthy family who liked fast cars and showing off. She came from a loving, poor family who liked tequila, target shooting, and ax-throwing contests. For some reason, he and Ruthie simply understood each other.

When he heard the next morning, through Harley, who had come to check on him, that Ruthie was going on *Marry Me*, he laughed.

"That's our girl," he said to Harley as he continued his wood carving of a blue heron.

Harley agreed. "Always a surprise."

They both chuckled.

Word got around. It was a small town.

When Ruthie heard a racket in front of her yellow farmhouse on Saturday morning about thirty minutes before she was to leave for the airport, she peeked out her door. Her house was surrounded! Family, friends, neighbors, and the teachers and students she had worked with at the high school until last year were all there! (Except not the principal with the hips of an irritated buffalo or the twenty-four-year-old twit. That's a story for later in this story.)

Dozens of Deschuteses, most of them on their motorcycles and in the backs of trucks, were waving and honking their horns.

"We're here to send you off, Ruthie!" Harley shouted. "Get your bags, you little minx, then get on my bike with me. Patty will take your bags to the airport in the car."

Ruthie laughed, head back. Her heart grew bigger as she stared, with unabashed joy, at everyone outside her home, cheering for her. She hugged them, and they hugged her back and wished her well and told her they would miss her.

Her heart grew a little stronger, a little wider that day, because she was taking in so much love. Many of her unofficially adopted thirty-one children were there, some with their children, and they all wished her good luck on *Marry Me*. Oh, how she and Russell loved all their kids.

"I can't wait to see you on TV," her daughter Halona said.

"I can't wait to tell everyone that my Nana Ruthie is on TV," Halona's daughter, Lizzy, five years old, said.

"I can't wait to see myself on TV!" Ruthie told them. "Let's hope I'm as sexy on TV as I am in real life!"

"Sexy!" Lizzy said. "You'll be sexy, Nana Ruthie!" She jumped up and down. "What's sexy?"

After the hugs, Ruthie checked her watch then ran back inside her farmhouse. She could not be late for her flight! One of her sons would be staying at the house with his family while she was gone. They lived in an apartment in town, so to move to Ruthie's big farmhouse in the country would be a treat. Their four children would love the open air, the stream in back, the geese and ducks, and the freedom. They would take care of the animals, too, so she wouldn't have to worry.

"Thank you, Liam," she said, hugging him, then his wife, Michelle. Liam had come so far from when she and Russell had taken him in when he was fifteen twenty years ago. Then, he'd been thin, scared, angry, and doing things he should not have been doing. Now, he was the head of a construction team and would buy his own home later this year.

"We're so happy for you," Michelle said. "You're going to make everyone laugh."

"Laughing is good for the bowels," Ruthie said.

"What's bowels?" their four-year-old daughter, Sheila, asked, bopping about. "I want bowels, Nana Ruthie."

Ruthie climbed the stairs to her bedroom, Liam and Harley behind her to get her bags, the dogs, cats, pig, and rabbit following, too. The animals were worried. They were anxious. The old dog, Atticus, snuffled and complained. His hips were especially achy today. Fitzwilliam was distraught. Whose lap would he sit on tonight? They all knew Ruthie was leaving, and they would be lonely.

The four kids who were here were noisy. They pulled their tails and chased after them. They were exhausting. Atticus, especially, didn't know if he was up for this. The rabbit was planning on hiding. If she had to, she would scream. The cats were distrustful, suspicious, as cats always were. This situation wasn't going well for them.

Ruthie hugged the dogs, the cats, the pig, and the rabbit, and then she was off. She had received a list of all the clothes she would need to wear while on *Marry Me*, but she'd ignored it and packed what she wanted to take. She was not going to buy all those fancy dresses. Why? She had the money, but that would be a waste. She would never wear them again, and that money could go to someone in need or the animal shelter.

"The bride is ready!" she shouted to everyone from the doorway, waving her hands in the air. Everyone roared their approval. Two Deschuteses started singing the "Wedding March," and everyone joined in as Ruthie pretended to elegantly walk down the "aisle" on her walkway, gripping an invisible bouquet.

They were not surprised that Ruthie was going on *Marry Me*. She had always been a daredevil and so much fun! Why, the family had heard the stories of how free-living and adventurous Ruthie had been when she was younger, and they admired her so.

Ruthie climbed on the back of Harley's bike and pulled her helmet on. The cheering got louder, deafening. The other motorcycles gunned their engines, people in cars and trucks gunned their engines, and they were off in parade-style, four police officers in the front, two fire engines, with their sirens on, in the back. Many of the police officers and firefighters were members of the Deschutes clan or were former students of Ruthie's. She stuck her hands in the air, waving.

Honking and engines roaring, the entire procession headed toward the center of their small town. Lining the streets were more excited people. They were holding signs that said, "Good Luck, Mrs. O'Hara!" and "Marry Me, Ruthie!" and "Mrs. O'Hara, You Got This!" and "I'll Marry You, Ruthie!"

A small band from the high school played on a corner. Ruthie, from her perch behind Harley, waved at everyone like she was a princess. Then she mimicked drinking from a shot glass. People laughed and clapped as the parade sped through town at a mighty five miles an hour.

Everyone agreed that they had never, and would never, see any member of the Deschutes family driving that slow again, especially on a motorcycle. No one knew they were *capable* of going that slow. Such a curiosity!

Even the owls woke up in their nests in the trees and watched, their heads swiveling back and forth. What a racket!

Later, Ruthie leaned back in her first-class seat on the plane, poured herself a shot of the Deschutes Family Tequila that she had smuggled onto the flight in a makeup bottle, then promptly went to sleep.

Leaving for *Marry Me* had been exhausting!

Marry Me had sent a camerawoman and an associate producer to Ruthie's house to film her getting ready to leave for the show. Unfortunately, their plane had been delayed, and they had not had time to interview her or film her packing her suitcases and wandering around her home, pretending to look nostalgic or nervous or hyper happy. They had rushed in at the last second and had had to fight their way through the crowds of people outside of Ruthie's yellow farmhouse. They got there in the nick of time.

They later agreed that the footage they got of Ruthie on her front porch, surrounded by dogs and cats and—was that a rabbit, and did you see a pig? —then sauntering down her walkway, hugging everyone, and climbing onto the motorcycle was pure perfection. The bearded and tattooed men in their pickups and the police and firefighter escorts and everyone else in their cars honking their way through town were much better than the emotional drivel they'd thought they would get.

Ricki, the camerawoman, called Shonda when she was done filming. "You are not going to believe what happened."

She sent Shonda part of the video that showed one of Ruthie's cousins playing AC/DC's hit "Big Balls" from a speaker in front of her house. The music blared as everyone started singing, Ruthie in the center of a circle. She knew all the words and the facial expressions to go with them, plus she played a mean electric air guitar. "And he's got big balls," she warbled out. "And she's got big balls."

The whole gang yelled, "But we've got the biggest balls of them all!"

Shonda was drinking her fifth cup of coffee as she watched the video. She laughed and spat it out in a mouth fountain.

Her stomach had been roiling for weeks as she'd tried to pull this show together. She thought she'd have an ulcer by the end of it. Or a nervous breakdown. There were a thousand details and a thousand problems every day. This was not helpful for her anxiety disorder.

They had left Hollywood weeks ago to come to Whitefish, Montana, and they still weren't ready for all the arriving bachelorettes. The bachelor was already here. He was chill. But this Ruthie...

"She rocks," she coughed out, in between choking on her coffee. "I need to be this cool."

"I think," Ricki said, "she's gonna be a hit."

No truer words had ever been spoken in the history of *Marry Me*. They just didn't know it yet.

4

Tony Beckett sat slumped in a chair on his wood deck in the modern rental home that *Marry Me* had provided for him in Whitefish, Montana. Normally, Tony did not slump. He had spent well over two decades in the military and had the bearing to prove it, but he could not prevent the slump tonight. He sighed and then bent over and held his head in his hands.

If it wasn't ten o'clock at night and if he put his tired head up, he would be able to enjoy the majesty of the Rocky Mountains. But it was pitch-dark, and the mountains were hiding within the shadows. Tony wanted to hide. He envied the mountains.

Three American goldfinches, two red-breasted robins, and a gang of chickadees surrounding him in the trees were tucked in for the night, as were a close-knit family of bighorn sheep. If he could, Tony Beckett would have turned himself into a red-breasted robin and flown on out of Whitefish, Montana, on the next rush of wind. He would head south and not stop until he was home.

He wondered what the hell he'd done. What had gotten into him? Why on earth had he said yes to being on *Marry Me*?

This was ridiculous.

He was ridiculous.

His mind was spinning like a top. He sat up and leaned his head back and rubbed his face. If he were at home, in his log cabin in a valley between mountain ranges in Eastern Oregon, he'd be in bed. He would have watched the sunset through his floor-to-ceiling windows after a day of working outside, and he would be reading, listening to his horses' neighs or his dogs settling in. Instead, he was waiting for a reality TV show to start, with him as the star.

He was *The Groom.*

Him.

Tony Beckett. *Good God.*

He sat up and exhaled...then inhaled. He told himself to calm down and get it together, *man.*

His two sons had signed him up to be the groom on *Marry Me.* They had filled all the paperwork out, uploaded photos, and even arranged a Zoom interview with the producers. They'd told him fifteen minutes before the interview began that they had nominated him. He hadn't even known what *Marry Me* was.

He hardly watched TV, unless it was sports or documentaries or if his favorite books were made into movies. He liked things quiet. He liked to be alone or with his sons or best friends. He liked to work. He sold farm equipment. He'd made a fortune, but he never talked about it. He was also outside on his property a lot. Being outside in the peace and quiet suited him best after the Army and the memories he had of machine guns, ear-shattering blasts and bombs, and dangerous poisons pouring out of planes.

Now he was going to be on a TV show being filmed in a lavish private lodge in Whitefish, Montana. He had recently toured it with the directors. The rooms were huge, the ceilings high, the views panoramic. You could fit ten families in there, and they would think they'd died and gone to heaven. This type of extravagance was anathema to him. It was outrageous. He and his late wife, MaryBeth, had given money away every month to those in need, and here... One person owned this whole home?

He didn't fit in here, he knew that. He didn't fit with the show. They had chosen the wrong man.

He wanted the mountain ranges and the blue, gentle stream running through his property. His home was in the midst of heaven, filled with fields, meadows, forests, and mountains. Why would anyone leave?

Why had *he* left?

He groaned.

But as he castigated himself for agreeing to be on—of all things—a *reality dating show*, something kept poking at the back of his mind. He could hardly go to town anymore in Grand Rivers. He avoided the street the grocery store was on as if it were lined with human-eating aliens. He had to shop in another town. Everywhere he looked, he was reminded of MaryBeth. *Everywhere.*

So maybe…maybe living in Grand Rivers wasn't the best place anymore. Why hadn't he sat down and asked himself if maybe it was time to move? He could move closer to his sons in the city. He wasn't a city guy, but maybe he could become one?

"No," he muttered. "No cities." Moving might be the answer. Being on this damn show was not.

His sons had begged him to do the surprise interview for *Marry Me*. Pleaded.

His oldest, Scott, became emotional. "Dad, Mom's been gone for almost five years. You have to get out, see the world, meet someone. Please, Dad. We're so worried about you. We don't want you to be lonely. We're worried you're lonely."

"I'm not lonely." He *was* lonely. Lonely for MaryBeth.

His youngest son, Will, also became emotional. "It'll be something new, Dad. You might even fall in love."

"I'm not going to fall in love," he retorted. "That is not going to happen."

"It could," Scott said.

"It might," Will said.

"It won't," Tony said.

"You haven't even been on a date since Mom died," Scott said.

"Not one," Will said.

"Who would I date? Your mom is the only date I want."

"Please, Dad," Scott said. "For us."

Tony sighed. "They're not going to choose me anyhow," he insisted. "This is a

damn waste of time."

They chose him.

The co-directors of *Marry Me* loved Tony.

As Shonda, a Black woman in her mid-thirties who was six feet tall and had

black hair with a fashionable purplish sheen, said, "If he doesn't find a wife on *Marry Me*, I'll marry him."

"Move over, sister," Pearla said, a half-Mexican, half-white woman in her forties with short black hair and huge eyes, who swore in Spanish, never in English. "I'm claiming that one as my own. He is a silver fox. A silver lover. A silver sex god."

They laughed, but Shonda and Pearla were serious.

Tony Beckett was a man. A *real* man. A gentleman. An honest-to-goodness polite male who, by the looks of him, would be most excellent, if maybe *too* polite, in bed. Those shoulders! That tall, broad, proud body. He was six foot, five inches tall! The way he stood! The way he listened! The way he talked, sparingly, but always with something intelligent to say.

He'd been in the military. He knew how to protect and provide. They did not think it was antifeminist to say that. Women could protect and provide, too. *But Tony!*

Those sharp, *penetrating,* very penetrating—they squealed a bit here—dark blue eyes. He gazed right at you, paying attention, as if everything you said was so important to him, he couldn't miss a single word. But he wasn't flirty. He wasn't suggestive like some older men could be who were losing their filters or who insanely thought a younger woman would be attracted to them with their big bellies and balding heads. *As if.* Tony was well-mannered, measured, calm. *Respectful.*

In fact, both Pearla and Shonda got a tad flustered around him, lost their words here and there, had to find their way back to being co-directors on the successful, but sinking, *Marry Me*. It was their job to boost ratings, and my goodness, Tony looked like he could "boost" a lot, including their heart rates.

Shonda and Pearla had taken the camera and lighting people

and other crew members out to Tony's ranch in Eastern Oregon after he'd passed, with flying colors, the Zoom interview. They'd marveled at the towering mountains, the clean, rushing river, and the quiet.

They'd interviewed him in his gorgeous log cabin. That interview was what later brought millions of viewers to decide they had nothing better to do on Thursday nights than to watch *Marry Me*.

Tony had a dry sense of humor. He was cryptic. Serious. Super smart. A leader. He was obviously well-off, his log cabin filled with windows and high ceilings, his kitchen modern. Why, most women in America would love that house and that view and that man in their bed. And yes, they showed the bedroom with the four-poster bed. Shonda and Pearla sighed. Oh, what kind of acrobatics could go on in that fluffy bed with a man built with steel? What romantic and tender moments could be had? They might have pictured this seventy-year-old man naked. They had never done that before. Any man over fifty was suspect in the naked department, but not Tony.

When Shonda and Pearla had the cameras right on him, where he sat, relaxed, on his leather sofa, Shonda said, her heart only fluttering a little, "What are you looking for in a wife, Tony?"

He thought about it, those blue eyes catching a ray from the Oregon sun, becoming almost luminescent. "I want someone who is unique."

"What does that mean?" Shonda asked.

"I want someone who is completely, utterly herself, honest, and kind. Strong when life gets..." He paused. "Challenging. Funny would help. Someone who likes to read. Someone who can live in the country and be happy."

The women viewers gaped. They held their breath. Those were the words they needed to hear. *They wanted to be themselves! They liked to read! They could live in that log cabin in the country!*

"What can you offer a woman?" Pearla asked.

Tony stared through the windows at the Wallowa Mountains, practically in his backyard, then focused again on Pearla. "I really don't know. This might be the shortest season you have. Twenty-four women will rapidly decide that they would rather date a bear, and I'll be headed back home."

The directors' and the crew's laughter later mingled with the laughter of the men and women watching at home.

"But you're a veteran," Shonda said. "You have a successful business. You're kind and insightful, and you even ride horses." Shonda stopped herself. Riding horses probably didn't have a lot to do with this situation. But she was thinking of riding... Oh, never mind! "Why would they reject you?"

Tony paused again. Everyone was getting used to his pauses as they waited, hardly breathing, until he spoke again. "Because I'm not unique enough."

Wow.

And that's how Tony Beckett ended up in a modern rental house in Whitefish, Montana, awaiting twenty-four women who would descend tomorrow night, move into a lodge, meet him, and decide if they wanted to marry him.

He was quite sure none of them would want to date him, much less marry him. He lived in the middle of nowhere, twenty minutes outside of a small town. He was not romantic. He didn't know how to do small talk. He hadn't dated in forever. His right hip wasn't real good. He spent a lot of time on horses or driving a tractor on his property or working at his farm machinery business. As he could barely stand to drive through town because of what happened to MaryBeth, he went the long way around to get to his office in an old building he'd bought and remodeled years ago. Otherwise, he was a hermit. Almost.

"I cannot believe I signed up for this," he said, caught on a hot mike later that afternoon. He'd thought the microphones were off. "No one is going to want to marry me."

America, shocked, laughed and leaned forward on their couches.

Oh, many women wanted to marry that hunk of sizzling manhood.

This was gonna be fun.

5

When Ruthie met the other potential brides in the awe-inspiring great room of the private lodge in Whitefish, with a drop-dead view of the Whitefish Range in the northern Rocky Mountains, and Big Mountain so close she could almost touch it, she felt no insecurity at all, despite how the other women looked. In fact, she hardly noticed.

The women were decked out. Stylish, expensive, and vogue. They had their own fashion sense, and it showed in sleek pants or designer dresses, knee-high boots, silky blouses, and jewelry that glittered. Ruthie clicked on in, wearing her red cowgirl boots, her best-butt jeans, and a white T-shirt that said, "Jane Austen Is My Guidance Counselor." In other words, she came as herself.

Ruthie had grown up hunting. She could shoot a bow and arrow and hit a fly out of the sky. She could get a fire going with two sticks, camp outside for weeks, make tequila, and sing bawdy songs. She swam like a fish and galloped away on horses. She had spent years in 4-H, winning awards for her animals.

She had read piles of classics and modern literature and the books that made life happy—thrillers, Regency romances, fiction, memoirs, and a little Stephen King, though his books made her spine tingle with fright. She could talk books with *anyone*, and that was something to be proud of. She hoped there were some book addicts in the group. She wasn't there to hunt for a husband, but she was definitely there to have a marvelous time, and if the women could talk about books, life would be peachy.

She was seventy years old and not afraid or intimidated by anyone—no matter how they looked.

After a dry and dull meeting about silly rules and regulations, which Ruthie had no intention of following, and mind-numbing scheduling information, which she almost slept through, the women had dinner at one long table set with flowers, white cloth napkins, silver, and china. The cameras were on to catch the dinner and the interactions between the brides.

It seemed a tad stuffy between the women, so Ruthie introduced the brides to Deschutes Family Tequila. She grabbed shot glasses, made sure limes and salt were on hand, expertly poured the tequila, one lined up glass after another, and said, "Ladies, here's to new friends who make you laugh."

Everyone raised their shot glasses with much enthusiasm. They wanted to make new friends! They wanted to laugh! They clinked their glasses together, standing to reach the brides who were farther down the table.

"Now, put your bottoms up!" Ruthie shouted, her arms out.

The bottoms of the brides did not poke upward—that maneuver might have cracked their backs—but they thought Ruthie was hilarious as they tilted their heads back and gulped tequila strong enough to burn hair off chests.

A few women made gagging sounds. Several coughed. All reached for limes.

"Oh, my ever-loving God, girl!" Dallas Grayson shouted, her Southern accent strong, her hand to her ample chest, cleavage deep. "I think my heart skipped a beat, and my pacemaker is supposed to regulate that!"

"What is that made of?" Susie Whitlock gasped. "The devil's fire?"

Velvet Hashbrune, a character herself, said, "Well, swirl me around a stripper pole six times. That woke me up. Give me another one to wash the first one down, honey."

For the second shot, Ruthie declared, "I want to make a toast to wild sex and passion!"

That was a popular one, too. The women wanted wild sex and passion!

Their third shot had Ruthie and the gals clinking glasses to, "La la la la, la la la la, tequila!" A few stood up to dance.

All the ladies forgot the cameras were filming the festivities as Ruthie later gathered them around the giant fireplace in the cavernous great room and taught them three songs about a gun-toting woman named Wanda, a striptease that got out of control in a honky-tonk town, and skinny-dipping in a pond with an alligator. The choruses were simple and raunchy, sexy, and funny, so everyone remembered the words, no matter how much tequila they tossed back.

They would soon be sung all over the nation by *Marry Me* fans, although a few words had to be bleeped out when the show aired.

Ruthie's Grandma Mabel, her father's mother, had taught her the songs. Mabel had owned a saloon in Triple Mountain when Triple Mountain had been a tiny, dirty spot on the map. Her husband, Dax Deschutes, Ruthie's father's father, had made the tequila. That saloon had had a reputation. There'd been fights, chairs thrown, people thrown, a couple of shootings, a few knifings, plenty of gossip, and too much drinking. It had added a lot of excitement in town and provided a lot of money for the Deschutes family.

The women loved Mabel's bawdy songs. Several of them sang in church or other choirs, and one had sung on Broadway, so they carried the songs beautifully. Ruthie swayed, semibuzzed, in front of the roaring fire, hands signaling like a choir director's when certain women had their solos and trilled things like, "If I had to choose between my man and tequila, I'd choose tequila," and, "Swimmin' at night, my body ain't a fright," and, "If I did a striptease, I'd break my knees."

The producers and directors and crew laughed themselves silly. If the show continued like this, they would be employed for years. Could Ruthie be their next "bride" again and again?

Most of the brides woke up with hangovers, their heads splitting.

They laughed. It was the best night they'd had in a long time.

"Welcome to *Marry Me*, everyone! I'm your host, Jackson Coleman, coming to you from Whitefish, Montana. Behind me is the private lodge all our brides will be staying in this season. The romance and magic will happen here, folks. It's a lodge for love! Yes, those are the Rocky Mountains behind me, and if you look up, you can see Big Mountain. Glacier National Park is right over there," he pointed, "and Flathead Lake is only forty minutes away! Is this not gorgeous? What an amazing setting for the launch of *Marry Me*.

"Tonight will be life-changing for twenty-five people—our groom and twenty-four potential brides. Will the groom find the love of his life? Will the bride say yes? Will there be a wedding? Will there be heartache and tears? You'll have to wait and see. However, I can tell you that this season of *Marry Me* will be full of twists and turns, excitement and, inevitably, dramatic blowups and meltdowns."

Jackson, in a tux, stared right at the main camera, though there were many cameras all around, directors, producers, assistants, etc. The area was crowded with crew members, as all reality shows were. Standing in front of the massive, hand-carved wooden doors of the lodge with hundreds of candles, the dusky summer evening appeared romantic and hopeful.

"We do have an exciting change for all of you, though. This season, for the first time ever, the show will be, well, *almost live*. Yes, almost! What we do here in Whitefish will be on your TV screen in seven days. Our crew will be working hard to make sure that all of our brides get time with Tony and that you are seeing what is going on here almost"—he paused and grinned— "*immediately*, instead of having to wait for months on end. And now, the big moment!"

He paused to heighten the tension, his arms outstretched.

"I'm excited to introduce to you our groom, Tony. Tony is seventy years old. I promise you, I truly do, you're going to love him. He's an incredible man, and he's ready to find that special lady with whom he can spend the rest of his life. All right, everyone, are you ready? Take a look. Here's Tony Beckett…"

"Cut," Pearla called. "Good job, Jackson."

"Whew." His shoulders sank with relief, and his face sagged, the beaming smile fading. "Thanks, Pearla. At least I didn't stumble over my words again like a drunken sailor."

"You definitely spoke English this time," Shonda said. "In the other takes, not

so much. It was like you were making up your own language."

Jackson laughed. It was true. He'd stumbled and biffed the intro repeatedly,

and he knew that his mistakes would end up on the bloopers part of the finale at the end of the season. Jackson was a tall, strong, Black man. He was built like a tank. He was a former NFL football player turned actor. He had been in several action movies, thrillers, and two romance movies. He was well known and popular.

Five years ago, some people had shaken their heads at him when he'd told them he was going to host a new dating show called *Marry Me*.

"What are you doing that for, man?" they'd asked. "Are you crazy? You've been in blockbuster movies. You're a movie star. What the hell?"

But Jackson knew he'd made the right choice. Ever since he was a little boy, and his mother, a doctor, and his father, a journalist, had given him two little sisters, he'd known he wanted to be a dad one day. His sisters looked up to him their whole childhood, and he took care of them. He loved his sisters' eight kids. They called him Uncle Jack Jack. Uncle Jack Jack and Uncle Henry, his husband, never missed their birthday parties or Christmas.

When Jackson met Henry, it was love at first sight. You could almost see cupids flying through the sky and angels singing. Henry was half white and half Hispanic and a stage builder for TV series and movies. Henry played piano. Jackson played piano. Henry loved Bach. Jackson loved Beethoven. Henry loved Formula One. Jackson also loved Formula One. Henry fought bouts of clingy depression. Jackson suffered from obsessive compulsive disorder sometimes. They got each other. Henry was his soul mate. They'd been together and in love for twenty years.

Henry and Jackson wanted children. Five, Henry said, if he could have his wish. Three, Jackson said, if he could have his wish, but if Henry was set on five, he could swing that, too. They married, they worked, they saved money, and then when they were ready, they found a surrogate named Tara Sparks. They loved Tara for her honesty, her (ironically, given her last name) sparkly spirit, and her generosity. She was white. She was married and had an indulgent husband and three of her own children. Jackson and Henry went to all her doctor appointments with her, then took her to lunch.

The day Jackson and Henry found out there were, *remarkably*, *inexplicably*, three babies sleeping inside Tara, was shocking. It was the most exciting, terrifying thing that Henry and Jackson had ever experienced. They both cried at the doctor's office. Tara comforted them.

"There, there," she said, patting their shoulders. "There, there."

The babies were all girls.

There was no way that Jackson could work the long hours in foreign locations that he had before. Same with Henry. They knew they would need to make changes, but they were utterly, blindly clueless as to how enormous those changes would have to be. When the babies were born, too early, they lived with the babies in the NICU for four weeks. The babies were never without their daddies. Tara and her husband came, too. They all cried, they held hands, and they held the babies' hands. They sang to the babies and encouraged them. They prayed the babies would live...and they did.

When Jackson and Henry brought the new babies home, this new family knew the truth: Their plans of how they would both go back to work when the babies were a few months old would never work out. It was the worst plan *ever*. The babies would not be in daycare. They would not be with a nanny all day. Henry, sniffling, crying, holding two babies at once, would not leave them.

"Maybe I'll go back to work when they're in first grade," he said, trembling with emotion. "But probably not. I want to be a parent volunteer and go on the field trips."

Jackson nodded. Someone had to be the parent volunteer and go on the field trips. "Okay, honey."

Henry and the girls, now five years old, rebellious, and willful, were in a home nearby that the show rented for them so the five of them could be together. The girls loved Montana and had even seen two bears.

Jackson getting the hosting gig for *Marry Me* was a gift for their family as it allowed for Jackson to work fairly normal hours. He was almost always home for dinner and story hour before bed, which was important because he was best at doing the "voices" in the books, particularly the voices of dragons and lizards.

Jackson liked the young contestants on previous *Marry Me* shows, in general, but they were also immature, selfish, reckless, gossipy, ridiculous, half-cocked, raving, and there had been a few lunatics who needed serious help.

This version of the show, for older people, was going to be...interesting. His sisters couldn't wait for it to start. Neither could his mother. "You should have insisted on older people long ago," she chided him. "I told you so!" Indeed, she had.

He had met the ladies already. Smart. Mature. Funny. They'd been on the planet for over six decades. They could think like rational people. They were not reckless, ridiculous, half-cocked, or raving. So far, no lunatics.

He and the groom, Tony Beckett, got along well. Tony was a man's man and a woman's man. Jackson and Henry had already been invited by Tony to stay with him in Oregon in the future. The girls would love all the animals on his ranch and his log cabin.

Jackson had high hopes for *Marry Me* this season. If the ratings continued to decline, that would be a problem. He could lose his job. He might even be blamed for the demise of the show. That could be career-ruining. He felt faint. He had a family to provide for!

He hoped—oh my, how he hoped—that this season, at the very least, held steady with the viewership. He inhaled, exhaled, inhaled, to calm himself down. He pressed the tips of his fingers and palms together and told himself to think peaceful thoughts filled with serenity. He thought of golden butterflies floating over a meadow.

"You okay, Jackson?" Shonda asked.

"You bet!" His fake smile beamed out again as the golden butterflies dropped to the ground, like *Marry Me*'s TV ratings.

On the evening the "brides" were supposed to meet the "groom," the women wore sequined, silky, fitted, high-end dresses, towering heels, glitter, and glamor. Their hair was brushed and curled and flattened to within an inch of its life. Their makeup was thick, their eyelashes unnaturally long.

"Tarantulalike," Ruthie muttered. "Eyelashes for women who like spiders."

The cameras caught that.

The women's boobs were hiked up so high that Ruthie said, "My God. Their boobs are going to hit them in the face if they jump an inch. They're going to get black eyes from their own boobs."

The cameras caught that, too.

The gang of makeup artists came for Ruthie as they had with all the women. She let them do their thing on her face, which took soooo long, Ruthie said, "Are you doing plastic surgery? Are you rearranging the placement of my mouth and nose? For heaven's sake, I could have read Faulkner's *The Bear* in the time it took to have my makeup done, and I so hate that book."

The makeup artists laughed. Ruthie was so entertaining! (The cameras? Yes. Still there!)

When they were done, they swirled Ruthie around in her chair so she could see herself in the mirror, and she released an ear-splitting screech.

The two makeup artists jumped in fright and screamed back, the multi-screams bouncing off the walls. One dropped a box of eye shadow. The hair stylist, a young man, also screamed, so there was a lot of screaming going on. They were experienced professionals, but this terrorizing response hadn't happened before.

"Hell's bells!!" Ruthie declared after the scary screech, gaping at herself in the mirror. "What have you done to my face? Who is that?"

One of the makeup artists had grown up in a tiny town in Oklahoma. Her family had a lot of edgy and over-the-edge people, so she was used to outbursts, but still. Screaming after a makeover?

The hair stylist had grown up in Los Angeles. His father was in construction. His dad hated that he was a makeup artist. He had told his father to call him Trix from now on. He knew it would make his dad mad, so he did it. His real name was Ryan. They were working on their relationship, but the "working" part was not succeeding. His father would not be happy to learn that his son had screeched over lipstick, but Ruthie's scream had reminded Trix of horror movies. He liked horror movies. His dad did, too. He later wondered if they could bond over horror movies in the future.

"I am not going to meet the bachelor as a clown," Ruthie said. "Is this a clown show? Did I sign up for the wrong show?"

The other brides crowded around. The shaken makeup artists and Trix gave up and went to fix the next bride. Hopefully, she wouldn't scream bloody murder and jangle their nerves.

Ruthie felt bad for what she'd said and for the scream. She didn't want to hurt anyone's feelings.

"I cannot wear all this makeup," Ruthie said. "I can hardly move my face." She tried to move her face with her fingers. "Did they secretly inject Botox into me? Do I have fillers in my cheeks? Does anyone see any stitches that would indicate a bad facelift?"

Oh, how the other brides laughed. Ruthie should have been a comedian, not a teacher!

One of the women, a seventy-one-year-old Black architect named Susie Whitlock, who had grown up on a farm milking cows, said, "You look completely different. It's like they took eyeliner and redrew you." Susie didn't mean this rudely. She was blunt. She was truthful. She'd owned her own architectural firm for decades. The sexism and misogynistic attitudes from men in other firms was nauseating, so she'd started her own. Owning a company made her extra blunt.

"I don't even look like myself. Whose face is that in the mirror? I look like an old, deranged monkey with garish lipstick!"

"No, you don't," one of the women said. Her name was Carol Washington. Her mother was Chinese, her father white. Carol missed her husband. They had been married for thirty-five years, then he disappeared. He'd packed two suitcases, his fishing pole, and camping gear and left. No one knew what happened to him. She'd thought they were happy, except for a dark-bear depression that would come clawing for him now and then. But he had been gone for ten years, and she knew she had to start over. She wanted a new husband who would not disappear. She was lonely. "But maybe we could blot some of this off…"

"My face looks thicker because of all this gunk! It's like I've gained another layer of face. I don't need another layer of face," Ruthie said. "I can't even move my lips." Indeed, Ruthie Deschutes O'Hara did seem to have trouble moving her lips. She stuck her fingers on either side of her mouth and pulled her lips up and down, making silly faces. The women around her started to laugh, then they laughed more and bent over.

"Oh, Ruthie," they gasped. "Stop!"

Dr. Benedetta Fields, a gynecologist, gasped, "My bladder

cannot take laughing this hard. Oh no! Oh no! Not in my dress!" She clenched her legs and waddled to the bathroom, yelling, "Get out of the way!" and "Coming through, ladies!"

Maria Gonzales, an artist originally from Mexico, leaned on the makeup counter, as she was laughing too hard to stand up. "Are you a plant on the show, Ruthie? Are you a famous comedian, and I'm the only one who doesn't know? Wait! Is this whole show a joke to make fun of me?"

"I was an English teacher," Ruthie said, standing. "Books are my hobby. And now I will use my words to declare my freedom from this makeup mask. Makeup"—she pointed in the air with both index fingers— "should never be the enemy of our faces!" She marched to a sink, filled it up, and dunked her entire face. She blew bubbles, sang a tune underwater, then reappeared with a gush of water, the makeup sliding off like she was losing her face, which made the women cackle uncontrollably with laughter, and another one had to skedaddle off to the bathroom. Two women snort-laughed and couldn't stop. One woman sounded like a stoned hyena.

"Is my second face gone yet?" Ruthie asked. "I can feel it sliding down my boobies." She reached down and grabbed said boobies and declared, "Hang on, girls! I will not let you be a hostage to makeup!" which set off another round of laughter.

In the end, Ruthie soaped up, dried off, and put on her own makeup, which was hardly anything at all. Lotion, "so my face will not be a prune," liner, mascara, blush so she wouldn't look "skeletal" or "vampire-esque," and burgundy-ish lipstick. "I want him to know I have lips and my dentures are not molting in a water glass somewhere."

She mimicked taking out her teeth and tossing them in a water glass.

"Why should I hide my face under makeup as thick as Play-Doh? If I end up sleeping with him, the poor man will see what I look like in the morning—an old witch corpse—so I might as well get him used to my wrinkles now. Lord in heaven, I don't want the man dying of shock when our faces are on the same pillow."

The cameramen and women laughed so hard the cameras shook. A week later, when the show aired, the crew could be heard chortling with glee.

The same would happen to the viewers at home.

Ruthie Deschutes O'Hara had no idea how popular she was going to be.

Shonda and Pearla, watching from a corner, winked at each other.

They knew.

That evening, Ruthie was driven to the lodge in the back of a shiny, black SUV with five other ladies—Sarah Whitemore, who had been stuck in a controlling polygamous cult starting when she was born until she escaped; Velvet Hashbrune, who owned a lingerie company; Dr. Benedetta Fields, the gynecologist; Maria Gonzales, the painter; and Pamela Topava, who was from Florida and liked alligators. They were headed to the lodge to meet the bachelor, and then, Ruthie thought, if she was rejected, she could leave and get a good night's sleep at the hotel in town. The brides called it Hotel Rejection, because if they didn't make the cut, they got kicked out of the lodge and banished to the hotel.

Montana was beautiful. After she was tossed out on her fanny, Ruthie figured she would stay a few more days, maybe a week, and take a look-see around. She would drive up to the ski resort and take the ski lift and gape at the view. She would go to Glacier National Park and swim like a fish in Lake McDonald. The next day she would head south to Flathead Lake and rent a speedboat. She would go as fast as possible, the wind flattening her hair. Woo woo! She loved speed. She would head out hiking with bear spray and kayak in the Swan River.

Most important, she'd have her story. She had been on *Marry Me*, and she could give Willow and Lucy the scoop on the other women and the groom, the lodge and the food, the directors and producers, the meetings she attended, and the rules she had to follow. As a Deschutes, she would follow the rules that she saw fit, as prescribed by her DNA.

"Cheers to you all, ladies," Ruthie said, raising a shot glass as they traveled through downtown Whitefish, galleries and restaurants lining both sides of the old western styled streets. "To tequila and big hot dogs!" Good Lord. She had only had two shots of tequila, but it was burning its way down to her stomach and making her relax.

Everyone laughed, way too hard, because the Deschutes Family Tequila did that to people. The hot dog was a suggestive joke involving the groom. The women had agreed on the way over that they hoped he had a big hot dog.

A parade of SUVs headed up into the hills outside Whitefish to the lodge. The lodge sprawled, the views of twinkling city lights stunning. A pool in back and an adjoining hot tub were ready to be frolicked in. There were eight bedrooms and a huge bonus room, so the ladies could spread out, getting more room as each woman was eliminated, her dreams of being a bride smashed to hopeless smithereens.

Ruthie was having the time of her life, even though she was not dressed like the other women in their sequins, silks, and satins, her boobs yanked up.

"What are they going to do? Meet the queen? Is that why they're dressed like that?" Ruthie asked one of the camerawomen.

"I do not have any fancy dresses," Ruthie had said to Shonda and Pearla when they'd told her she would need to wear one of her fancy dresses to meet the groom. The show did not provide the brides with seductive clothing. They had to buy their own.

Shonda's and Pearla's jaws dropped.

"Fancy dresses were on the list!" Pearla said, her voice nervous, squeaky, like a perturbed bird.

"We talked about it," Shonda said, her voice irritated and

alarmed, like a moody bear.

"I know it was on the list," Ruthie said. "But I'm not a fancy-schmancy kind of gal."

They started to scramble to find her a fancy dress with sequins, silks, and satins, their voices pitching up in fear, as if this were the worst thing in the world, and, indeed, the world might implode because of a missing ball gown, but Ruthie stopped them. "I am not wearing an expensive, showy dress that would cost more than most people would spend on clothes in a year. That is not me."

"It is you," Shonda said, begging.

"Shonda," Ruthie said with a pointed, reprimanding stare, shoulders back, ever the strict English teacher. "Never tell a woman who she is. She already knows."

"Yes, ma'am," Shonda said, head down, in a whispery voice.

"I will be myself tonight, as I will be on all the other nights," Ruthie said.

"Yes, ma'am," Pearla said.

Ruthie wore her red cowgirl boots that her daughter, Willow, had given her, a jean dress with square silver buttons, and turquoise earrings, bracelets, and a necklace from her granddaughter, Lucy. Ruthie knew Willow and Lucy would see her secret signs to them in the boots and jewelry, and hopefully, they would call her when she got home from the show, and she could mend this mess.

The SUVs arrived at the top of the hill in front of the lodge. *Huh,* thought Ruthie as she examined the groom from behind the darkened windows of the SUV. He was quite tall and in a tux. He was...handsome. Definitely a looker.

She didn't regret not wearing a fancy dress, but she undid another button on her jean dress and yanked up her bra straps so her cleavage poofed up. She glanced down at her bosom and said, "I've been blessed in the bosom department." She winked at the camera. "These are from my mama. My grandma and great grandma were blessed by God with the same...endowment." She gave her bosom a lift with both hands. "Come on up, girls!" she called out. "Stand tall and at attention! There's a man out there!"

Later, the TV audience would watch that scene and dissolve into more laughter.

That Ruthie!

"Hello. My goodness, you're a tall drink of water," Ruthie said to Tony. He was, she thought, resplendent in his tux. She briefly imagined what was underneath that tux besides the broad shoulders. "I'm Ruthie Deschutes O'Hara." She said this with pride and a smile, two dimples flashing, as she tilted her head up and stared into the tall, dark blue-eyed drink of water in front of her.

At first, Tony Beckett couldn't speak. He had seen twenty-three women get out of the black SUVs in front of the lodge. He had greeted them near the front door. They were beautiful. They wore the fanciest dresses he had ever seen. They sparkled and shimmered and shone. Yes, he'd been to some posh events during his years in the Army because he had risen in rank, but this was another level entirely. The women looked like they were going to some important, expensive party with important, expensive people.

In truth, Tony was wealthy. His house and land were paid off. He had his Army pension. He had Social Security. He had a thriving farm machinery business. But he never lived or moved or spent money like a wealthy person. MaryBeth had been a nurse for decades. She had never wanted to live or move or spend like a wealthy person either. They both thought displays of wealth were obnoxious, low class, and ostentatious. Above all: *very un-Oregonian.* True Oregonians just didn't do that.

In fact, MaryBeth had been in charge of giving their money away. But Tony was, at heart, a kid from Portland who grew up in the "have not" section of town and worked hard from a young age like almost everyone else he knew. His "have not" mentality was still within him.

These women were out of his range. They were not in his

sphere on this planet. They were not in his galaxy. They were not the type of women he would ever date. He could not imagine any of them on a horse or camping or feeding animals or living out in the country. They wouldn't want to marry him either, he was sure of it. He had rarely worn a tux. He wore jeans, T-shirts, flannel, a cowboy hat, boots. That was the extent of his fashionable clothing. The tux felt like a lie. In fact, the tie was choking him.

The women smiled at him as they introduced themselves. They hugged him. Smiled again. Perhaps he was judging them unfairly. He should not be making snap judgments, but good God, they all wore a lot of makeup. Was there a face under there? What would their faces look like without makeup? And their perfume was like a lasso cloud wrapped around him too tight.

He couldn't imagine them in a small town either. Some of them seemed wealthy. It was the ease in which they wore their dresses, he thought. The jewelry. The appearance of wealth hung on them like cash. He had seen Army wives like this, too. With their perfect teeth and perfect skin, they had a superficial shine.

He didn't like a superficial shine. It felt fake to him.

They were friendly, polite, eager. He, too, was friendly and polite.

But this woman, this—Ruthie, was it? He couldn't remember because he suddenly found himself unable to speak. She was *different*. She was—and there was that word again—*unique*.

She wasn't wearing an expensive dress. She wore a denim dress and red cowboy boots. She wore turquoise jewelry. Her hair was gold and white, blended somehow, in waves around her face, her eyes so blue he wondered if she had blue contact lenses in. But it was that smile. It took up half her face, braced by dimples. He thought he'd never seen a prettier smile...except for MaryBeth's, of course.

But then MaryBeth's face disappeared, and Ruthie's was there in front of him, as if he'd been in a mirage, and now he was back.

"Ruthie," he said, his hand outstretched to shake hers. "I'm

Tony Beckett. It's very nice to meet you." Had she called him a tall glass of water? What did that mean?

"Pleased to meet you, too."

And then they stared at each other, holding each other's hand. Their eyes locked. Light blue and dark blue.

They hardly blinked.

They felt the other's energy, their spirit, their soul.

Did they know then?

Somewhere deep inside, did hope flare, a golden light, tiny but shimmering? Was there a warmth melting even a tiny part of both hearts that had been previously battered and grievously wounded? Did one soul recognize the other as if they had been waiting for that exact person for eternity? Was it attraction, that base level that was hard to understand, impossible to scientifically explain, but was it there, bubbling and hot?

Was it lust?

Was it all of it?

Ruthie and Tony were both seventy years old. They knew they were on borrowed time. Anything could happen at this point.

Things could end rapidly. One bad doctor visit. An X-ray that was suspicious. An operation that didn't go well.

Or something could begin. Something...*miraculous.*

Something happy.

Something hopeful.

Something sexy.

Friendship. Companionship. Love.

They kept staring and smiling and holding hands.

The viewers watched, stunned, then delighted. They laughed gently.

As one woman, Melda Zamborini, eighty years old in Omaha, Nebraska, said quietly to her wife, "Get those two a room."

The inside of the private lodge looked even more glamorous at night. The lights of Whitefish glittered below. The rooms were gracious, very Montana-y, and filled with candles. A fire danced in the huge river rock fireplace. The kitchen was modern, the wood floors shone, the wood beams on the ceiling brought one's gaze way up high, and a long wraparound deck had plenty of room to hide in the shadows with a new lover. If you didn't mind the cameras four feet from your face, that is.

The lodge was packed with two dozen potential brides, a nervous groom who was deeply questioning his decision-making skills, and tons of camera people, directors, production assistants, and others with a whole host of titles that will not be listed here, as that would be dull.

The women had been told to never, ever look at the camera. This made Ruthie turn to the cameraman closest to her and say, "I'm not gonna look at you, Tyson!" Then she made a funny face.

They had been told to "open your heart." This, Ruthie knew, was code for, "Say something sappy and personal, something you've never told anyone before" that would then be broadcast to the world next week.

They'd been told to "be honest about your past." Which Ruthie knew meant, "Have any juicy secrets? Oh, ladies, divulge those *immediately*."

They had been told to "speak boldly about your feelings. If you're in love with the groom, tell him!" This, Ruthie knew, meant, "Let's all fall in love. It will be excellent for ratings as one heart after another is broken."

Finally, they'd been told, "Don't hold back your emotions," which Ruthie knew meant, "Cry like hyenas when you get rejected. If you don't want to cry, get mad!"

No way.

Ruthie would do what she damn well wanted, and no producers young enough to be her granddaughters were going to change her mind. She hadn't come on this show to look like a love-desperate fool, and she certainly wasn't going to disgrace the Deschutes family name by doing anything disgraceful. She was participating in hopes that her daughter and granddaughter would see her on the show, forgive her, and talk to her again.

She hadn't eaten in hours, so she headed to the kitchen as soon as she'd met the dapper groom. She didn't like anything she saw. Fruits. Vegetables. Something called quinoa, which she thought was pronounced "*keen*-wa," but it was spelled Q-U-I-N-O-A. She said this while looking straight into the camera. "What is this *keen*-wa? Is it edible? Is it food? It looks like circular worms to me."

She didn't like the kale salad either. "Don't eat kale," she said, looking straight into the camera again. "Kale is meant for rabbits and mice. Not humans. What are you? A mouse? A rabbit?"

Ruthie opened the fridge and started pulling out real food. Eggs. Cheese. Mushrooms. Avocados. Tomatoes. Onions. Bacon.

She chopped. She whipped. She minced. She sizzled. She put four huge skillets on the six-burner stove and cooked up omelets. The scent floated all over the house.

One after another, the brides wandered in after they'd grabbed some time for themselves with the groom, who they all agreed was "smokin' hot," and "kind," and made them feel "seen and important."

They fixed themselves a plate. Pretty soon, most of the women were in the kitchen chatting, not in the cavernous great room of the lodge, the night dark and sparkly with all the lights that had been strung across the backyard.

"This is delicious, sugar," Dallas Grayson said.

They all learned that Dallas's late father had been an oil baron in Texas. He'd been born in Dallas, hence the name. Dallas spoke with a drawl. As a teenager, she'd been a debutante. "I was presented to polite society. I felt like a cow at auction. I did not want to be a debutante. I did not want to be a cow at auction. I did not want to wear a dress that made me look like a virgin and a hooker at the same time. I was neither. When asked to introduce myself in front of everyone, I said, 'My name is Dallas Grayson, and I will not be marrying for years, as I think the institution is an archaic prison for women that benefits men only. I don't want to be a maid. I don't want to be strapped to one man the rest of my life. How dull. I don't want to lose my independence and slowly suffocate. Wifehood is not for me.' Some of the women clapped. The men didn't. You have to remember—this was over fifty years ago. My honesty did not go over well with my parents, but I had warned them on multiple occasions that I didn't want to be there, and they did not listen."

The women all appreciated this rebellious story.

"Ruthie," Pamela Topava said, "I could die happy after this omelet. Honestly, it is better than sex."

Everyone laughed, which began a conversation about what foods were better than sex. Chocolate made the list. Buttered popcorn. Bacon—duh. French fries.

Pamela, the one from Florida, mentioned that she regularly found gators in her pool, but it didn't seem to bother her much. Her mama was "from the wrong side of the tracks" and taught her how to use a gun. She had shot off her gun at the gators, deliberately not hitting them, as she was a huge animal-rights supporter, and they slithered away. She even had names for two of the gators—Big Teeth and Claws.

Pamela divorced one husband because he "relentlessly, continually" made her feel like "pond scum." She escaped through a back window when things escalated and "ran like hell." She stayed married to the next husband for thirty-three years, until the day he died.

Ruthie had a wonderful time with the other women. This was exactly what she had pictured! New friends, yummy food, free champagne, and a pool.

"Who hasn't talked to Tony?" Carol asked, the one whose husband disappeared into thin air with his camping gear.

It was then that Ruthie remembered that she should talk to the gallivanting, gorgeous groom. She held up a finger and announced, "Whoops!" She didn't want to be sent home, at least not tonight. She grabbed a plate, put an omelet and a biscuit on it, clinked two glasses of champagne together in one hand, and said, "I'm off on my love journey, ladies! I shall go and hunt down our mutual male and enthusiastically pounce on him. I will report back shortly."

Her timing was perfection. But then, Ruthie had a habit of perfect timing. Even when she was born, she was right on time, not early, not late.

She spotted Tony with a woman named Audrey out on the deck. Audrey reminded her of three snobby, wealthy, entitled girls she had gone to high school with. They had looked down their noses at her because she belonged to the Deschutes family, who had a reputation of lawlessness out on their homestead. Audrey was already talking behind the backs of some of the women there.

Ruthie paused. Audrey and Tony were sitting on a bench. Audrey was leaning forward, talking a mile a minute, her boobs almost popping out of her dress. Tony looked exhausted. Ruthie was exhausted listening to Audrey prattling on.

She waited for ten minutes, not wanting to intrude, and ate a strip of Tony's bacon. Then she walked over with the champagne and omelet, dawn breaking in the distance. The clouds were still dark, but the sun, rising in the east yet again, was bringing with it stripes of cotton candy pink, emerald green, and golden yellow.

"Hello," Ruthie said.

"We're still talking," Audrey snapped.

"Ah, well, I'll wait inside," Ruthie said. "I believe we're going to start a poker game." She turned to go and said, "Come find me when you're done, Mr. Tall Drink of Water."

"Audrey," Tony said, as if awoken from a stupor of verbal vomit, "I'm going to talk to Ruthie for a few minutes. I was recently informed that we're going to have the I Do ceremony soon, and I think Ruthie is the only one I haven't talked to yet." He turned his attention to Ruthie. "I heard she makes an amazing omelet." He stood, and so did Audrey.

"I do," Ruthie said.

Audrey huffed, then wrapped her arms tightly around Tony and lifted her head to kiss Tony on the mouth. He turned his head before she could lip-smack him. "Thank you for the conversation and for being vulnerable with me and opening up and sharing your heart with me," Audrey gushed. "I think our souls have connected."

Tony blinked. It was clear he didn't know what in God's name she was talking about.

Ruthie hid her laugh behind the champagne glasses. (The camera caught this, too.)

"I'm so glad we had this time," Audrey kept on. "You're really special, Tony."

"Thank you. Ruthie? Would you like to talk?"

Audrey hmphed and walked too close to Ruthie, glaring at her. Ruthie stood her ground. The camera, once again, caught her smile. The viewers laughed. Wasn't hard to stand tall in those cowgirl boots, plus Ruthie never liked "giving ground." She was a Deschutes. They did not give ground at all, to anyone. (Unless it was the husband giving ground to his wife. That was a rule to be followed, too.)

"Here," Ruthie said as they sat on the bench, camera people and crew surrounding them like locusts, though she was supposed to pretend they weren't buzzing about. "You need an omelet."

"Thank you," he said. His gratitude was apparent.

They sat in silence while Tony ate. They were both comfortable. Why did everyone talk so much these days? There was so much noise all the time. This was better.

When Tony was done, he said, "Best omelet ever, Ruthie. Thank you."

"Thanks. All they had to eat was kale. Do you know what kale is? And something called keen-o-a." Ruthie laughed, and he joined her.

"I am not going to eat kale or keen-lo-la," Tony said. "I need real food."

"I always need real food. So, Tony, tell me about yourself."

Tony wasn't naturally open. The less said about his personal life, the better. He gave her an outline. His childhood in Portland, Oregon. Military service. Long marriage. Two sons. His farm equipment business in Eastern Oregon. "Tell me about you."

She gave him an outline, too, including that she also was an Oregonian. They disagreed on which university to cheer for during football games, but otherwise agreed on everything else, including their favorite places in Oregon to visit, including Bandon; Central Oregon; the Metolius, Fall, and Deschutes rivers; Lincoln City in the North End; Mount Hood; and the Wallowa and Steens mountains.

"What do you want out of life, Ruthie?"

"What I want to do is to embrace living again," Ruthie said, impressed by the depth of his question. "I want to live without grief, without having to battle every day the sadness I feel over losing my husband, Russell. I have been in pain for long enough. I want to laugh. I want to have more adventures. I want to see new places and meet new people. I want to be brave and helpful to others and to be a kind and kickass mother and grandmother. I want to leave a lot of love here when I'm gone, before I'm burned to dust and thrown through the wind."

Tony nodded. He was serious, thoughtful. "I think I need the same. It's time, isn't it?"

"Yes," Ruthie said, and she understood everything he meant when he said that. No one got through life unscathed. All lives had downpours of rain that ran down your face like tears. But by the time one was seventy, there had been many blows and hardships and a lot of downpours. They knew they needed to embrace life for as long as life allowed them to embrace it.

It was there, in that moment, the white moon tilting, the Big Dipper dipping, Orion's Belt gliding, that they understood each other. They shared the same feelings, the same goals, the same wishes for a new life. It was deep, and it bonded them.

He smiled at her, and she smiled back.

In the forest on the mountain, two deer kissed, two brother foxes wrestled, and two mountain goats admired the night sky together. They were coupled up outside, and here, inside, were two humans coupling up.

Ruthie and Tony chatted about life and what they wanted to do and see in the future. They talked and talked, as if they'd known each other a hundred years but were still fascinated by each other, until Shonda and Pearla knew they had to split them up to stay on schedule.

First, they tried to split them up politely, as it did not appear that these two would ever stop talking. "Tony, Ruthie," Pearla said, "I think we can give you five more minutes, then we'll need to move on," and they nodded amicably and went back to chatting about the best way to win at poker, why life living in the country is best, and who their favorite bands were in the sixties and seventies.

Pearla came back a half hour later and said ever so politely yet again, "Okay, you two. That's it. We're going to have the I Do ceremony soon."

And Ruthie and Tony smiled and said they understood, and they stood—Ruthie first, then Tony reluctantly—but they were in a conversation about fishing on the Deschutes River and the importance of not stepping on rattlesnakes on the banks. Soon, they moved on to their love of golf.

"A terrible sport created by the devil," Ruthie said.

"Mind-numbing in its frustration," Tony said. "I hardly know why I do it."

Ruthie agreed. "It's like willingly putting yourself through torture."

Pearla and Shonda, increasingly stressed about their schedule, started to walk them toward the great room of the lodge, through all the candles and crew members, city lights twinkling in the distance. Ruthie and Tony kept chatting, and then they were physically, softly, separated.

Ruthie said, "Nice talk, cowboy."

Tony laughed and said, "Thanks, cowgirl." He studied those red boots.

Ruthie turned to Pearla and winked at her. Pearla grinned. Ruthie headed for the lodge.

Tony turned to Shonda and winked at her.

Shonda grinned and looked up at Tony. "We like her, too."

"Doesn't everyone?" Tony asked. "How can you not like Ruthie?"

They were both so…likable, Shonda and Pearla later agreed. Solid. Super smart. Ruthie was fun. He was serious.

Pearla and Shonda winked with great exaggeration at each other, then chuckled.

"This is gonna be interesting," Pearla said.

"Indeed," Shonda said.

Ruthie couldn't see them, but in the forests, along the hills, and up the mountains outside of town, animals and birds did their business as the darkness lifted and dawn began. They flew, they hunted, they tried not to *be* hunted. Bears, coyotes, wolves, hawks, eagles, bunnies, mice—all trying to survive outside, while the brides tried to survive inside.

One coyote, one bear cub, and one blue jay briefly wondered about the spectacle in the lodge, but they moved on. Humans were complex, and it was always best not to know too much.

It was time for the I Do ceremony. Tony was to choose which women he wanted to continue the "walk down the aisle" with him. In other words, some women were stayin', and others were headed on outta there to Hotel Rejection.

The mountains were sleeping, but the birds weren't. They chirped as if they were in choir practice. The sun was up over the horizon. The women wanted to be in bed. They'd stayed up partying and barhopping this late when they were younger, but not now! Their feet hurt, their hips cracked, their knees were creaking, and they were done smiling and trying to appear attractive with all that makeup caked on their faces. They wanted to take off their push-up bras, which made them feel like they were stuffed into a corset, and lie down, preferably with Tony.

Each bride had a light, like a mini spotlight, hanging discreetly over her head to symbolize her "golden" years. For the I Do ceremony, they stood under the light, which was currently off, in the great room, the fire roaring in the fireplace. So many candles flickered it was a wonder the house didn't burn down. Surrounding the women was an army of lighting technicians, cameramen/women, Shonda, Pearla, Jackson, production assistants, etc.

When the ladies were all under their lights and ready to go, Tony greeted them, thanked them for coming, said he was so impressed with all of them, and it was so hard to choose, yada yada, blah blah. Jackson, standing next to Tony as his "best man," told the women what to expect during the I Do ceremony. "If Tony wants you to stay so you can continue your walk down the aisle, the golden light will go on over your head."

All the women tipped their heads up. That damn light. They wanted it on right now!

"Let's begin. Ladies, I hope your walk down the aisle continues," Jackson said, then stepped back.

Tony pressed a button on a board in front of him. The light went on over Benedetta's head.

Tony said, "Benedetta, do you wish to continue our walk down the aisle?"

She smiled and said, "I do."

The women could say "hell no" if they didn't want to continue. But no one with a brain would do that with Tony Beckett, embodying Redford, Washington, Selleck, Newman, and Smits standing right in front of them.

Pamela, Sarah, Dallas, Susie, Carol, Maria, Velvet...one woman after another smiled with relief and walked down the aisle—a strip of pink carpet—to Tony and received a bouquet of flowers with ribbons. The bouquet resembled a bridal bouquet. They each hugged Tony—some daring ladies planted a smacker on his cheek—then they returned to their place under the spotlight, victorious and breathing better. Their feet still hurt from their high heels, which felt like mini torture chambers, but at least they got their wedding bouquet, and soon they could get their slippers on.

The process of eliminating the "brides" was humiliating, as all eliminations on reality TV shows were, but someone had to go home, because there had to be a wedding at the end of this shindig.

When Tony asked Ruthie if she would like to continue their walk down the aisle, she said, "Oh, hell yes, cowboy," and headed right on down that pink carpet, proud in her red cowgirl boots.

In the end, Tony did not turn on the golden light over four women's heads. Audrey was one of the unlucky ones, and everyone could tell she was pissed off by the way her face scrunched up like a gnome's. She even said, "Shit. This is stupid," and, "I cannot believe this."

Jackson said to the four unfortunate women, with heavy solemnity and regret, "Ladies, you will not be Tony's bride. I'm so sorry."

The women said goodbye to the brides who were saved by their golden lights and then left after giving Tony a hug. Well, not Audrey. She didn't give Tony a hug. She said to him, "I thought you would be smarter than this." He did not reply, so she said, "You made a mistake." Again, he did not reply.

"And then there were twenty," Ruthie muttered, her golden light shining over her head. She loved Agatha Christie! Her favorite Agatha book was *And Then There Were None*. She didn't think the ending of *Marry Me* and Christie's book would be the same. There would be no murders here because there were too many cameras. Why, you'd be caught before you could make a run for it!

<hr>

"Tony made a bad and surprising error," Audrey said to the camera, in front of the lodge, the sun continuing to rise, saying hello to this side of Earth. Audrey's mascara was smeared. Plus, insert any more Botox into that face, and nothing would move except her eyes. And the fillers. Sheesh. She was unnatural. The viewers definitely thought that Tony had not made an error.

Maybe Hollywood did "that type of thing," but most of America did not buy into shooting a dead botulism virus into their faces to become perpetually younger, nor were they comfortable with "fillers"—who knew what was in that crap? What exactly was a filler? Did God give you Botox when you were born? No, He didn't. So why shoot it into your face?

George, an older gentleman from Idaho who had been wrangled into watching *Marry Me* with his wife, Yolanda, in exchange for sex, said, "I could never sleep with a woman like Audrey who progressively got younger with all that stuff in her face. I would feel like I was in the middle of a horror show and would expect her to turn into a cannibal and eat my guts when I wasn't looking."

It was worth having sex with George to have him watch *Marry Me* with her, Yolanda thought. He was always so clever in his responses. "She does have an aura of cannibalism about her, George." She patted his knee. "Nice choice, Tony. You two are not a match. Audrey needs a Ken doll with a lot of money to pay for that face and those boobs and those teeth. Those teeth are blinding, aren't they? Practically need my sunglasses."

"We could both wear sunglasses to bed tonight," George suggested, wiggling his shoulders. "We could pretend we're spies and can't reveal our real identities to each other."

"I'll do it!" Yolanda said. "I'll play the spy game with you again."

But Audrey was not yet done with her sulky speech, and George and Yolanda, future spies, leaned forward toward the TV.

"There's no one in there who will be a good wife to Tony," she said vehemently, her forehead not moving at all. "I know that for a fact. I'm a stellar judge of character, and the other women are..." She waved her hands in dismissal to express her disgust. "My God. Where was the vetting? He needs a wife at a higher intellectual level than them. He needs people who have traveled. He needs someone sophisticated. Well, this is a stupid show and a stupid idea, and I can't believe I even came." Her face remained frozen. "There are plenty of men in New York for me to date, and who wants to live in the backwoods of Oregon anyhow?" She pushed her hair back. It had fallen out of the elegant chignon it had been in. "And Ruthie. How on earth did she get to stay over me? She's wearing cowgirl boots, for God's sake." Audrey crossed her arms over her fake, expensive boobs. "She goes in the kitchen and starts to make omelets, and then she steals Tony away from me. He'll find her boring and silly, I guarantee it. Boring and silly small-town woman."

The scene flipped to Tony smiling down at Ruthie and Ruthie smiling back up at him, fascinated with each other.

"I don't think he finds her silly," George from Idaho said.

"I don't think he finds her boring," Yolanda said.

"And look. Ruthie's face moves like a normal woman's should. She has a pretty smile, doesn't she?"

"She sure does," Yolanda said. "If we ever did a threesome, we could invite her."

George, a conservative man, though he was game for pretending he was a spy tonight, stared at her in shock. Yolanda knocked him in the ribs with her elbow and handed him the popcorn bowl.

"My God," he muttered. "You will never stop surprising me, Yolanda."

She did not tell him that he hadn't surprised her in four decades plus five years. But she still loved him. She leaned over and kissed his cheek.

He smiled, reached for her hand, and kissed it. Best wife ever.

After the twenty women came together with Tony, delighted they were staying another week, Ruthie said, "I think I need to jump in the pool and cool off."

The brides gasped, then giggled. Tony laughed. He was so devilishly sexy in his tux.

"Come on, everyone," Ruthie cajoled. "Haven't you ever

wanted to jump in a pool with your clothes on? What are we waiting for? Is anyone here getting any younger?"

They agreed that no one was getting any younger at all.

"Then let's go! Let's have some fun." Ruthie led everyone out to the pool. The women glanced at one another, their faces lighting up. It was so warm out. They were sweaty from stress and adrenaline. They'd been so worried about not being chosen. They wanted to get rid of the stress. Who wanted more stress? Not them.

Tony was right next to Ruthie as they stood about six feet from the pool. The other brides lined up beside them in all their glitz and glamour and started laughing.

"On the count of three, brides and groom!" Ruthie shouted. "Be cool! Everyone in the pool!"

"One..."

The women and Tony kicked off their shoes. Tony took off his jacket.

"Two..."

The women hiked up their lavish dresses.

"Three!"

The women and Tony ran for the pool and jumped.

Later, when the photo—all the women and Tony freeze-framed jumping into the water—was posted to social media to advertise the new *Marry Me* for older adults, it caught on fire, flames leaping everywhere. Interest for the show hit an all-time high. Newspapers, social media, and talking heads for different shows all discussed it.

Marry Me was soon to become a megahit.

Willow and Lucy sat together on Willow's leather couch, watching Ruthie on TV. A bottle of Deschutes Family Tequila sat next to a framed photo of the three of them on a side table. They were all dressed as giant poodles.

The moon winked through the blue and white plaid curtains,

and an owl hooted outside. It was the same owl that Ruthie heard, too, at her farmhouse not far away. That owl got around as he minded the humans' personal business.

"I can't believe she went on *Marry Me*," Lucy said.

"I can," Willow said. "That's Mom. She does daring and outrageous things."

"Yes, that's Nana."

Willow sniffled.

Lucy sniffled. Lucy's brown cat, Nancy Drew, jumped on her lap. Nancy Drew liked to watch *Marry Me* with them, so Lucy put a leash on her and brought her to her mom's each week.

"She shouldn't have done what she did," Willow said, but her voice was gentle, and she patted her daughter's hand. She had been caught between her mother and her daughter.

"No, she shouldn't have," Lucy said, some fire in her voice.

"It was wrong. But I understand why she did it."

"Mom, stop." She turned toward her, frustrated. "I know you don't like him either."

"I tried."

"No, you didn't."

They sat in silence, then laughed at something Ruthie said on the show.

"I miss her so much," Willow said.

"Me, too," Lucy said.

Willow wiped a tear.

Lucy did, too.

"She wore the red cowgirl boots that I gave her," Willow said.

"She wore the turquoise earrings, necklace, and bracelets that I gave her," Lucy said, honking her running nose into a tissue.

"She did it on purpose," Willow said. "It's her way of saying hello."

"Yes, it is," Lucy said. "She's loving like that. But, Mom, what she did… It wasn't right. It wasn't her business to interfere."

"We're Deschuteses, honey. We always interfere."

Lucy honked in reply.

The owl hooted in response.

6

Marry Me

Interview: Tony Beckett

Interviewed by: Tyler, the associate producer, who went to Stanford and will say that shortly. He's so annoying.

Tyler: How was your first night, Tony?

Tony: Wet.

Tyler: Uh, wet?

Tony: Yes. We all jumped in the pool.

Tyler: I saw that. What do you think of all the women you met?

Tony: They're wonderful.

Tyler: I think they think you're wonderful, too. I went to Stanford, and there were wonderful women there, too.

Tony: Huh. Well. I want the women to be glad they're here. I don't want them to feel like they're wasting their time.

Tyler: The brides.

Tony: What?

Tyler: Uh, the brides. We call them brides.

Tony: I call them women.

Tyler: But, uh, we'd like you to say… Okay. Any favorites?

Tony: All of them. They are talented, smart, honest, sincere, and kind. I have enjoyed all my conversations.

Tyler: Do you think you can find your bride here?

Tony: I am hoping to find a wife here, yes. If she'll have me.

Tyler: If she'll what?

Tony: If she'll have me.

Tyler: What does that mean?

Tony: I think I'm going to get out of this tux. It's soaked. Have a good night and thank you for the interview.

7

After the pool party, the sun peeping up, Shonda and Pearla agreed over wine and mini wieners that Ruthie was "spectacular." They had been stressed out, trying to corral all these women and get them in their rightful places to launch the damn show, and now they could breathe for a moment and eat in the staff building in front of the lodge.

"Ruthie refused to wear a fancy dress, but she outdid the other women," Shonda said, flipping back her black/purple hair. "She was natural and stylish and funny... It was like watching Betty White. No matter what Betty wore, no matter how prim she appeared, no matter who she stood next to, it was always Betty's show."

They both agreed Ruthie had that same Betty White charisma. Shonda and Pearla reached for more mini wieners and cheese cubes set up for the crew, most of whom had limped off to bed.

"They had the best time in the pool," Pearla said. "I laughed all the way through filming. They acted like they were twenty."

The brides and groom had had chicken fights. They had jumped off the diving board cannonball-style and slid, in train formation, down the slide, ankles up. Too much wine and beer and tequila had been consumed. They'd sung Ruthie's raunchy songs and done handstands in the pool and leaped from the deck onto floating doughnuts in the water, often belly flopping, their dresses dripping.

The viewers, when they saw the raucous pool party, were in rapture about the whole event. It was one scene after another of "old" people having a marvelous time. It gave people hope that they could do cannonballs and slide down slides with their friends in a train formation when they were old, too, ankles in the air.

"These wieners are a lot better than the real ones," Pearla said.

"No comparison," Shonda said. "I'll take these wieners over the others any minute of any day." She put three in her mouth, letting them stick out like, uh, wieners, and said, "Yummy!"

The ladies slept in the next day at the lodge. They shared bedrooms and the bonus room, which also held beds. The rooms were light and bright, filled with windows, the log walls giving off some serious comfy vibes. The beds were soft, the blankets softer, and the fireplaces created a calming mood.

But they were hungover. As in brain-splitting pounding in their heads, aching bodies, and exhaustion that felt like a wet blanket.

It was a huge problem-o. The directors and production assistants and associate producers and even the in-house chef had to beg the women to get up the next morning. They pleaded with the brides. They prodded. They insisted.

"I think someone is slapping a stripper pole against my cranium," Velvet Hashbrune complained, moaning. She pulled the blanket over her head. Her mother used to be a stripper before she started making stripper lingerie.

"I have not been this hungover since I escaped the cult," Sarah Whitemore said. "I need to rest because my head won't stop spinning. Is the room spinning? Are we in a spinning earthquake?" She flipped over and went back to sleep.

"My stomach hurts from laughing too much," Dr. Benedetta Fields said. "My privates hurt, too. An odd symptom, but not abnormal given the fact that I landed, legs splayed, on a floating dragon in the pool. I think I squished one of his horns. I don't think I'll be able to stand up today." She stumble-crawled to the bathroom, whispering something about dragon curses.

"I'll make Bloody Marys," Ruthie said, rolling out of bed in slow motion so as not to jangle her brain. She very rarely drank too much. Two shots of her family's tequila were plenty. (Most of the time. Unless the party was rockin'. Or it was Rattlesnake Lake Jump Day.)

Ruthie struggled up and clutched at her back. "Bloody Marys will demolish these hangovers."

By eleven o'clock, the women had eaten, downed Bloody Marys, showered, and dressed, but many could hardly stay awake. They were no longer used to this type of ruckus and merrymaking.

Outside, it was another blue-sky Montana day. Unlike the brides, many of the animals in the forests were back in their dens, their caves, their trees, their hiding places. Some animals had been predators, others prey, the night before. None of them was hungover. A few birds chirped, perhaps talking about all the singing and celebrations last night by the pool.

Jackson strolled in. He was looking as fine as ever, even though he, too, had been up late with them and had jumped in the pool, too. The women had all agreed that Jackson and Tony were "hotter when wet," and "men you could lie on and cuddle" at night.

"Good morning, ladies. You all had quite the time last night!"

"Blame Ruthie," Pamela said, holding her head. "My poor head. It feels like an alligator bit it. No one talk above a whisper."

"I had the best time in my ever-lovin' life," Dallas, the rebellious Texas debutante, drawled. "I was drunk as a skunk. I remember being in the pool, twirling around in the inflatable doughnuts, and singing the song about skinny-dipping that Ruthie taught us. Did we do that for real, sugar?"

"Yes, we did," Pamela said. "You have a voice like a lusty angel, Dallas."

"Thank you. I was a lusty angel. Could not help myself as a

young, hot-blooded American Texan woman. Bless my own heart, I had to sing in the choir at church when I was a teenager. The night before, I'd be in the back of my boyfriend's truck, rolling around naked like a little blonde angel, then I had to look all holy up there singing Christian songs about loving Jesus. I was a darling little angel my daddy was so proud of. He thought I was a virgin on the morning of my wedding. I was on man number seven, praise the Lord."

Ruthie, sitting on the couch with her new friends, laughed. "How was the wedding?"

"That's a funny story," Dallas said. "I—"

"And...back to our day!" Jackson said, knowing he had to get control of this conversation. "I talked to Tony, and I have good news for eight of you." He read out the names of the women who would be accompanying Tony on a date. Ruthie's name was not one of them.

Some of the women cheered. Pamela, the alligator lover, said, "Will we have time for a nap first? I must get this alligator to let go of my poor head."

Sarah Whitemore, cult victim, said, "I cannot be up until seven in the morning again. My uterus will shrivel."

"You still have a uterus, honey?" Dallas asked. "I got rid of mine years ago. For some reason, my sex drive went up after that." She snapped her fingers. "It was like magic." She did a little shimmy with her shoulders.

"If we're going bungee jumping, I need to know so I can grab my special diaper-panties," Velvet said.

Two other women nodded. Yes to special diaper-panties if there was going to be any jumping whatsoever. Even bitty jumps.

"Same with parachuting. I've seen these shows with all their bladder-leaking activities. Last thing I want to do is pee myself," Carol said. Peeing herself wouldn't be attractive to a new husband, she knew that, she did. He might disappear on her like her last husband on his camping trip. She briefly wondered if he'd been eaten by a cougar in his tent. An animal cougar, not an older-lady cougar.

As soon as Jackson left, the lucky women wobbled up the stairs to get ready. Ankles popped and knees cracked. Two hips made grinding noises. They ignored it as best they could and hoped their hangovers would subside. They were going to put their faces on and change their clothes and brush their teeth to get rid of their nagging tequila breath. God Almighty, what was in that tequila? Hellfire?

The eight brides had a marvelous time with Tony. They went zip-lining. The specialized diaper-panties were needed for two women who screamed. They had brought them in their bags and quick as a lick changed into them when presented with the possible urine-inducing zip-lining activity up in the mountains.

Afterward, the brides and groom ambled down to the lake on a short hike and had lunch at picnic tables. By the time they returned to the lodge, a few of them were pretty darn sure they would become the next Mrs. Beckett. The others were totally willing to climb out a window, with the special panties on in case they fell, to escape the cameras and run off with Tony *tonight*.

Oh, they loved Tony. He was handsome. Smart. Independent. Thoughtful and measured. He made them feel welcome and appreciated. He listened. Oh my, he listened, and most men listened with, at best, half an ear. Maybe a quarter of an ear. Most men, the women thought, were selectively deaf, but not Tony. He'd been married until death did they part. If he married them, they would not have to worry that he would run off with a blonde bombshell. He was a true man. He even dressed like a stud. Those jeans fit him well. They liked the T-shirts. They liked the cowboy boots.

A coyote, covered so well in shrubs she was invisible, watched from the top of a hill. Humans were quite strange, she thought. Quite strange. She liked to study these two-legged animals, but she had no desire to join them. She fluffed her tail and disappeared into the woods. She had a boyfriend and wanted to find him.

When the eight lucky women were on the date, the other women stayed home. Ruthie read part of a book by Eloisa James to get the spirit of romance back in her life, then popped into the pool, the hot tub, and back to the pool with her new friends. They talked about their favorite books, which meant that Ruthie was in high heaven.

In the afternoon, all the women took naps. Ruthie completed the *New York Times* crossword with her new bride friends. She and Pamela made chocolate chip cookies with a dash of lemon and cinnamon and drank hot toddies. The other women crowded around, and they told funny stories about their lives—the good and the bad.

The youngest was sixty-five years old. The oldest was seventy-five.

They could live decades. They could live two weeks.

They were not wasting any time. They did not worry about calories. They did not worry about the alcohol and its impact on their liver or kidneys.

"Cheers," Ruthie said. "To life."

"To life," they said and clinked glasses.

Ruthie was utterly enjoying herself. After being forced out of her teaching job last year by a sanctimonious twit and a buffalo-hipped woman, and her daughter and granddaughter not talking to her, she needed this happiness, these new friendships, this change of scenery.

And the groom, well, he was not hard to look at.

She told him that, too, at a dinner party the next night at the lodge.

"You're not hard to look at, Tony," Ruthie said.

"You aren't either, Ruthie," he said, a smile on his rugged face, but his voice was serious. He had a deep, gravelly voice. The kind of voice that people listened to with respect. "In fact, it's a pleasure. I like your smile. I like your dimples."

Tony had asked Ruthie to come outside the lodge with him and sit in two Adirondack chairs overlooking the city lights. The cameras followed, but the other women didn't, as it was Ruthie's turn to spend time with Tony.

Off in the distance, a bear foraged for berries. A fox slunk through the trees and watched a wolf. The wolf howled so he could find his pack. The deer shrank down in the foliage to avoid the wolf pack, and a curious hawk surveyed the whole scene, wondering what would happen next.

"Thanks, cowboy."

"Thank you, sunshine."

"Sunshine?"

"You're like the sunshine, Ruthie. Golden. Happy. You make everyone laugh, including me."

Ruthie tilted her head. "You are quick with your compliments, slick."

"No," Tony said. "I am not slick. I'm telling you the truth."

"Then tell me the truth with this question: How did you come to be the groom?

You don't seem like the type of man who would be on a reality show. You're very different from all the young grooms who have been on before."

"How am I different?"

"They did not appear to have functioning brains."

He laughed. "I might not either. I'm here because my sons signed me up." Tony

sighed and smiled, the smile crinkling the corners of his eyes.

Many viewers would later say, "He's got that Robert Redford look, doesn't he?" And their hearts would pitter-patter.

"I didn't even know what *Marry Me* was. I'd never seen it. A producer called me—Shonda. I thought it was a joke and hung up. My sons were over, and they looked guilty, and I said, 'What the hell did you do?' And they told me. I was shocked and told them I'd never do it. But..."

"Yes?" Ruthie asked.

"I did it because they begged. Because they both seemed disappointed when I said no. I haven't dated since my wife died. I had no desire to date. But they convinced me. My son said to me, 'Dad, you're seventy. What have you got to lose?' So I called Shonda back and said yes, I would talk to her, have an interview. I still can't believe I'm here. What about you?"

She told him she thought it would be entertaining. She didn't want to tell the truth on television, as she did not want to embarrass or pressure Willow or Lucy. But she had let her clothing do the talking again tonight. She was wearing a light green dress with colorful embroidered flowers and birds around the neckline. The neckline was quite low, and Ruthie had worn a red push-up bra underneath to highlight her "assets." She wore a leather belt around her waist and leather sandals with a wedge, as the top of her head barely came up to Tony's shoulders.

She, Willow, and Lucy had each bought an embroidered dress at the same shop in Mexico last year. She felt a sad ping and a ding in her heart at the memory, but she was hoping that Willow and Lucy would know she was sending a cheerful signal to them that she loved them and was sorry. (She wasn't *entirely* sorry, though they didn't need to know that.)

"After my teaching career ended, I needed something to do. I knew I would be staying somewhere new with free food and wine and women to become friends with, and after seeing you on TV, I thought you might be okay." She laughed so he would know she was joking.

His lips curved up. His jaw was hard, his face kissed by the sun. "Thanks, Ruthie. I feel special. Tell me about your family."

Ruthie gave the highlights of the Deschutes family, starting with their history in a window-shattering brawl in a seedy bar in Missouri and a quick escape on a train to Oregon. She talked about her family's traditions for Christmas. "We have a huge bonfire, and then we sing traditional Christmas songs, only we've changed the words. For example, 'Jingle Bells' becomes 'Jingle balls, jingle balls, jingle all the way. I've had too much to drink in town, and now I've got the sways, hey! Jingle balls, jingle balls, jingle all the way. Tequila is my best friend, and now I'm on my sleigh, hey!"

She sang a few more Deschutes family Christmas songs, showing him the corresponding hand and hip movements, and Tony was utterly amused.

She did not talk about what happened when she was eighteen and how her life took a steep nosedive into a tar pit of fear and sadness. That was private. She didn't want to talk about it on camera. Maybe, she thought, if they became friends, she would tell him. Later. No cameras.

She told him about her dogs, old Atticus and Mr. Rochester, who liked to walk Ruthie on her leash; cats, Fitzwilliam, Darcy, Elizabeth Bennet, and Lydia Bennet; the pig, Gatsby; and the scary, screaming rabbit, Scarlett O'Hara.

He told her about how his old dog tried to follow him around the house. He would sit down so the dog could rest. "Poor guy. When I see him sagging, I go to the couch, lift him up, as his hips don't work well anymore, and pet him until he goes to sleep. As soon as Herman's asleep, then I can go back to work. He likes me to sing to him."

"And do you?"

He looked askance at her, but he laughed. "Of course I do. He's been a good dog. He's probably the only one who likes my voice."

"Sing me his favorite song."

"No." He shook his head, quite vigorously, those laugh lines deepening.

"Please. I sang ballsy Christmas songs for you about drunken elves. I can't sing either. You can't be worse than me."

"Oh yes. I am worse. I sound like I'm being choked by a python. Especially not on TV. My sons would die of embarrassment. I'll sing it when we're alone."

"They deserve it for trapping you into applying to be the groom." Ruthie pretended to pout. "You could call it revenge singing."

He put his face in his hands. "Fine." He sang the song. It was one he and MaryBeth had made up. It was hilarious. It was about an old dog who had a romantic heart and fell in love with the dog next door. The song detailed all the antics and funny tricks he desperately tried so he could be with his love, including digging under the fence and jumping off the roof of a truck, his tongue wagging around, his mind on fire with passion, his legs hopping like a rabbit's. The whole thing rhymed.

At the end of the song, even the camera people were laughing. People at home laughed, too. It was a hit. They started singing the song to their dogs.

Ruthie hugged Tony. He hugged her back, and then they had a long stare between them. Ruthie kept smiling. So did he. The tension sizzled, the attraction on high. He bent to kiss her, and she kissed him back. That kiss was a doozy! A lusty smack! A lip-lock to end all lip-locks!

The viewers clapped and cheered as Ruthie and Tony smiled at each other and kissed again. Fireworks practically crackled between them! It was a wonder angels were not heard strumming their harps in the sky.

"Get a room," Melda Zamborini, eighty years old in Omaha, Nebraska, said quietly, again, as her wife sat beside her, giggling. "Get a room, you two. You need it."

8

Marry Me

Interview: Susie Whitlock

Interviewed by: Tyler, the entitled associate producer. Let's see how long it takes before he mentions Stanford.

Tyler: Hello, Susie. Thanks for talking to me. Can you tell me about yourself?

Susie: Sure. I grew up in Georgia on a farm, milking cows. We had a small dairy farm. We also grew corn.

Tyler: I understand that you have a degree from Cornell in architecture. I went to Stanford.

(See?)

Susie: Yes, I went to Cornell, but I don't brag about it because that's obnoxious. After I graduated, I worked for an architecture firm in Atlanta. I'm a woman, I'm Black, I was twenty-five years old, and I was good at what I did. That was a huge problem for many people, mostly men, in that firm at that time. Many were kind. Some were welcoming. But I heard the n-word more than once and endured other overt and covert racial attacks.

Tyler: Wow. Uh. I am sorry that happened to you.

Susie: I was, too. Sometimes I would imagine these misogynistic, sexist men as cows, and I would pull on their nipples until the nipples almost reached the ground. When they were explaining something to me that I already knew, as if they needed to educate me, or when they were condescending or stole my ideas and passed them off as their own or used my architectural plans secretly to get themselves promoted, I pulled on their nipples extra hard in my head.

Tyler: Sounds awful.

Susie: The nipple pulling or working with those people?

Tyler: Working with those people. The nipple pulling would be bad, too, but they deserved it.

Susie: I didn't mind the constant hard work. I minded the unfairness and the unkindness. I trained many of the men who were then promoted over me. They became *my* boss. Why? Because I was a woman and Black. My bosses would tell me that their clients "wouldn't listen to a woman, especially a Black woman," as an excuse not to promote me. That was legal then.

The men who were promoted over me often couldn't be trusted to build something with Tinkertoys. And there they were, my bosses. On the first day after his promotion, a man named Stel, who I had mentored, who was the son of one of the owners, which is how he got the job in the first place, said to me, "Honey, get me some coffee."

Tyler: Uh. Just because he was the owner's son doesn't mean he wasn't qualified. He was probably…uh…excellent. Skilled. And, uh, educated at an important college.

Susie: No. You are incorrect. He wasn't qualified at all. Stel got the job because he was the owner's son, like I said. He got into the college he did because his daddy and granddaddy made a significant donation as an alum. His grades were awful. He was as dumb as a turnip. If you dumped him in a shopping cart, he would be unable to figure out how to get out. Why are you blushing?

Anyhow, another young man I mentored, Xander III—he always stressed the "third" part—said, "Get me the Harrison and Miller files, Susie." He treated me like his servant when he leapfrogged over me, but I did all the work.

The owner of the firm said to me, "You're lucky we hired you, Susie. We're not racists here." But they were. Racism can be in your face, dangerous and hostile and violent, but it's also subtle, secretive, hurtful, controlling, and damaging.

Tyler: What did you do when those men told you what to do?

Susie: I gave Stel a cold cup of coffee swimming in salt and told him he had been promoted over me because he was a spoiled white male and the son of the owner, not because of his skills or work ethic, and he should remember that. I reminded him that he had flunked out of college his sophomore year and no other firm would have hired him.

I told Xander he was one of the most incompetent architects I'd ever seen, and he should stick to baking Bundt cakes so no one would die when his buildings collapsed. I told the owner that the entire place was filled with racists and that he couldn't see it because he was a white, dense man who didn't want to see it, who wouldn't allow himself to see it, and that he was a racist himself, which prevented him from seeing the truth, and then I left and started my own firm.

Tyler: How did it do?

Susie: We're very successful. Most of the women I hired at the start are still with me. I have forty people who work for me currently. Funny enough, several of the men who were promoted over me later asked me for jobs. I had been propping up a number of lazy, untalented men at the previous firm with my work, and when I left, the quality of their work dropped like a bomb, lawsuits were filed, and their clients came over to my firm. One of the buildings they designed literally collapsed during construction. It was all over the news.

The owners of the firm asked me to come back. They came to my office. I told them absolutely not. I explained how their behavior toward me had been appalling and hurtful. They were shocked. Then they apologized. Their firm crashed about six months later amidst two lawsuits.

When Stel came to me for a job, big smile, loud and friendly greeting, like we were best friends, I said to him, "Honey, get me some coffee." Xander came for a job, too. I said to him, "Xander, get me the Harrison and Miller files." Xander laughed—nervously—as if I were kidding. I asked both of them to apologize to me for how they treated me. They did. I told them that I would sooner hire drunk camels than their pretentious asses and to get the hell out of my firm.

Tyler: Let me look at the next question Shonda and Pearla gave me to ask you… Where is it… Here it is… Wait a second… Here… I've read that your firm designed and helped build a dorm for homeless people.

Susie: Yes. We spend billions on helping homeless people every year in this country, but we don't build them homes. What kind of craziness is that? My firm, pro bono, designed a dorm-style building for homeless people. A hundred dorm rooms, about one and a half times the size of a standard dorm room at a college. We also donated money to have them built. The city, the feds, and other philanthropists also pitched in. Each room has two huge windows. They have a bed, couch, table, and two chairs. There's a microwave and small fridge. Each room has a bathroom.

I cannot tell you how grateful these people are not to be riding subways all day, not to be living outside in a tent, not to be beaten up and attacked, not to have to worry about freezing to death or going hungry. They have a roof. They have heat and air conditioning. They have a bathroom and food. How can people who are homeless, who are often suffering from mental health issues and/or addiction, or from PTSD, get better if they don't have their own home to be safe and warm in? It doesn't happen. The dorms make new lives happen.

Tyler: Why did you decide to apply for the show?

Susie: I want to fall in love. If not here, maybe somewhere else. I wanted to do something outrageous, too. What is more outrageous than going on a reality TV dating show? I want to open up my mind and step away from the stress of life and see who I am now. Who am I in my older years? Who do I want to be in the future? What do I need to change about myself? What do I need to rethink, reanalyze? I want to live more, worry less. I want to have fun.

Tyler: Thank you, Susie. I learned a lot from you today.

Susie: Thank you.

9

That night, there was another I Do ceremony at the lodge.

The golden spotlight turned on above Ruthie's head. She walked down the pink carpet "aisle." Tony said to her, "Do you wish to continue our walk down the aisle?"

"I do, Mr. Handsome." He handed her a bouquet of purple orchids with lavender ribbons. They smiled at each other, warm as hot chocolate, as if they shared a secret. The smiling went on for a little bit longer than one might expect.

Jackson, beside Tony, beamed at Ruthie.

Four women went home.

"And then there were sixteen," Ruthie said under her breath. She thought again of Agatha Christie. At least the women here were not being poisoned. You could live through a rejection.

Tony came up to her right before the end of the evening. He winked at her. She grinned.

"Good night, Ruthie."

"Good night, Tony."

She lay in bed that night, staring at the ceiling. She hadn't come on the show to fall for the groom. She'd come because she wanted forgiveness and reconciliation with Willow and Lucy.

But...Tony Beckett.

He was a manly man built like a tall tank. He would keep a woman warm at night. Her heart might have skipped a beat. Her breath might have caught in her throat. She might have imagined him naked. She might have imagined him in bed naked but with his cowboy boots on. She knew she did not have a perfect body. She had a feeling that he would not be expecting perfect. But she was too old to worry about that stuff anyhow, and she knew it.

"Stop it," she told herself. "Don't daydream about a romp in bed. There are gorgeous, smart women in this lodge. He'll choose one of them."

She went to sleep, but Tony Beckett danced through her dreams, smiling at her as he twirled her waltz-style inside a library, their horses out front.

Tony couldn't sleep that night. He was staring at the ceiling, too.

He kept thinking about Ruthie. There had been an instant attraction from the second he smiled down at her the first night. *Instant.* What was the word he was searching for, he who would not consider himself a romantic? Electricity. Fire. Connection. Passion.

What was it? Why would one feel electricity and fire with one person but not the next? How did you explain it?

Ruthie was so feminine. She would keep a man warm at night. His heart skipped a happy beat. Every time he was around her, his breath caught in his chest. He imagined her naked. He imagined them naked together in his huge bed in Eastern Oregon. She had a perfect body. He felt guilty for thinking that. He knew there were a thousand more important characteristics about Ruthie, but she was beautiful. Significant cleavage. Curvy.

He tried to think about how he felt about the other women.

He couldn't concentrate. His thoughts immediately turned back to Ruthie as if she were a magnet to his brain. It reminded him of when he'd met MaryBeth. It'd been a rush. She'd taken over all his waking moments. He'd smiled and laughed more. He couldn't wait to see her again.

It was, miraculously, happening again, with Ruthie.

He was a practical, sensible, pragmatic, reserved man.

But what was going on with Ruthie, well, he'd been here once before.

He fell asleep, and in his dreams he and Ruthie were riding his horses through his ranch, a sunset in the distance, books ready to read when they returned to his log cabin.

"Ruthie needs a lot of face time," Shonda said late that night, back at the hotel.

"Definitely," Pearla agreed. She passed over a bag of potato chips, which were on their list of "healthy foods." Potato chips were better than the jellybeans they'd eaten for breakfast.

"We got stats in on the first show already. The viewers are loving her," Shonda said. She drank from her wineglass.

"She's sincere," Pearla said. "She's taking a chance, a dare, to be on the show. She says the most outrageous things."

"I wish she were my grandma," Shonda said. "I want to be a crazy grandma."

"I wish she were my mother," Pearla said.

They watched the most recent film together. They smiled and fist-bumped each other.

"Most successful season ever, I'm betting," Shonda said.

Pearla chuckled when she watched the scene again where Tony kissed Ruthie. "Damn…"

"It's encouraging to know that at seventy years old I'll still smolder with a man," Shonda said. "That I'll still feel lust. I mean, if Ruthie does, there's hope for me."

"Those two could catch on fire together," Pearla said. "Poof! Keep the fire extinguishers ready to go."

They laughed and ate more healthy potato chips. Then they went to their own hotel rooms and collapsed into bed and slept like mummies.

10

Tony's wife of forty years was shot during a robbery at the local market by a young man who was high on a drug that had been laced with another drug that turned people's brains inside out. MaryBeth died immediately by the apples.

Allen thought he was in a video game. He was an addict, but he was a gentle and sensitive soul who had never hurt anyone. When Allen sobered up and was told that he shot MaryBeth, he couldn't forgive himself. He was beyond despondent.

MaryBeth and Tony were friends with Allen's mother, Lisa. Their hearts had broken as they had watched Allen, whom they had known since he was three, fall to pieces because of drugs. Lisa was devastated by what her son had done.

Tony's best friend from childhood, Carl, who was the police chief, and his wife, Rosa, came to his home to tell him about the shooting, along with the fire chief, Connie, and her husband, Zane, also close friends. They held him as he cried and raged.

Life cratered for Tony, and he tumbled into a dark spiral of grief. His sons' grief, a tsunami of pain, nearly overwhelmed him, and he held the boys close. He thought he had left senseless deaths and violence on the battlefield years ago, but he hadn't. A bullet had caught up with him, only it had blasted through MaryBeth instead of him, yanking the light straight out of their lives and enfolding Tony in a black, suffocating blanket.

He was hardly able to function that first year, but he put his head up and shoulders back and toughened up because he'd been toughening up his whole life. His sons needed him. His business and his employees needed him. He did what he had to do, then spent hours riding his horse through his ranch with rain, snow, and sleet mixing with his tears.

Tony grew up in Portland, Oregon, poor and struggling. His father, George, was a factory worker after he'd served for three years in Europe during World War II. George had been a sharpshooter in the Army and had been taken captive during the Battle of the Bulge for long, hungry months where he was routinely beaten up by the Germans.

Tony's mother, Eileen, was a maid. They lived in an apartment across from Carl and his parents. Tony and Carl became best friends, their mothers always said, when they were both one year old.

When Tony and Carl were twelve, they had paper routes so they could earn money for their parents. When they were fourteen, they worked at a grocery store after school and sports and on the weekends.

Tony's parents almost burst with pride when he earned his high school diploma and was the valedictorian of his class and a star athlete. His mother had graduated from high school, but not his father, as needing to work to help support his own parents and siblings had been more important. They hugged Tony tight while tears flowed. When he left for the Army and then, later, for Vietnam, they hugged him tighter, tears flowing then, too. Carl, who won first place in the state chess competition his junior year and first place in the state science fair his senior year, followed suit.

George and Eileen, along with Carl's parents, spent much of their time praying for the health and safety of the boys when they were shipped out to the jungles and tunnels and hell of Vietnam. When they found out two years later that Tony would soon be home because of a severe leg injury, they were so grateful they could hardly stand. They were horrified that he'd been critically hurt, but he was alive. Carl soon followed him home. He, too, had been injured. He had almost lost his left arm in an explosion. It would never work the same, but he was alive.

Carl and Tony understood each other. They understood the clawing demons that followed them both home. They understood the vivid flashbacks and night terrors they both suffered from. They were best friends for life.

Tony met MaryBeth at a bar in Portland when he was twenty-four. He was in Portland for Carl's wedding. She was in town, too, for the same wedding. MaryBeth's best friend, Rosa, was Carl's bride.

Tony proposed to MaryBeth six months later, down on one knee and almost begging. She smiled and said, "Stand up, hot stuff. Yes. I'll marry you."

It was hard being an Army wife, moving from one base to another, enduring long stints apart, but MaryBeth had an adventurous spirit, was endlessly social, and made new friends quickly. It was harder on their sons to move every two or three years. But, as adults, they appreciated it. They had traveled widely around the world.

On the Army's dime, Tony earned bachelor's degrees in English and business and a master's in history. He figured he should take advantage of a free education. Tony had learned a lot in the Army. Discipline. Hard work. Self-control. How to think while under fire. How to survive. How to grieve and cry and keep in his heart the Army buddies he'd seen die. He had served on many secret missions all over the world. He had retired as a lieutenant colonel. He was proud of his service, but it had beaten him down, too. His injured leg was hurting him more and more, a reminder of booby-trapped jungles and tunnels he wanted to forget.

Tony and MaryBeth moved to MaryBeth's hometown in Eastern Oregon after he retired. After all the moving around she had done with him, she deserved to be home, he thought. Carl and Rosa were there, too, as Rosa had grown up in Grand River, friends with MaryBeth since kindergarten. Tony had a built-in best friend from childhood. Carl had left the Army after Vietnam and entered the police force.

Grand River was a small town where everyone knew one another and their grandparents. Families were friends for generations. As MaryBeth was one of six siblings, and both sets of grandparents had grown up in Grand River, she knew almost everyone. As MaryBeth's husband, Tony was enthusiastically accepted.

For years, before he'd met MaryBeth and started a family, Tony had had half of his military pay sent home to his parents so their lives would be easier. Decades later, he found out that they didn't spend any of the money. All of it was in an investment account in his name.

He bought land and a small house outside of Grand River. An older gentleman was selling his farm machinery business and moving to Florida. Tony knew nothing about farm machinery, but after Vietnam and some of the missions he'd been on, nothing scared him.

He moved his parents to Grand River and into the small home on his property after he built a larger home for himself, MaryBeth, and the boys. George and Eileen loved MaryBeth and adored being close to their grandsons. After many years of joy, they died one week apart.

Sometimes Tony would swear that he saw his late parents off in the distance on his ranch, right under a big-leaf maple tree, smiling at him, waving, looking young and in love. At first, he'd thought he was losing his mind, but he didn't see himself losing his mind in any other area of his life, so he took peace in the visions and smiled back, tears burning, grateful he'd had his parents' enduring love for so long.

After MaryBeth died, he and the boys, Carl and Rosa, Connie and Zane, and about three hundred other relatives and friends watched as the boys and Tony spread MaryBeth's ashes under the maple tree. Tony thought he would be dead in a week from grief, but that wasn't the plan for him. Carl laid his arm over Tony's shoulders. They had been friends when they were in diapers, friends through high school and through Vietnam. They had buried both sets of parents and now this. Carl and Tony cried together. Two tough men not afraid of tears.

At dusk that evening, with everyone gone except his sons, a river of tears soaking the earth from all who loved her, Tony swore he saw his parents under the maple tree, MaryBeth standing right beside them, waving at him. She looked...ethereal. Serene. Relaxed. There was a glow around all three of them, a golden mist. She blew him a kiss, and her face crumpled, and he saw that she loved him, missed him, that her pain was as jagged as his, and then the golden mist dissipated, and they were gone.

That night, Tony slumped down, alone, in one of the two Adirondack chairs on his deck, the chairs that he and MaryBeth used to sit in and hold hands and cried until he thought his heart would stop beating.

He was achingly lonely, crushed, and completely lost without his wife.

Life is so utterly awful sometimes.

11

Ruthie slept in until eight the next morning. She had to be downstairs by eight thirty. She had a quick shower and washed her hair. She put on a little makeup, not much. She looked at the camera before she put on her makeup, her hair pulled back in a pink band. "I look like death without my makeup, right? Maybe I'll come and haunt you," she said in a scary voice, raising her hands like a zombie and making ghostly sounds.

The viewers did not think Ruthie looked like death. They liked her and could clearly see her warm, friendly glow.

She headed downstairs in jeans and a turquoise T-shirt that said "Be Smart. Read Books" in silver, sparkly letters. She wore silver hoops in all four of the piercings on her ears, six silver bangle bracelets on one wrist, her silver watch, and a silver twisty bracelet on her right. A turquoise stone, surrounded by an intricate silver design, hung from a chain. The turquoise stone was from Lucy.

"Morning, ladies," she called out, but not loud, not perky—everyone always found perky people so grating.

The women said, "Good morning," and smiled. Some were eating. Others were drinking coffee.

Ruthie grabbed the largest mug she could find and filled it with coffee. "Now that's a brain starter," she declared.

"Coffee gives me gas," Pamela said.

"I get it from popcorn," Sarah said.

"I get it from watching Keanu Reeves in movies," Maria said. "I don't know why. He's so sexy."

Everyone paused on that one. Watching Keanu gave Maria gas. Huh.

"Okay, ladies," Shonda said, hurrying into the kitchen. "Please come into the living room. We're starting. The gang's waiting."

The brides were soon surrounded by assistants, camera people, grips, gaffers, boom operators—a range of people looking busy and others holding all sorts of paraphernalia.

"These lights are reminding me of my failed debutante season," Dallas said, slow and easy, no rush to her southern words. "Remember I told you about that? Afterward, my mama took to her bed for days. My father grounded me for months. He was livid. He later tried to force me to marry a man when I was nineteen. It was his best friend's son, who was as slick as a weasel, like his own corrupt daddy. I said no, repeatedly, but no one listened—again. Morning of the wedding, I snuck into the florists' van and hid. They unknowingly drove off to town with me in the back, and I caught myself a bus to Vegas. I won four hundred dollars at the tables. The gambling gods were with me. I used the four hundred dollars to start my new life as a realtor and yoga instructor. I had to waitress for two years, but I made it. I can help y'all buy a house and calm you down about the cost, no extra charge. We'll do down dogs together."

"You were kick-butt brave, Dallas," Ruthie said. "You broke free."

"Like a Tasmanian devil, though I was a Tasmanian Dallas," Dallas said. "I have an aversion to men telling me what to do." She paused. "But I think I'd be okay with Tony taking the lead in the bedroom. I'll bring the candy handcuffs and licorice whips. He can bring his smile."

This comment incited a conversation about sex toys and massage oils and, for some reason, leather.

Jackson did his regular spiel, the barely awake brides perched on leather couches, the fire roaring, even though it was summer, as the cameras filmed. Jackson had to start and stop a few times, because he'd been up with the triplets most of the night, and the poor man could hardly speak. They all laughed, and he apologized, but he finally got it right.

"Ladies, once again, eight of you are going on a date today."

They cheered.

The names were read. Ruthie was chosen.

"Hallelujah!" she said, arms in the air. "I'm going on a date with my sister wives and our groom."

Ruthie was so funny. The viewers at home laughed. Sister wives!

"I could be your sister wife," Susie said. "You build a mean Bloody Mary, and I like things that are built well."

"I could be your sister wife," Maria, the artist, said. Her work was well known in the Southwest. She'd come to the US from Mexico when she was ten, with her parents and five siblings. They'd escaped a cartel's gang that'd been trying to kill her father, a policeman who'd been trying to arrest the cartel's leader for drug and human trafficking. "We'll paint together. Maybe we'll paint naked ladies as warriors. It will be a metaphor for women being proud of themselves and their bodies and ready to fight for their own truth."

"I heard you have dozens of children, Ruthie," Velvet said. "If we were sister wives, would I have to be an aunt to all of them? Would I have to babysit? I don't think I have enough patience for that anymore. No offense."

"Dozens?" Several of the would-be sister wives turned to Ruthie.

"It's a long story," Ruthie said. She would tell them the next day about her adored children, and they would love Ruthie all the more. "And I have to go and get ready for my date with my seven sister wives and one sex god."

"As someone who was in a cult who had sister wives," Sarah said, "I'm telling you, it's a nightmare. My husband was a nightmare, too. May he rot forevermore. Even though I love you, Ruthie, I've already done the sister-wife thing and don't want to do it again. But I'm glad we're on the date together."

Ruthie whipped around to Sarah. "Oh, dear me. I hope I didn't offend you, Sarah. I'm very sorry."

"No offense taken!"

"Whew," Ruthie said. "Thank you."

"Should we leave that in?" Shonda asked Pearla later.

They decided yes, because Sarah got to have a voice and say what being a sister wife was like. They would show her personal interview directly after this scene. Tyler would need help with the questions he'd ask Sarah, as he was an imbecile with a rich daddy.

12

Marry Me

Interview: Sarah Whitemore

Interviewed by: Tyler, the associate producer, who needed help figuring out what questions to ask for this interview, as usual. He may or may not remember to ask them. Get ready for the braggy Stanford comment.

Tyler: Hi, Sarah. Thank you for being one of our brides on *Marry Me*. Uh. We're happy to have you on the show.

Sarah: Thank you. I'm happy to be here.

Tyler: Can you tell us about yourself?

Sarah: I have six children, eighteen grandchildren, and I grew up in a cult.

Tyler: A cult?

Sarah: Yes, you know what that is, right?

Tyler: Yes. It's a group of people who are brainwashed. They have a leader. It's abusive. I learned about it in a book I read in an English class at Stanford.

(You were warned!)

Tyler: How long were you in the cult?

Sarah: Until I was thirty-two years old. I finally found the strength to take my kids and leave. I couldn't tolerate my life. My oldest son was fifteen years old, and my husband told me that he was soon going to be expelled from our home and from the cult.

Tyler: Why was he going to be expelled?

Sarah: Because in our cult, all the girls were married off young. If the girls were going to be married off—forcibly married, required to marry—they wanted to marry a young man. That wasn't permitted. In our cult, the older men chose younger wives. They were given the girls as a reward for being loyal to the cult leader and/or making a lot of money for the cult in construction or concrete or real estate or some other type of business.

Tyler: Men were given girls to marry?

Sarah: Yes. They were given wives. Plural. Like one might be given cattle. I was sixteen when I was forced to marry a man named Rowland. He was forty-five. I was his fourth wife. This was not uncommon at all. They did it under the umbrella of a religion they invented and forced us to believe the leader's rules were God's words and truth.

Tyler: That must have been awful. He was so much older than you! Gross. Yuck.

Sarah: Yes, it was awful. I didn't even know Rowland, but I had to follow the rules of our religion. I was told that if I didn't, I would burn in eternal hell. My husband was an unpleasant, difficult, argumentative, egotistical jerk. I couldn't stand him. But I didn't know better in terms of having any different kind of life. We were living in a cloistered, gated community. No one was allowed in who wasn't a member of the cult. We were told that everyone outside the compound was evil and dangerous. My mother was the fourth wife of my father. She was kind but beaten down and always exhausted. I have eight full siblings and, at least, forty half siblings.

Tyler: All from the same father?

Sarah: Yes.

Tyler: To clarify again, at sixteen, you were a wife?

Sarah: Yes. I didn't even know what to expect on my wedding night, except for what my mother whispered to me in about five minutes right before our leader married us. Sex that night was horrifying. It continued to be horrifying. It hurt. I was humiliated. I was traumatized. There was no love or tenderness, only old, creepy hands grabbing at me. I became a mother nine months later. I gave birth at home and almost died because I hemorrhaged. My husband wouldn't give permission for me to go to the hospital because he didn't want the authorities to know that I was a minor and that he was a polygamist, which was illegal. Better to let a seventeen-year-old girl die.

Tyler: Let me find what Shonda and Pearla wanted me to ask you… Hang on… Oh, got it. Here's the question: How did you gather up the courage, and the means, to leave?

Sarah: I got myself and my kids into our twenty-year-old van and drove off, away from the cult. I told my husband that I was taking the kids camping. He didn't care. He told me to be home on "our night." I lived in the basement of a sprawling, ramshackle home that would never have passed inspection. The basement was dark and damp. There were mice. Rats. It was disgusting and unsafe.

Tyler: Then what did you do?

Sarah: My aunt escaped from the cult years ago after she was forced to marry a sixty-two-year-old man at seventeen. She snuck off the compound with help from one of her half-sisters who had escaped earlier. We were not allowed to talk to her. I found her number and called her. She had made a great life for herself, despite several years of hardship. She had a new, kind, and loving husband. She and her husband helped me and the kids. She hired an attorney for me, and she arranged housing for us in a three-bedroom condominium. We got new clothes at Goodwill and enrolled the kids in school. We were all so excited to have those new clothes, and we could not believe how beautiful the condo was after the trash heap we'd been living in. The kids loved school, too.

My husband was absolutely furious. He found me and stalked me, followed me in his truck, yelled at me. Banged on the door of my condo. He insisted I come back. He threatened me with a gun. Told me he would tell the police I was mentally ill and needed to be in a mental ward. Told me when he dragged me back to the compound that he would have me locked up forever, and I would never see the kids again. This had happened to other women, and I was terrified.

He told me he would fight me for custody of the kids, and then he would hide them, and I would never see them again. My attorney and the police got involved and arrested him for harassment, among other charges. Being arrested was the only thing that made him back off.

I started working at my youngest children's school in the cafeteria as a lunch lady and, later, as an aide in the classroom. I started to provide for my children. I even provided their health insurance. I was very proud. My attorney and the courts forced my ex-husband to pay child support and alimony. We made it.

Tyler: Your children must be proud of you.

Sarah: I hope so. I love them all so much, and my grandchildren.

Tyler: Do you think your ex will watch *Marry Me*?

Sarah: No. He was murdered two years ago.

Tyler: Oh no.

Sarah: Why do you say, "Oh no"? He was a horrible person. He hit all his wives. He hit his children. He gave his young daughters away to old men. He kicked his sons out onto the streets, as he was directed to do by our leader. He died after he got in a fight with his brother. They literally killed each other. Shot at the same time. The brother was equally terrible. We're told not to speak ill of the dead, but why not? Why should we lie, or dismiss, or minimize the destruction some people brought to others during their lifetime, simply because they're dead? We need to stop doing that. For their victims, it's extremely hard to hear them being praised for anything.

Tyler: I didn't mean it like that. Sorry. Sometimes it felt like I was in a cult at Stanford.

Sarah: That is absolutely ridiculous.

Tyler: Yes, you're probably right.

Sarah: I am not probably right. I am right. Did you not listen to what I said?

Tyler: I listened. Uh. One more question. Did you ever marry again?

Sarah: God no. All I could see was a dangerous trap and

psychopathic control. But I saw a photo of Tony, and then I read about him, and I thought, "Why not?" He sounded awesome. And here I am. I've already met women I really like. Especially Ruthie. She makes me laugh so hard every single day.

Tyler: Good luck with Tony and thank you for being a bride on *Marry Me*.

Sarah: Thank you. And never make that comment again about Stanford being a cult. Sheesh.

13

Willow and Lucy sat on Willow's couch again. Nancy Drew lay across Lucy's shoulders like a cape. She purred. It sounded like a drill in Lucy's ears. There had never been a louder cat in the world, Lucy thought.

In the blue-black night, the stars flashed, in and out, the shadows of the pine trees shifting as *Marry Me* came back on after a commercial break for tampons and another medicine that had side effects that included sexual dysfunction, hives, constipation, heart palpitations, dry mouth, and death. It certainly didn't make a person want to take drugs.

"She's wearing the turquoise necklace I gave her," Lucy said. She wrapped her arms around herself. She had never had an estrangement with Nana before. Never. They loved each other. They talked about books all the time. They talked about everything. She sniffed. She had been so mad at Nana for what she'd done. It had been so manipulative and sneaky. She was still a little mad, but maybe it wasn't all at Nana. Maybe she was mad at herself, too.

"I noticed," Willow said. "The silver bangles are from me. It's a message to us. Here, have some lemon cake. I watched a cooking video by Olivia Martindale where she whipped this right up, and then I made it with her recipe."

"I love Olivia," Lucy said. "She makes cooking and baking fun. When she set her stove on fire accidentally last week, I laughed until I cried." She started to snuffle and sniffle. "I'm not laughing now. I don't want to be in a fight with Nana." Being in a fight with Ruthie wasn't the only reason that Lucy wasn't laughing. There was another issue, too. Another person. She'd had a fight with him, too.

"We'll talk to her when she gets back."

"I was so mad, Mom," Lucy said. "She shouldn't have done that."

"She overstepped. Went too far."

"She did, but..."

"It was all out of love and concern for you."

"I know." She put a tissue to her nose and made that honking sound. Nancy Drew purred like a jackhammer. Outside, the owl hooted. Lucy thought she heard its wings through the trees. "Here, let's have a shot."

They clinked their shot glasses half filled with Deschutes Family Tequila.

"Bottoms up," Willow said.

They put the bottoms up.

"It's like watching a comedian who is also a movie star," Willow said as they both laughed so loud at something Ruthie said that Nancy Drew meowed in protest, nearly blowing out Lucy's eardrums.

Lucy burst into tears. Her mother slung an arm around her.

Nancy Drew missed Ruthie. This time she meowed in sadness.

It was a shiny, sunny day in Whitefish, Montana. The mountains showed everyone who was boss as they towered over the town. An art show in the park brought out hundreds of people. Boats puttered around on the lake, and people set out on hikes.

The bears in Glacier National Park were alive and well, searching for berries, and only one hiker had to make a run for it when he turned a corner on a trail and nearly bumped into a papa bear. The bear wasn't that hungry, so he didn't pursue the petrified hiker. Plus, the hiker was too thin. Almost all bones. Not worth the trouble. He would catch fish instead. Certainly better than eating that piddly human.

The first activity for the groom and his eight brides?

Ax throwing.

Ruthie wore a dark blue T-shirt with golden daffodils from Willow and a silver charm bracelet from Lucy. The bracelet had the following charms: dog, rabbit, pig, cat, lamb, heart, book, pencil, girl and boy (for her kids), cowgirl boots, tequila bottle, a D for Deschutes, an O for O'Hara, and a rattlesnake for Rattlesnake Lake. She wore dark jeans that "plumped up" her butt, and she carried a puffy red jacket in case it cooled down in the evening. She, Willow, and Lucy all had puffy red jackets.

Their ax-throwing guide, Charlie, a six-foot-tall woman who formerly competed in the Olympics in archery, took the nine brides out to the woods. Jackson was there, as were Shonda and Pearla and a pile of crew members. Charlie showed them how to throw an ax at the bull's eyes of a target. Charlie hit that target like, well, an ax-wielding warrior.

One woman after another failed, the ax being thrown straight into the ground or way off to the left or right. It was a wonder no one was beheaded.

Then it was Ruthie's turn.

"You can do it, lady!" Sarah called out.

"Come on, Ruthie!" Susie said.

Ruthie smiled. Then she stopped smiling. She stood still as Tony watched. In fact, he'd been watching Ruthie carefully from the moment he met the ladies at the front of the lodge. She was always so cheerful. The other women liked her. That was important to him. Other women had liked his first wife, too. He knew women were smart and discerning and could see things that men couldn't. That they liked Ruthie told him a lot.

Ruthie threw that ole ax like it was nothing. It spun through the air, handle over blade, and whack—it landed smack in the middle of the bull's-eye. The other women jumped up and cheered. Tony smiled.

"Don't ever tick me off when I'm holding an ax, Tony," Ruthie told him as he gave her a hug.

"You can be sure I never will." He held her longer than he did the other ladies, but not too long—that would be impolite.

He and Ruthie had about twenty minutes alone after the ax-throwing activity, the cameras catching all, as they did with Tony's other conversations with the other brides.

They talked nonstop, quickly, as both wanted to tell the other about their day, their thoughts, and they wanted to hear what the other's thoughts were, how their day was going. If you had asked them later what they had talked about, they probably would not have remembered, but they would have remembered that the energy was electrifying. Tony snuck a kiss. Ruthie snuck one, too. The electricity went up a hundred notches. One could almost see lightning strikes in the shapes of hearts between the two.

The groom and his brides went to lunch at a brewery. Ruthie had the best time. She didn't sit by Tony, but then, she hadn't wrangled herself into a seat by his, as other women had, with only two elbows flying and one hip swinging. She'd thought two of the women might get in a shoving match in their eagerness to eat their salads by Tony.

She sat by Velvet and heard her stories about being the daughter of a stripper. She asked questions of Maria about her art and how she made it. She talked to Pamela, and Pamela told her how she'd had to climb out a back window of her home with her children to escape a bad marriage in her twenties. "I prefer the alligators that sometimes swim in my pool over my first husband."

Ruthie had pasta with tomatoes, pesto, and Parmesan and then ordered dessert—chocolate pie. The other women were passing on dessert, not wanting to seem like they ate like whales in front of Tony, and Ruthie said, "Come on, ladies! Let's live and enjoy! Dessert is a stimulant for the libido anyhow. Everyone knows that."

Not everyone knew that, but the ladies grabbed the menus again and ordered desserts. They wanted stimulated libidos! They traded desserts to sample one another's and passed them around the table.

"That," Sarah said, "was the best meal I've ever had with other women. Had my sister wives been like this, my life would have been so much better."

Then she teared up, and Ruthie and Maria gave her hugs.

Tony, at the end of the table, was bowled over by Ruthie. Every time he saw her, he learned something new. He could feel himself opening up to her. He was starting to trust her. There was something genuine, authentic, and completely honest about her. He looked forward to talking to her again. He wished they could talk without cameras lurking like vultures.

He listened to the women around him chat. He tried to talk equally to all the women, but eight women at once was so intimidating. He had never talked to this many women at one time. He hadn't talked to more than two women at a time, he didn't think, ever. He was interested in them and their lives and how they thought, so he asked questions, but at the end of the table sat Ruthie.

He could tell that she hardly remembered he was there. Well, a couple of times, she beamed at him, like sunshine, and he smiled back, but she was busy talking to the other women, laughing, listening, completely engaged. That was another thing he liked about her—she was completely engaged in life. She made everyone feel important when she talked to them. All her attention was on that one person. She listened, and she was... What was the word? Vivacious.

Ruthie laughed then, full throttle, full of vivaciousness.

It was like getting hit by a bull. But this bull was short and had blondish-whitish curls and waves in her hair and deep dimples and a smile that said, "Let's go have fun and maybe get into a little trouble."

He tried not to stare, but she was...stacked. He wondered if they were real, and then he wanted to hit himself in the face. It was not his business. But her figure... She was a knockout. No question about it. Her legs were long, too.

Stop it, Tony. She is not here so you can assess her body.

He swallowed hard. That was true, but he hadn't really *noticed* any woman at all in decades, since he met MaryBeth. Ruthie was the first.

He glanced away and focused his attention out the window for a minute. The mountains were awe-inspiring, the sun glinting off patches of bright white snow. They were taking the ski lift up. He would sit by Ruthie. Shonda and Pearla had asked him to choose someone. He would ask Ruthie for her company. Hopefully, she would say yes.

Ruthie was making him feel like he still had life to live, that he could be happy once more.

She laughed again. He laughed, too.

"Ruthie," he said as they stood in the lift lines at Whitefish Mountain Resort. "How about you and I take a gondola up together?"

"Yay!" she said, putting her fists in the air. "Yay and yes."

The other brides standing in line with Ruthie and Tony wanted to groan or throw a tiny fit, but they knew not to. The cameras were rolling. It would be so embarrassing if their grandchildren saw the fit!

The gondola whipped around, and four brides got in, the next gondola took three, and then Ruthie and Tony climbed into the third gondola with Shonda, Pearla, and a camerawoman named, appropriately for this occasion, Valentina.

The mountains stretching far and wide were spectacular. Nature was spectacular. If the five of them could see around a bend or two, they would see a cougar sleeping in a tree, an owl's eyelids closing, and a rabbit burrowing down in a hole. Nap time on the mountain!

Ruthie turned around and peered behind them to see the Rocky Mountains in the distance, one rising after the other, their tips jagged or triangular, the blue sky and mountains meeting in the middle, clouds puffing about here and there. The Swan Mountains, gray, white, and blue, stretched alongside, while the charming town of Whitefish lay below, right out of a postcard.

"It's incredible. I love being outside," Ruthie said. "Nature is so peaceful. You can think when you're in nature. Your thoughts are calmer, clearer. I love to read my books on my back deck. The quiet does something to your soul, don't you think, Tony?"

"I could not agree more," Tony said, and that was the truth. This was one more thing he liked about Ruthie: She was a country lady. They talked about Ruthie's yellow house, and the animals and birds she saw flying and trotting through her property.

"I love being outside on my ranch," Tony said. "I watch the weather coming in, the storms and rains and snow. The changing seasons are right in front of you when you live in the country. They're not blocked by cities and freeways and buildings. I've seen bears, bobcats, beavers, elk, mule deer—"

The gondola suddenly screeched to a halt with a grinding noise, metal on metal. They swung back and forth, like a crystal on a chain. Shonda, Pearla, and Valentina, not country ladies, gasped.

"Huh," Ruthie said, smiling. "Is this when we realize we're in a horror movie, and the gondola wire is going to snap, and soon we'll be plummeting down the mountain while I'm incoherently screaming?"

Shonda, Pearla, and Valentina froze in fright at the image. They did not want any snapping wires. They did not want to scream incoherently.

"I don't think we're in a movie. I think we're on a reality TV show. At least that's what they told me," Tony quipped.

Pearla made a squeaking sound, like she couldn't get air through her throat. She sounded like a scared mouse.

"I don't think it's anything. They're probably letting more people on," Tony said, his voice low and reassuring. But he wasn't sure. They were halfway up the mountain, and that grinding noise had been loud. He'd been here before, and he'd never heard a grinding noise like that, even when people below were being loaded up.

Shonda grabbed Pearla's hand. Pearla squeezed it. Valentina couldn't hold anyone's hand, because she was holding the camera, but she would have if she could have. The three of them lived in Los Angeles and never skied. They didn't like chairlifts, and this gondola, to them, women raised on the beach, was like an open-air nonmoving airplane. The sky could almost be touched. The mountain was *right there*. When they dared to peer over, whoa! They were up *way too high*. The only time they wanted to be this high was in an elevator that opened up into the lingerie section at the mall.

The gondola swayed again.

Shonda and Pearla tightened their grips on each other. Shonda held her breath. Pearla exhaled, a mouselike whimper escaping.

Boom. Their anxiety was triggered and running loose.

"Do you ski, Ruthie?" Tony asked.

"Yes. My motto when I was younger was 'the faster the better.' The motto now is 'don't fall and break your tailbone, as you still need your bottom.'"

Tony laughed, and the gondola lurched again, then stopped, the grinding noise deeper, heavier. The gondola, once again, lurched forward, then back.

"Do you still think this is normal?" Pearla asked Tony, hope in her voice.

Ruthie didn't think this was normal, but no need to alarm anyone.

"I think everything is fine," Tony said, so calm, like a hot toddy. But he was less sure than before. They were swaying too much, especially since there was little wind. He wasn't worried, though. Tony would need to have something far scarier happen for him to become worried. "But remember, we're definitely not falling. We're securely attached. There may be a slight mechanical issue. That's it."

They didn't know it then, but Tony was right. There had been a breakdown below. Something to do with the thingies and ring-a-lings and contraptions and gadgets and levers that made the gondolas and chairlifts go up and down.

They swayed again, swoosh, swoosh. Pearla clasped her hands together and started to pray, her voice trembling. "Look, God, I've made some mistakes. Some of those mistakes were fun, and I know you'll forgive me, but I'm hoping we can get things squared between us about the other things before I die..."

Shonda started singing a children's song about a lonely kitty and a lost butterfly who became best friends. "It's what I do when my anxiety gets away from me," she whispered, then went back to the song, her knuckles white on her seat, her knees knocking together. "Meow, meow!" she purred as the sweet song continued.

Valentina clenched her teeth and tried to keep the camera straight. She'd put two more mini cameras up in the gondola to get all the angles, but she needed her hands to stop shaking so the viewers wouldn't get seasick.

Marry Me would want her footage, especially if the gondola tumbled down the mountain. She vowed to herself that she would not scream out vulgar obscenities, if so. She would die gracefully, with immense bravery, especially if it were caught on camera. She didn't want her last moments to be filled with the f-word. What would her grandmother Thelma say? Thelma would be so embarrassed. She was a Christian woman and read her Bible every night. If the f-word wasn't in the Bible, then it should not be said aloud!

"Are you three all right?" Tony asked Shonda, Pearla, and Valentina, his voice so concerned and gentle.

The gondola wobbled up, then wobbled down, then side to side. A scraping sound, like steel nails on a chalkboard, was added to the grinding noise. It was as if they were in a deathly snow globe, and some bratty kid was shaking it.

"It's going to be okay," Tony said. "It really is. The gondola is not going down. It's hooked into cables. Totally secure. It will be fixed within minutes. These things happen, and they know how to fix it." He glanced at Ruthie. She didn't seem worried.

"Oh dear," Ruthie said. "You all look a tad pale. Everything will be fine." She reached over and patted their knees. "I'm sure we'll be on our way in a few minutes, and we can get up to the lodge, and you can have a series of beers."

They nodded at her. A series of beers would be calming. Maybe they'd pour one over their heads to cool the anxiety down.

Valentina's hands shook again on the camera.

"Why don't you take a break and put the camera down, Valentina, and breathe? You'll feel better," Ruthie said.

"Okay," she said. "I will. But don't say anything interesting, you two. I want it on camera."

Ruthie and Tony agreed to be boring and talked about their lives in Oregon, what their hobbies and interests were, their favorite TV shows and movies. They had so much in common, including a love of reading. They talked books, too, which was like verbal sex to Ruthie.

When Valentina was calmer and did not believe her graceful death was imminent, and the gondola stopped its knee-knocking swaying, Shonda asked if they could talk about their former spouses so the viewers could get to know their life stories better.

"Sure," Tony said as Valentina hoisted the camera back up, her hands still trembling a bit. Tony turned to Ruthie. "Can you tell me more about your husband, Ruthie? His name was Russell, right?"

"Yes." Ruthie paused. She didn't know if she wanted to talk about her *first* husband, Wayne. Russell, her darling second husband, had known all about Wayne. He'd been there to literally sew up the damage, and later, when they met again, she had told him everything. She'd told Willow, too, as she had a right to know about her father. Two of her best friends, Helen and Alice, knew what had happened with her first husband, and so did members of the Deschutes family, but she rarely talked about that part of her life. It was in the past where it belonged, locked away, like secrets in a box.

But now she was seventy years old so she reconsidered. Would her story help other women? Would it give them courage? If she didn't mention what had happened to her, would she be lying to the viewers of this show by omission? Were they owed that information? If they didn't know, would they think she'd had a perfect life with a perfect doctor husband? It wasn't true. No one had a perfect life.

She took a deep breath.

"Russell was not my first husband."

"No?" Pearla rasped out tightly as the gondola shuddered.

"No, he was my second husband. My first husband beat me."

Shock showed on Tony's face, then fury, then sorrow. "I am so sorry, Ruthie."

"Me, too." She told her story.

Ruthie Deschutes O'Hara had not had a perfect life. In fact, her first husband had nearly killed Ruthie and their daughter, Willow.

14

On the day that Ruthie met her first husband, two vultures were circling in the air above her, diabolic and creepy. It was strange to see them in the city, floating amid the tall buildings of Portland. One would have thought they would be out in the country, up in the mountains and hills, waiting to feast after a kill by a cougar or wolf. Ruthie didn't notice them, though. If she had, she might have seen them as a mystical warning, a message of doom. Her family often looked to nature for warnings, but she had more important things on her young mind.

Ruthie was busy being swept off her feet by a man named Wayne Millson. She'd met him at a music festival on the riverfront the day after her high school graduation in early June. She was eighteen years old, had piles of blonde hair, bright blue eyes, and a curvy figure. She was with her best friends Helen and Alice. It was 1967. Their skirts were short, their beads colorful, their headbands groovy.

All three girls would be headed off to the University of Oregon in the middle of September. They were excited. They heard the parties were a blast and the boys cute. They would be free from the small town of Triple Mountain! They were going out into a wide new world filled with adventures. They were not abandoning their protests against the Vietnam War. Too many of their friends had been drafted and shipped off. Two would never come home. They *all* needed to come home. The government needed to stop lying to them, and the corruption needed to stop, too.

They also supported the Civil Rights Movement. They were

appalled by how the police, how politicians, how people in general fought so hard to keep Black people down and in "their place." They were against racism, discrimination, segregation, and sexism. The country was burning, and they leaped into the fire. They were aware, and they cared.

They would get an education, they would wear their go-go boots, and they would work to make the world a better place. They didn't know if they would get married. They probably would. They probably would have homes and children. Someday. But they vowed to one another that they would remain independent. They would be different from so many of their mothers—although not Ruthie's. Ruthie's mother was a fearless warrior woman. But they would not allow their male-dominated culture, or the church, to dictate who they were and who they could be in the future. They would not allow a husband to smother them and smash their dreams.

Wayne, swoon-worthy and sexy, was twenty-three years old. Ruthie met him when she and her friends were dancing in front of the stage, a rock band banging away, their short skirts swirling.

Wayne flattered Ruthie with love and compliments…and then smashed her

dreams—but he did it slowly, carefully, so she wouldn't know the evil that was descending. Ruthie was intellectually smart, but she was not smart enough to recognize and do battle with a malignant narcissist. Who is?

She had had no experience dealing with a narcissist. She had come from an untamed, rowdy, and happy family. She had never been in love. Yes, the boys at high school had asked her out on dates, and they had been kind and fawning, but they hadn't been *men*. Wayne's attention was unrelenting, romantic, passionate. He talked to her during the whole festival, asked her questions about herself, her plans, her dreams, and he was intensely interested in her answers. He told her she was "the most beautiful thing I've ever seen."

Wayne was older than the boys she knew. More sophisticated.

Suave. Smart. He had graduated from a fancy college, he said. He worked in Portland, the big city with the big lights. He had a fast car. He said, with superficial embarrassment, that his family was wealthy. They lived in a mansion in the hills of Portland. They belonged to a country club. They belonged to a golf club. After the music festival, Wayne showered Ruthie with flattery and gifts, indulgent smiles and kisses, when he came to visit her in Triple Mountain.

He met her family in their three-bedroom log cabin home overlooking Rattlesnake Lake. They didn't like him.

"He's a snake," Grandpa Jovie, her mother's father, barked out. "Stay away from him." He crossed his arms over his massive chest and glowered.

"I don't trust him," Grandma Maybelle, her mother's mother said as she warmed herself in front of the stone fireplace. She was famous in the family for her outdoor survival skills. "You can do better, young lady. Much better."

"Go to college," her mother, Hazel, said, wielding a spatula. She was flipping steaks. She thought about flipping Wayne onto his butt. "You're smart, Ruthie. Don't mess this up by staying with slick Wayne. Go find out who you are and what you want to do with your life. Did I already say do this without Wayne? I did? Say goodbye to Wayne."

"Drop him," her father, Raymond, said. His eyes strayed to his gun cabinet, as if to reassure himself they were still there. He had built this solid house with his wife and brothers, uncles and aunts, and he didn't want Wayne in it. "He's dangerous."

"Ruthie, what the hell are you doing?" her cousin Buddy asked. He had a deer in the back of his truck. On the front seat he had his beloved violin. "There's something seriously wrong with him. It's like the guy has rabies. He stares at you all the time. He follows you around. He's possessive, like he doesn't trust you to be out of his sight. He's a snob. We were talking to him, and he talks like he knows everything. He smirks. He brags."

"He even started telling us how we should run our tequila

business," her cousin Hilda said. "As if he would know anything about it." She grabbed a blue quilt off the couch and wrapped herself up tight in it. She did that when she was upset.

"Or that we would need help," her cousin Shaley said. She was a whiz with numbers. "He talked to Hilda and me as if he had to tell us what to do because we're silly little women who would need his knowledge and wisdom. We disagreed with everything he said, because he was wrong, and he got all flustered and angry. He even said, 'Look, ladies, I know what I'm doing. I'm trying to teach you something.'"

"I told him we didn't need him to teach us anything," Shaley said. "His face turned bright red, and he clenched his fists, and I told him if he took a swing at me, he would end up half dead and ready for our pet possums to eat him."

"Wayne's smart," Ruthie said, her voice wobbling. This wasn't going well at all. "He was trying to be helpful. He has a degree in business."

"He should not run any business," her father said. "He doesn't know what he's doing. I'd hire my horse before I'd hire him."

She pleaded with her family to come around.

They would not come around.

The Deschuteses were all stubborn. It was in their blood. Everyone knew it. There wasn't a compliant, obedient, shy, or unopinionated Deschutes on their homestead anywhere. That's why they had a wee bit of trouble getting along now and then.

Wayne kept pushing Ruthie to have sex. He grew angry when she said no…and no, and *no* again. She was a virgin. She was waiting until she was with someone special. After he simmered down, he went back to being charming and attentive. He told her she was "smart enough," that she "didn't need college," that they would conquer the world together.

Three weeks before Ruthie left for college, he forced himself on her. He took her to dinner, continued to pressure her to have sex, saying she had to "put out" if he was still going to be interested in her.

Ruthie said, "Don't tell me what to do," and, "I'm sick of you pushing me to have sex," and, "I've already told you that I'm not ready to have sex with you."

He backed off, apologized, then drove down a deserted road so they could make out. Ruthie would make out, but nothing more. She was, finally, seriously questioning her relationship with him, wondering if she had temporarily lost her mind. He started kissing her, and the physical attraction she had for him bubbled to the surface. It didn't boil, like it used to, but there was a bubble. Maybe three bubbles.

The bubbles burst forever when he unclasped her bra and shoved his hands up her shirt, gripping her breasts too hard, his fingers pinching.

"No, Wayne!" She started to fight. "I said no!"

"Don't tell me no." He reached under her purple miniskirt and ripped off her underwear.

"Stop it, stop it! Damn it. Get your hands off me, Wayne. Let go!"

He panted as he told her he loved her (as if that were a reasonable excuse), they would be married soon (as if it didn't matter that he was forcing himself on her, because she would soon be his wife), and to "relax, you'll like it" (because he believed his potent sexual power would be amazing, and she would soon forget, in mindless ecstasy, that he was assaulting her).

She didn't like it.

She fought. She cried. She kicked and pushed him. She tried to slap him, but he wrenched her arm back so hard she thought it would break. He yelled at her, held her down, and said through clenched teeth, "If you will stop fighting, you'll have the night of your life, Ruthie, goddammit." He was so strong.

She tore. She bled. She ached. She continued to fight and then gave up when she couldn't breathe. He collapsed on top of her, panting and groaning, his breath hot and rancid on her face, and she rasped out, her throat raw, "Get the hell off of me."

He berated her on the way home. Called her a tease. "This was your fault, Ruthie," he insisted. "You're always flirting then pulling away. What was I supposed to think? Do you admit that you led me on? You wanted it. You know you did. See how you're dressed? You owe me an apology. I don't owe you one."

She pulled herself into a miserable ball by the car door, then didn't say another word, though he continued to berate her, telling her how it was all her fault. She was responsible.

At the first stop sign in town, she leaped out of the car and sprinted away from him as he hollered at her and insisted she, "Get back here right now, damn it!"

She ran the back way home, dodging his headlights as he tried to track her down and hiding behind trees and bushes, blood trailing down her legs. She snuck into her house through the back door and darted to her bedroom. She pulled the blankets over her head and sobbed, then took the longest shower of her life. She should have told her parents. They would have hunted Wayne down with shotguns, but she was so ashamed. They had told her not to date Wayne, and she had. Was she at fault? Did she bring it on herself? Was she a tease? She didn't think so, but she knew she would never see Wayne again.

It wasn't long before Ruthie missed her period.

She didn't know what to do. She felt trapped. Near hysterical. Overwhelmingly depressed. It was 1967, and abortions were illegal. She had heard of two girls who'd had abortions. One died in Mexico. One could never have children because the doctor who'd performed it, who had lost his license, had been drunk and caused internal damage and scar tissue.

Ruthie would be an unwed mother. She would give birth out of wedlock. She would be seen as a disappointment. An embarrassment. A disgrace. Not to her family—they were unconventional and didn't like laws or rules—but to everyone else. It was a small town. Everyone would know. She had been a standout student at school, involved in so many activities...and now she was pregnant.

Pregnant.

She refused to take any of Wayne's calls. She told her father and grandpa to tell him to go away when he arrived on their land. But Wayne waited for her to come to town. He stopped her at the grocery store and begged her to marry him. He bought an enormous diamond ring. He proposed on one knee in the ice cream aisle. He apologized a hundred times for what happened in the back of his car.

"It will never happen again, Ruthie. I am so sorry. You're beautiful. You tempted me. I got carried away."

Ruthie, angry and scared, hopeless, only eighteen years old, said no, ran to her car, and sped off. But Wayne was relentless, as narcissists are. He had to win. He had to make Ruthie say yes. He had to break her. He cried in front of her, begged. He sent flowers and love notes and letters. She started to weaken.

Maybe they could make it work. If not, she would move home. But at least she would not be an unmarried mother when her baby was born.

Wayne was delighted she was pregnant. He wanted to keep her pregnant so she would never have time to look at another man. He would forever own her. It was perfect.

They were married at the courthouse in town, just the two of them, with two random witnesses, because she knew her family did not approve of Wayne and would not provide a wedding. She told her family about their marriage that afternoon. Wayne had "business" to take care of, so he'd dropped her off on the Deschutes property after kissing her and shoving his hands up her shirt and squeezing her breasts again, too hard. She'd shoved his hands away. Wayne feared her family and their reaction. He thought they might shoot him. Best if Ruthie faced it on her own.

Her family was furious.

"You did what?" her loving, caring father said, his hands on his hips as he
stalked around their home, his face flushed. "You married that fool? You're supposed to go to college in a couple of days! And that sniveling crook dropped you off so you could tell us yourself, without him. What a coward."

"Damn it, Ruthie," her mother said. "I cannot believe you married him. He's your

first boyfriend! You shouldn't marry your first boyfriend!"

Her husband was not offended. "She's right, Ruthie. Why didn't you listen to her?"

Grandma Maybelle sat close to her and held her hand, calm, but sad. "You're pregnant, aren't you, honey?" she said with sympathy.

Her parents froze in shock.

Ruthie burst into tears. She could barely stand up in the morning because of the nausea. Her breasts hurt. She was so tired all the time. The hopelessness, the grief, and the fear were wearing her down.

Her parents both started swearing up a storm and threatening to kill Wayne.

"Did Wayne force himself on you?" Grandpa Jovie asked with rage.

At the expression on Ruthie's face, Grandpa Jovie joined in the swearing.

"We got…" Ruthie trailed off, crying, not wanting to admit the truth because what was done was done, and she was still so filled with shame and disappointment in herself. Did she fight hard enough? Could she have done something to escape his clutches? "We got carried away. I'm so sorry."

No one believed her.

Her four brothers, Stanley, Turner, Vincent, and Warner, started to cry. They were emotional. That was another trait the Deschutes family had: They showed their emotions. No need to bottle them up. Men could cry, too! They were devastated for Ruthie. They hated Wayne!

"When a man forces you, Ruthie," Grandpa Jovie said, "you are not getting 'carried away.' He attacked you."

Ruthie's favorite uncle, Garth, was so mad he went to the field and shot his revolver into the air. No one flinched. They were used to gunfire.

"Stay here," her mother said. "Get divorced. Get an annulment! Have the baby. You know we'll love that baby."

"That's right," her father said. "We'll get you divorced. Your cousin Zippy is a judge. He'll take care of this." Ruthie's cousin Zippy's real name was Patrick. He was fast as a kid, so everyone called him Zippy. "You want an attorney? Call your cousin Diggy." Diggy's real name was Douglas, but he'd liked to dig as a kid, so the name stuck. Unless he was in court. Then his name was Douglas.

"I'm staying married," she said.

The silence was deafening. Then everyone told her their adamant opinion again, complete with hand gestures and pleading. No one thought she should stay married.

"Don't go, Ruthie!" her brother Vincent said. "We'll miss you! Don't leave us for Wayne the snake!"

The other brothers burst into tears again and begged her to stay home. "I'll hold the baby for you, Ruthie!" Warner said, the youngest brother, the "surprise" in the family. "I can milk it, too!"

That comment caused another moment of silence, but only a moment as the vociferous arguments began again.

In the end, as Wayne's car pulled in, her father said, "I love you, Ruthie, and when you need rescuing, you call me, and I'll come get you." He hugged her tight.

Her mother said, "Please stay here. I'm begging you. No? You are welcome anytime. Do not bring him. He is not welcome. We love you. We're here for you. I am trying not to shoot, Wayne. It is taking all my strength."

Ruthie packed her suitcases.

When she was done, her heart heavy, she trudged outside, scared, feeling like she was entering the beginning of the end of her life. She reminded herself she could leave him at any time.

Wayne was out of his car, surrounded by her father, mother, Grandpa Jovie, Grandma Maybelle, and her brothers. His face was pale. He nodded, nodded again as they let him have it, told him they did not approve of the marriage, of him, that he'd better shape up and "act like a man."

He said, "We're in love… I will always be kind and gentle with Ruthie. I always have been. I love her. She's the love of my life. Yes, I'll be a caring father." He stumbled over his words, but pride and fury were beneath them, his chin tilted up, shoulders back.

Ruthie could tell he did not like being questioned. He didn't like anyone telling him what to do. She hadn't known him long, but she knew that.

Ruthie stared bleakly out of Wayne's car, the scene of that horrendous crime, as they drove away. She left her sweet childhood home, her loving, extended family, and Rattlesnake Lake. Her family waved. She saw her father crying, her brothers hugging one another in despair.

Wayne was fuming at how her family had told him—*him*—what to do. "Who the hell do they think they are to talk to me—*to me*—like that?"

"They're Deschuteses," Ruthie said. "And they don't like you. They don't want me to stay married to you." Ruthie felt like she was riding away with the devil himself. She could see Helen's house in the distance. Alice's home was in town. They were preparing to go to college without Ruthie. She was crushed. She was depressed. She was lost.

"Why would I care?" he shouted. "They're farming hicks! Low class and poor. Uncouth and absurd. You're lucky I'm with you. Do you understand who my family is? The power and money they have? Do you know their reputation? Do you care?"

What a joke.

Deschutes Family Tequila was already successful. In the future, they would all be wealthy and employ dozens of people.

Soon, Ruthie and her family would learn the truth about Wayne's "reputable" and "wealthy" family, but it would not be in time. The damage would be done.

The vultures were back. They circled above Rattlesnake Lake, then followed Wayne and Ruthie as they drove off.

"That's a bad sign," Grandpa Jovie said, devastated, as he watched them.

"A very bad sign," Grandma Maybelle agreed, worn down to the core with grief. Their poor Ruthie!

"She'll be back," her mother said hopefully, starting to sob.

"And we'll be waiting," her father said, his voice grim, his stomach in sick knots. He hugged his wife.

The Deschutes family nodded. They prayed. They hoped.

They had a couple of straight shots of tequila.

Wayne and Ruthie headed to Wayne's dingy apartment in Portland. At first, Wayne was the same as he had been in the past—giving her adoring attention, smothering her in love and sweet words. He was better in bed in that he didn't force himself on her, but he was inconsiderate and thoughtless. Ruthie was not impressed with the sex. In fact, she didn't like it and started to wonder if she was gay. Or if she was a person who simply didn't like sex.

Wayne went back to work at his family's car dealerships, and Ruthie stayed home and vomited in the toilet from morning sickness, her back beginning to hurt, her breasts still aching, partly because of the rough way Wayne handled them.

Ruthie knew she couldn't go, pregnant, to the University of Oregon, as Wayne would never allow it and would follow her down and harass her, but she told him that she wanted to take classes at a local community college.

"Absolutely not," he told her.

"Why not?" she said. She put the dish towel on the kitchen counter.

Wayne liked dinner ready and hot by six each night. She should meet him at the door, in a dress and heels, looking sexy, a Scotch on the rocks in her hand, he told her. Every night. "That's what my father does for my mother, and you should, too."

Ruthie refused. She wore jeans and tennis shoes and T-shirts. It was her own form of rebellion.

"Why can't you take college classes? Because you're my wife, and you don't need to go to college. You'll be a mother and a housewife. You don't need an education."

"Yes, I do," Ruthie said. "I want to go to college. I want to learn. I have a lot to learn. I want to read more and write and study English and history and art—"

"Shut up! I said no! You're not going," he said, his rage flaring dynamite-quick, as if a switch had been flipped. He threw a ceramic pitcher across the room, and it shattered against the wall. He grabbed both of her arms, stuck his face in hers, and told her to, "Stop arguing. You are not going to go and sit in a class with a bunch of men who only want to get their hands up your dress. No, Ruthie. Do you hear me? No."

It wasn't long before everything was Ruthie's fault. She wasn't good enough, the apartment wasn't clean enough, she wasn't enthusiastic in bed. He compared her to other women and found her lacking. Ruthie had been raised with love all around her. She hardly knew what hit her. She soon learned.

His fist slammed into her cheek when he found out she had signed up to take

three community college classes when he was working. She stared at him in shock, pain ripping through her head and neck as she collapsed to the floor. No one had ever hit her. None of the men in her family hit women.

She moaned and wiped the blood from her face, leaning against the wall she'd crashed into as dizziness and nausea competed against each other.

Wayne's face collapsed. "Oh my God, Ruthie. I am so sorry."

But he wasn't sorry, and it kept happening. It was the story that happens millions of times, all over the world. The violence, the apology, then the makeup sex, which Ruthie never liked.

Ruthie hid the bruises behind makeup. She stopped going home. When her family came to check on her, she added more makeup and long sleeves and pants. Ruthie knew she would have to leave Wayne, but he threatened her, as violent, controlling men with personality disorders do. He threatened to kill her family if she left him. He showed her his gun, then locked it back up. He told her he would take the baby from her. He would have her committed to a mental health institution. He would tell people she was crazy.

"My father will hire an attorney, and you will be locked behind doors for years. Do you want that? My father has money and influence. We will win, Ruthie. You. Will. Lose."

She was petrified. She had not met his parents yet. He'd said they were in Paris for several months, but she didn't doubt him, her mental health shredded, her body racked with pain. Her sweet baby needed to be protected, and she worried he would punch her stomach.

Ruthie went into labor with their daughter six weeks early because of another beating. Wayne thought that Ruthie was flirting with a man in the grocery store near the lettuce and tomatoes. The beating started on her face, then he shoved her, and she landed on her stomach. Wayne left her on the floor, told her she was a "slut" and a "bitch."

Their neighbor came flying over when she heard Ruthie's bloodcurdling scream through the paper-thin walls. As Wayne slammed the door and left the apartment, he said to the neighbor, "Mind your own damn business."

The neighbor did not mind her own damn business, and she and her husband, a minister, drove Ruthie to the hospital as Ruthie bled on their back seat in the woman's arms. The husband prayed out loud, through tears, begging for God's intervention.

Ruthie gave birth in the emergency room, but the baby was blue and not breathing. The doctors and nurses thought the baby was dead, and they worked hard to save her. Finally, the baby, beloved Willow, howled in outrage.

Ruthie collapsed with relief as the doctors and nurses then turned to save Ruthie's life, blood gushing out of her like a river.

She remembered one doctor. He was young, but he was the best one there. He was competent and quick. He encouraged her, told her everything would be all right. He told her to hang on, to stay with him even when her vision went black around the edges. He was tall, wide shouldered, but lanky. He wore glasses.

As Ruthie's heart slowed, her breathing labored, she saw the white ceiling above her turn to a pure blue sky with puffy white clouds. A golden staircase shining with twinkling white lights climbed upward through the clouds.

As a girl, she had envisioned heaven, and this staircase came right out of her childhood imagination. She smiled. Heaven was real! She saw, she felt, dear relatives who had passed away surrounding her. The doctors and the nurses and the cacophony and the panic in the emergency room faded away, and she felt the love and safety of their collective embrace.

One of her relatives, Great-Grandmother Dot on her mother's side, said, "We love you, honey, but don't break your mama's heart. You stay right where you are."

Great-Uncle Micah held her hand, kind but worried, and said, "There, there, sugar. You breathe for me now. You hear me? Breathe."

Erroll Deschutes patted her shoulder. She'd never met him, but she recognized him from old black-and-white photos. He said earnestly, "Fight now, little Ruthie. *Fight.*"

His wife, Lavender, brushed her hair back and said, "Oh, my love. Be strong…"

But Ruthie couldn't fight anymore, and she closed her eyes.

Her heart stopped. She died.

The doctors and the nurses were heroic in their efforts to save the young mother. They yelled out directions, worked at lightning speed, and slapped instruments and supplies into the young doctor's hands as he frantically worked. They were a dedicated, trained, lifesaving machine.

Ruthie would not be able to have more children—she had an emergency hysterectomy—but their top goal was to save her life. When Ruthie started to breathe again, they breathed again. When Ruthie's eyes fluttered open, their eyes closed briefly in relief. When

Ruthie's head moved back and forth as she came back to life, they sagged. What a night!

The head doctor, exhausted, looked at everyone with triumph. "We did it," he said, panting. "She's going to live."

They smiled back at him, weakly. Lord, that was close! They'd almost lost her.

The doctor was young, he was new, and he was brilliant.

Ruthie later learned the name of the brilliant doctor: Russell O'Hara.

The gondola was making grinding noises again, steel on steel, scraping back and forth. The swaying started up again, too, as if the gondola wanted to swing itself through space, right in front of the mountain goat watching curiously from below.

As Ruthie told her jaw-dropping story, Shonda, Valentina, and Pearla had stopped fearing that they would soon fall to their untimely deaths. They were hanging on her every word.

"Is that enough for today?" Ruthie said, smiling. "I'm afraid I've been monopolizing the conversation."

"I'd like to hear more, Ruthie," Shonda said. She was intrigued, and crushed for Ruthie, but she needed to listen to the soothing sound of Ruthie's voice so she didn't have a panic attack. Same with Pearla. Both of them had dealt with the mental whirlpools anxiety brought on and panic attacks. They didn't like panic attacks. They didn't like hyperventilating. They liked breathing normally.

"Tell us more, Ruthie, please," Pearla said. Poor Ruthie! She stroked her throat because it felt like there was a rock in it, one of her most common anxiety symptoms, then settled her hand on her heart. A therapist had told her to place her hand over her heart when she felt herself being pulled up onto that roller coaster of a panic attack. She was to say to her heart, "Be calm. Be still. Everything is fine."

"Are you sure?" Ruthie said. "I don't want to bore you."

"Even if you tried, you could never be boring," Tony said. "Tell us the rest, but only if you want to. I'm sure this is tremendously hard to talk about."

"I would also like to know what happened next, Ruthie," Valentina said. "You're so brave." Valentina didn't have a history of anxiety, but she did have a history of depression, and she wanted to know how Ruthie found her happy ending with her doctor husband. She wanted to be exactly like Ruthie when she was her age—adventurous, funny, witty, and, most important, young.

Ruthie smiled, but it was sad. "Okay, then. Get ready. It's not pretty."

When she was done, they were in tears in that swaying gondola, but at least no one had a panic attack. Those things are terrifying.

When Wayne, drunk, returned to their apartment two nights later and started yelling for Ruthie, he was stunned to find no one at home. He pounded on the minister's door to find out where the hell she was, but he and his wife refused to answer the door. The wife muttered that she hoped God dropped him straight into hell headfirst and kept him there on a maggot diet.

Wayne had no idea that Ruthie was in the hospital. He tried calling Ruthie's parents, but no one answered his calls, which was so frustrating! Hillbilly hicks! White trash! Finally, he called the hospitals in the area. Maybe Ruthie had been in a car accident.

Thankfully, Ruthie's family had rushed to the hospital as soon as they found out she was there and stayed to protect her. When they arrived, Ruthie didn't bother to hide the bruises on her face and body, as she was exhausted from giving birth and trying not to die. Plus, she had given up the charade. She had made a life-threatening mistake. She should have listened to her family. She would divorce Wayne, despite his threats. He would kill her if she stayed, and she had a daughter to protect. She would tell her family about his threats. Her family had their guns, she had a gun, and they would be safe.

Her family saw the mortifying marks of abuse when she was lying in the hospital bed, as white as her sheets, the beloved, tiny baby in intensive care. Ruthie's mother collapsed. Her husband caught her. Her aunts sobbed. Her father and uncles looked like they all might lose their collective heads. Her oldest two brothers cried over her face, their tears dripping down her cheeks. The youngest ones were not allowed to come.

When Ruthie saw Wayne strut in, she instinctively screamed. It was a scream of sheer terror, as if every moment of the beating, every punch, had come back to strike her. She thought he would smash his fist into her face again. He might have his gun!

Wayne tried to get to Ruthie, prepared to be humble and devoted, as narcissists were so talented at pretending, but her family wouldn't let him. They stood in front of him, arms crossed, yelling, swear words flying. A nurse ran out to get the doctor and to call security, because she knew a brawl would soon start, fists flying, blood spurting, bones breaking.

"Let me see my wife. Move out of the way!" Wayne said pompously, but they refused.

The family closed ranks, their faces grim and deadly.

"Get out, Wayne," her mother, Hazel, said. "Get out before I put you in the emergency room myself."

Wayne stared at Hazel. She frightened him. Did she have one of her kitchen knives hidden behind her skirt? Still, he would get his way and get control of this situation. He would especially get control of Ruthie. This could not go on.

His superficial attention went to Ruthie. "You had the baby, honey? It's a girl? We have a daughter? Oh, Ruthie. I'm so glad. I'm so happy. The doctor said you had some problems." He did not apologize to her. He did not apologize for causing those problems. Wayne didn't pay any attention to the bruises on Ruthie's body. He didn't care. She deserved them. She had a lot to learn about how to be a good wife.

Dr. O'Hara came running in as soon as he was alerted that

"the husband who beat his teenage wife almost to death is here and furious."

Three security officers barreled in behind him and separated Wayne from the family, as the pushing and shoving, threats, and cursing, had started. The room was soon jammed, the mood throbbing and tense with the Deschutes family articulately expressing a desire to both strangle and shoot Wayne to death.

"You'll need to leave," Dr. O'Hara told Wayne. The room was not in total chaos anymore, but it was a matchstick away from another explosion.

Wayne, panting with exertion, his slicked-back hair messed up, was unnerved by the sizzling anger he saw on the doctor's face. He was also confused. What was the doctor so mad about? Dr. O'Hara, at six foot four inches tall, was broad and strong. He dwarfed Wayne not only in height but in size. The doctor didn't blink when he stared down at Wayne.

Wayne started to argue with Dr. O'Hara. "This is my wife. I haven't seen her in two days because I've been away on a business trip. I want to see her, and I want to see our daughter, alone. In fact, I demand that you all leave immediately." He glared at Ruthie's family. "Step away, please. In fact, go out into the hallway. I'll let you know when you can come back in if I allow it at all."

Several of the Deschutes family members snapped, their control gone, and lunged toward Wayne. The security guards, nurses, and two other doctors had to restrain them. More yelling and cursing ensued as Ruthie cringed in bed, trembling.

"No," Dr. O'Hara said, pushing Wayne flat against a wall with a bang. "You will not stay. Absolutely not. Did you not hear your wife scream when you walked in the room?"

Wayne rolled his eyes. "My wife is very emotional and dramatic. She has some"—he tapped his head— "mental issues. But I love her anyhow. I am trying to manage these problems along with her psychologist. I don't want to say she's crazy, as that's demeaning, but if you knew what I've been through behind closed doors, well, you might use that word, too. We all want what's best for Ruthie, me especially. She's had a breakdown and is suffering from a nervous disorder, so it has been a trying time for me."

"You are lying pond scum," Hazel said, breathing hard after being restrained by a security guard who did not want her to get hurt. "Ruthie is completely sane. It's you, Wayne. You are the one who should be locked up."

"No one believes a word of the verbal vomit shooting from your mouth," Raymond said, standing by his wife, fists clenched, face flushed. A security guard had a hand on Raymond's shoulder. He had a lot of sympathy for this father. If it were up to him, he'd let Raymond take that slick man apart for what he did to the poor girl in the bed.

"I saw the bruises—new and old—on her body when she came in," Dr. O'Hara said. "So did the nurses. She's covered in them. We photographed them. You did that. We also talked to the neighbors who brought her in after they heard her screams and found her bleeding out in the apartment. She went into preterm labor because you beat her."

Wayne's mouth dropped open. He was not going to take the blame here. No way. "That is not true. When I left, she was fine."

"I was on the floor, bleeding, Wayne," Ruthie rasped out, fear tearing through her at his very presence, but she would be brave. Her family was here now. She was protected.

"Please, Ruthie, don't lie," he scolded her. "You need your medication, and you need help. I am getting you that help, but I will not tolerate the lies." He glared at Dr. O'Hara. "Do you know who I am?"

"Yes, you're a wife beater," Dr. O'Hara said. "You're a criminal. No more than that. You almost killed her, and you almost killed the baby. You should be in jail."

Wayne seemed shocked! Baffled! "Who are you to talk to me like this? I'm calling my father. I'm calling our family attorney. By tomorrow, you will not have a job at this hospital! You will be fired for your incompetence." He pointed a finger at the doctor, but it shook.

"I will explain to the board, and to your father, the nature of the problem here," Dr. O'Hara said. "I have already called the police and explained the situation to them, too. They have been unable to locate you. You said you were on a business trip, but no one at your used-car lot could back that up. I'll let the authorities know you're here now."

Wayne swallowed hard, and his skin whitened. "There's no need to get the police involved."

"Oh, but there is," Dr. O'Hara said. "Your wife almost died in the emergency room because she hemorrhaged. You don't seem very bright, so I'll explain this situation to you in a way that even you can understand. She almost bled to death. She flatlined. Her heart stopped. She was clinically dead. *Dead.* Because of you, Wayne. We brought her back to life, but you nearly killed her."

"That's not true," Wayne whispered.

"How would you know?" Dr. O'Hara said. "You weren't here. You simply caused the injuries."

Raymond asked Wayne, suddenly so polite, if he could speak to Wayne outside. He put his hand on his shoulder. "For a moment, Wayne. How about we clear some things up? Man to man. We'll get this thing calmed down."

"I'll talk for five minutes, Raymond, then I'm coming back in to see Ruthie, and you all…" He pointed at all the seething, barely controlled Deschutes family members. "You will be gone."

The security guards decided they did not need to follow Wayne, Raymond, and a couple of other Deschutes out of the hospital. It would be better if they went to the nursery and wiggled their fingers at the sweet new babies in their cribs behind the glass.

Raymond took a swing at Wayne outside the hospital as soon as they rounded the corner of the building, knocking him flat to the ground. When Wayne got up, Raymond slammed him down again. And again. Raymond had had to resist hitting Wayne in Ruthie's hospital room, because he hadn't wanted to upset his dear daughter. She'd been through enough.

"How do you like being hit, Wayne?" Raymond asked, his

voice a roar of fury. "How does this feel?" He pushed and Wayne went sprawling. Wayne was a bully and a coward, and he was no match for Ruthie's father who everyone said was made of steel and nails. Wayne was facedown, bleeding, on the grass when Portland police arrived to arrest him.

The chief of police in Portland was a member of the Deschutes family. Chief Richard Deschutes, Dickie to the family, adored sweet Ruthie. He remembered her as a little girl wearing a beaver hat and butterfly wings while riding a horse.

There were no charges filed against Raymond outside the hospital where Wayne lay groaning like a pig. None of Raymond's or Hazel's brothers or sisters had seen anything, they told the chief. Nothing.

Wayne, who'd had trouble with the law many times, was "not credible," the chief decided, when Wayne alleged that Raymond had beat the tar out of him for "absolutely no reason."

"I think he did it to himself," Raymond said to Dickie and the other police officers. "If I had beaten up a woman, I would beat myself up, too."

"I agree," Raymond's brother Bill said. "I'd knock myself out before I knocked a woman out. Wayne's got some strong fists there, and that's how he did damage to his face and broke his own nose."

The brothers and sisters agreed. The chief agreed. The police officers thought it was highly plausible Wayne had beaten himself up.

"The man punished himself after what he did to our sweet Ruthie, poor girl," Dickie said. He clipped the handcuffs on and arrested Wayne for assaulting Ruthie Deschutes.

Still weak, still sore, still scared to death, Ruthie was released after a week in the hospital, but little Willow had to stay for another week. Ruthie never left her side. She sang to Willow, told her all about the magical books they would read together and how much fun they would have swimming in Rattlesnake Lake, hiking, riding horses, and writing stories. She told Willow all about her relatives.

She cried over her tiny miracle baby, her overwhelming love bringing her to tears. She was so beautiful, her little butterfly, Ruthie could hardly look away.

Days later, with her parents, two uncles, and two aunts who carried guns in their purses, Ruthie went home to the Deschutes family homestead, carrying Willow.

"I love you, my sweet daughter," she whispered to her. "I will always keep you safe."

Wayne was released from jail after two weeks. He posted bail. He was told to stay away from Ruthie, but he didn't want to, so he didn't. Rules did not apply to him. The bone-chilling stalking and harassment began. Wayne waited for her outside the family homestead one rainy day and followed her to town. She was with her mother and Willow. Outside Lionel's Hamburgers, he grabbed Ruthie, insisted that she come with him, that she was still his wife, and she was to obey him. Ruthie's mother pulled out the longest knife most people had ever seen, and she lunged for Wayne. He ran off.

But he didn't leave town.

Another day, when Ruthie was at the beauty salon with Willow, her mother, and cousins, Wayne was waiting outside in his car. When he saw her leave the salon, he charged up to her, his face red and tight with barely controlled wrath. A cousin called the police as Wayne shouted, "You're mine, Ruthie, so is Willow. You get in this car and come home with me right now!"

But Ruthie was ready this time, and her mother was holding Willow. "Get away from me, Wayne!" she warned. "Don't make me shoot you!"

Wayne froze, wondering if she would do what she'd threatened.

He didn't have to wonder for long, as Ruthie pulled her gun out from her pink purse. Her daddy had given it to her when she was ten. He'd taught her how to shoot.

The police were on their way, the sirens on, and Wayne took off, telling her, "This isn't over, Ruthie. Far from it!"

He sent her a letter.

I will never let you go, and you're damn stupid if you think otherwise... If I can't have you, no one can...You think you're going to divorce me? You are mine, and I will never let that happen. If something happens to your family, you're at fault. You understand that, right? Are you able to understand that you stupid girl? That baby? She's going to be mine, and you will never see her again.

Soon there was an outstanding warrant for Wayne's arrest because of the stalking and threats. He was not at his Portland apartment. He was not at work. Everyone knew he was still lurking around.

Ruthie stopped leaving the Deschutes family homestead. She shook with fear. She was always on alert, waiting for an ambush, a disaster, fearing that Wayne's chilling threats against her, her family, and her angelic baby would soon be carried out.

At three on a Monday morning, as a pack of coyotes skirted around Rattlesnake Lake and a pair of wolves slunk through the inky darkness, Wayne snuck onto the homestead and started a fire in the barn where Ruthie kept her beloved horse, Daffodil. Daffodil and the other horses were saved by two Deschuteses, Lexi and Scarlett, though the barn burned to the ground.

The Deschutes family knew this had to end.

They would defend themselves.

They would defend Ruthie and baby Willow.

Only three Deschutes family members knew *exactly* what happened to Wayne—two men and one woman. There were others who guessed that Wayne was...uh...hmm...no longer a threat to their Ruthie, but no Deschutes family member would ever reveal the secret to an outsider. Ever.

No one searched for Wayne except his employer, Terrence Marring, who owned a used-car business. Wayne had worked for him for three months, and two women—one an employee, one who wanted to buy a car—told him that Wayne tried to grope their breasts. Terrence was trying to find Wayne so he could officially fire him.

Wayne's family didn't look for him either. Wayne's parents lived on the East Coast, not Portland, as he'd said. They were not wealthy. His father was a bricklayer. His mother worked as a receptionist. They did not belong to a golf club or country club. It had all been a lie. The parents had had to call the police on their own son multiple times because of physical altercations he'd gotten into with his father when they fought because Wayne had repeatedly stolen money from them. His sister was in hiding with her husband and five children because Wayne wouldn't leave them alone.

The Deschutes family owned hundreds of acres with flower-filled meadows, rolling valleys, and forests with impossibly tall trees. The view of the mountains was awe-inspiring. There were four ponds with frogs galore, horseback-riding trails, and, at the way, way back of the property, another lake. They called it Bottomless Lake because it was so deep. Bottomless, in fact.

Concrete blocks and iron chains worked well when one needed to keep a dead body under the surface and away from Ruthie forever.

A bear watched, but he was uninterested. He was hoping he'd mate with a pretty lady bear this year. A hawk glided down and around, but she didn't care much either. She needed a mouse for lunch. A rabbit hopped away. Rabbits are sensitive about these things.

(Ruthie did not share the part about Bottomless Lake with the ladies and Tony in the swinging gondola.)

***

Diggy Deschutes rapidly took care of the paperwork, as Wayne had clearly abandoned and abused Ruthie, and the divorce went through quickly. The family line was that Wayne had moved back East after Ruthie and he had broken up.

"Good riddance!" they said.

Then the Deschutes family never spoke of Wayne again. It was as if he'd never been there.

When Willow turned one, Ruthie, who was still mentally recovering from her disastrous marriage, called the admissions office at the University of Oregon. The woman she talked to said, "Well, sure, honey. You can come and be a Duck! We'll mail you information. Do you still want to be a teacher?"

She did! Though Ruthie loved the family's tequila business, and her family had always encouraged her to work at Deschutes Family Tequila, she had a heart for kids and teaching. She herself loved school, learning, books, and talking about books. She wanted everyone to love books as much as she did. Life was nothing without books—she knew that for a fact.

She lived with her friends Alice and Helen in an apartment off-campus. They had a delightful time living together and were friends forever. Willow called Ruthie's friends Aunt Alice and Aunt Helen.

Ruthie, trying to regain who she had been before she'd met Wayne and his fists, left Willow with her mother and aunts and arranged for her classes at the university to be only four days a week. She came home for three days to see her sweet Willow and cried buckets of tears as she returned to college on Sunday night because she knew how much she would miss Willow. She majored in English because of her love of books and became a high school English teacher.

Willow, at five years old, was so proud of her mama when she graduated.

"And that was it," Ruthie said. "I never should have married Wayne. We divorced. He was not involved in my life from then on out."

Tony, whose eyes had flooded twice with tears, blinked, then blinked again. "I'm so sorry you went through that, Ruthie. You ran into a sociopath. A dangerous man."

"Yes, he was," she said.

"He's dead?" Shonda asked.

"He is," Ruthie said. "Long ago. I heard he was in a car accident back East and passed away." Ruthie did not cringe at the lie. She only briefly thought of Bottomless Lake and wondered if his skeleton was still intact.

"Good," said Tony. "Then he can't hurt other women."

The four women in the gondola nodded.

As if to conclude the story with a bang, the gondola, with another clank and shuddery, popping noises, resumed its ascent up the mountain. This time, it didn't stop. Shonda, Pearla, and Valentina sighed with relief, their anxiety fizzling away. They were shocked that over an hour had passed.

"Thank you, Ruthie, for sharing your story," Pearla said.

"You're welcome," Ruthie said. "I'm surprised I did. I hadn't planned on it. But I decided to share it because I want other women to know that the only possible way to a happy life is to leave your abuser as safely and as quickly as you can. Things will not get better, no matter how sincerely he apologizes and begs for forgiveness. He will not change. Get out. Your face is not a punching bag. Your stomach was not created so he can kick it. Don't wait until your partner beats you so hard you go into preterm labor and end up hemorrhaging and seeing your dead relatives up in the blue sky smiling at you, welcoming you to heaven. Don't wait until his rage makes you infertile. Leave."

Tony nodded.

Brave, determined Ruthie Deschutes O'Hara was his heroine.

Eight brides, one groom, and piles of employees from *Marry Me* gathered together at the top of the mountain and studied what lay below and in front of them. The view was exquisite. It went on forever, making everyone feel small, like a whisper, or a tremulous love song. Words escaped them as they stood in stunned admiration at the wonder of nature. They knew that when they died, these mountains would continue their march across the land, the sun would still rise, and the ancestors of the animals and birds now roaming the land and soaring in the skies would still be here. Surely this was a picture of eternity.

That night, the sunset would streak across the sky, a swirl of luminescent colors, magical and everlasting. A fox would stop and marvel at the display with his new partner, and a mama bear's cubs would snuggle in beside her as she admired the new sky painting. A wolf pack would watch indulgently as the little ones rolled and played together.

Love was in the air, for humans and animals.

15

Marry Me

Interview: Tony Beckett

Interviewed by: Shonda, the co-director. She's a very chill person, even with the anxiety issues. We all have our problems, right?

Shonda: How was the trip up the mountain yesterday, Tony?

Tony: As you know, we got stuck. But that ended up being a lucky thing.

Shonda: I think we all thought that we might die. The gondola kept swinging back and forth like it wanted to jump off the cables. You kept your cool, though. How did you do that?

Tony: I knew we'd be fine.

Shonda: Seriously, you weren't worried at all?

Tony: Would worrying have helped?

Shonda: No.

Tony: I was also talking to Ruthie the whole time.

Shonda: I can see by your smile that you enjoyed that part.

Tony: Yes, I did.

Shonda: How is your relationship with Ruthie?

Tony: She is… She is…one of a kind. She will always be one of a kind. Unique.

Shonda: What are three characteristics about Ruthie that are special?

(Long pause.)

Shonda: Do you need more time to answer?

Tony: I can give you a list of a hundred things that are special about Ruthie. What I'm trying to do is cut it down to three so we won't be here all day. One, Ruthie is courageous. Two, Ruthie embraces life. She sees life as full of possibilities, full of love, full of joy, and when life is heartbreaking, she fights back to that joy. She never gives up. Three, she's damn funny, and she's damn smart. You know how sometimes you're around someone and you recognize that they are much smarter than you? That's Ruthie to me.

Shonda: She's highly intelligent, that's for sure. The other women at the lodge say she's a tricky poker player and always wins.

Tony: That is not surprising.

16

The next week, when the show aired, women all over the country—women with bruises and scratches, women who had hidden their secrets from their mothers and sisters and best friends, women who were rich and women who were poor, women who were scared of their partners and how they would respond if they snuck away—finally found the courage to do what they knew they had to do.

They listened to Ruthie.

If she could do it, they could do it.

They left.

Others cheered for Ruthie. Look at this lovely, classy, hilarious, dignified, seventy-year-old English teacher. She'd had to fight for survival, too.

Everyone loved her.

Willow and Lucy sat together on the leather couch, watching *Marry Me* with Nancy Drew cuddled between them. The cat was snoring, and it sounded like a jet engine.

Willow and Lucy passed the tissue box back and forth as they sniffled and cried over Ruthie's tragic, painful story. The windows were open, and they could hear the owl hooting. It sounded mournful. Maybe the owl was upset, too.

Lucy honked. "I didn't know all that. I knew…" She dried her tears. "I knew that Nana's first husband was bad, but not that bad."

"You mean my biological, sperm-donor father?" Willow clarified. "The attempted murderer?"

"Yes, your bio father, my grandfather, the sociopath," Lucy said.

They ate Julia's Chocolates from the gold and pink box between them. They knew Julia, and she made the best chocolates they'd ever had. Chocolate was therapy, right?

"What really happened to him, Mom? You've been vague. You always said he went back East to his family. Nana said he did, too. And there was a car accident, and he died."

"It wasn't true."

"No?"

Willow shook her head and told Lucy the truth. She was an adult. She could handle it, and she knew never to tell Deschutes family secrets.

Lucy cried when Willow was done. She understood Nana a lot better now. She shouldn't have done what she did—that was invasive and overbearing, but...

"I want to talk to Nana," Lucy said. "I miss talking to her. I miss sitting here watching *Marry Me* with the three of us together."

"I miss her every day," Willow agreed as the show continued, and Ruthie said something outrageous and wise. "She's so funny..."

"Oh, she's hilarious," Lucy agreed. "Funniest person I know. No offense, Mom."

"None taken, honey."

"She's wearing the daffodil T-shirt from me," Willow said, her voice quavering.

"She's wearing the charm bracelet from me," Lucy said over a sob.

"She's wearing her sexy jeans," Willow said. "She must mean business."

"And she's wearing our puffy red jacket," Lucy said over yet another sob.

"I hope she and Tony get together," Willow said, blinking back her tears. "I like him, and I don't want her lonely and alone anymore."

"Oh, Mom," Lucy said, ingloriously wiping her tears. "I do, too."

They clinked their shot glasses and tipped the bottoms up.

That night in bed, for hours, Lucy stared out the window at the darkness and the shifting shadows, the light shining from the moon as hot tears streamed down her cheeks. Nancy Drew stood on Lucy's chest and stared down at her and purred, the noise as loud as ten buzzing bees.

Nana's story was making Lucy think.

She allowed herself to compare Ruthie's life with Wayne to her own situation as a wave of fright, sharp and prickly, swamped her.

"I could be Nana, couldn't I?" she whispered to Nancy Drew, her voice trembling.

Nancy Drew was a sharp, intuitive cat. She knew that Lucy was in the same sad situation that Nana Ruthie had been in. That was not a mystery. She meowed, three time in a row, to indicate agreement.

Lucy's phone rang. She didn't answer.

He sent a text. She ignored it.

He kept bothering her, and finally, she turned her phone off and went to sleep.

17

Marry Me

Interview: Dr. Benedetta Fields

Interviewed by: Tyler, the associate producer, who is going to be terribly embarrassed about the topic of this conversation. His education at Stanford will not help.

Tyler: Hello, Dr. Fields. Can you tell us about yourself?

Benedetta: I'm a gynecologist. I'm sixty-five. I have my own medical clinic. We serve and welcome everyone. My goal is to offer medical care to women of all ages and help them to live healthier, happier lives.

Tyler: You're a what?

Benedetta: A gynecologist.

Tyler: Wait a second. Is that spelled G-I-N-E? G-Y-N...? Is it C-A-L-L? And you spell the last part as J-U-S-T? No? Got it. Thanks. Okay. What made you interested in becoming a gynecologist?

Benedetta: I was curious about my vagina from a young age.

Tyler: Uh. Okay.

Benedetta: Are you blushing? My comment shouldn't embarrass you, young man. I'm sure you were curious about your penis and testicles.

Tyler: Uh. No. Yes, uh. No.

Benedetta: We all need to speak more bluntly about the health of our whole body, pregnancy, birth control, our sex lives, and desires and wishes in the bedroom. That's part of what I do. I help people advocate for themselves and their needs. I help women to shed the mantles of shame that we're often raised with, hammered into us through religion, strict family rules about sex, or a repressive society that insists women hide their sexuality and strength in favor of catering to men. Above all, I want women to be physically and mentally healthy.

Tyler: Okay. Uh. Can you tell us about your family?

Benedetta: We are descendants of slaves, on both sides of my family. We come from Sierra Leone and Ghana. We were brought over in the bellies of ships, where my ancestors suffered and often died. They were beaten, starved, raped, and chained. That was the beginning of my ancestors' hell. They were brought to a plantation in Mississippi, where they were again beaten, starved, raped, and chained. Not all of them survived. When slaves were freed by President Lincoln, we were still not free, especially when the KKK rampaged through with their pointed white hats and attacked. A racist society joined with the federal and state governments to discriminate and control and to keep Black people down legally, psychologically, economically, educationally, and physically. My great-great-grandparents were sharecroppers. That land was stolen from them. They were literally burned out of their home. They fled to Detroit with nothing. They started over. That land is now owned by a well-known computer company. It's worth millions.

Tyler: Uh.

Benedetta: Were you hoping I would say something lighter about my family? Something amusing or entertaining? Why? This is my family's truth, and you asked about my family. There is nothing amusing or entertaining about our history or slavery. As slaves, my family made white families extraordinarily wealthy on their plantations for over one hundred years. That money, that land, and their businesses were passed down from generation to generation. My family received nothing.

Tyler: We had to read a book about slavery in a history class I took at Stanford. We watched a film about it, too, so I do know a lot about it.

Benedetta (sighing): It would take more than one book and one movie to understand slavery.

Tyler: I got a solid education at Stanford. **(Laughs in a fake way)** I think most people would say so.

Benedetta: Dear God.

Tyler: Moving on. Can you tell us a little more about yourself or your life?

Benedetta: I was married for thirty years. Stephen died during a diving accident. He had a doctorate in biology and was a professor at Harvard. He was the gentlest, most intuitive, gracious, polite man I have ever known. He was a gift, and he was excellent in bed. Everyone deserves a Stephen. I have not been married in eighteen years because I have never met a man who I could imagine living with. Honestly, the men I've dated—even thinking about them moving into my home gives me heartburn. I prefer my friends, my cats, and my books.

Tyler: Do you feel differently about Tony?

Benedetta: I do feel differently about Tony. He's the most interesting male I've met in a long time. But I'm not twenty-five anymore, so I haven't walked into this reality show already in love and creepily possessive of the groom, as your younger contestants are. He may be for me. He may not be. Same with him toward me. We have to get to know each other. If I decided I wanted to have a serious relationship with him, I would still have to weigh that against my love for my cats and books, and he might not fit in. We'll see. He does give off healthy sexual vibes, though, which informs me he would be acrobatic and enthusiastic in bed.

Tyler: Acrobatic?

Benedetta: Yes. I'm going to go now, Tyler. This interview has gone on long enough. But one more thing: Ladies, don't neglect your Pap tests, mammograms, and colonoscopies.

18

Two nights later, there was another I Do ceremony. Before the ceremony, Ruthie and Tony snuck off to talk, like two teenagers, holding hands, only they were trailed by a wave of people—some holding cameras, some holding lighting and other stuff.

It was like the wave of people wasn't there. Their world was the two of them alone. Their conversation flowed. They talked quickly, as if they couldn't waste a blasted second. They laughed. They stared at each other. They shared. They trusted each other. It was there. They could feel it. Light blue eyes to dark blue eyes, they stared into the essence and spirit of the other and felt…a dollop of hope. A sizzle of attraction. A blast of energy, as if they were salsa dancing on the same rainbow together.

Shonda and Pearla had to pull them apart because their time was up.

Later that evening, Tony and Jackson got into place at the "altar" for the I Do ceremony. Jackson looked like he might keel over after welcoming the women and wishing them good luck. Two of the kids had ear infections. He had hardly slept in days. He could hardly speak.

When the golden light turned on above her head, Ruthie walked down the pink carpeted aisle and smiled up at Tony. He said, his voice low and manly, "Do you wish to continue our walk down the aisle?"

Ruthie said, "Yes, cowboy," and took her bouquet. It was a mix of purple freesia, white baby's breath, and pink roses.

Four women went home.

One woman was angry, and she called Tony an asshole. He seemed sad, not angry. The viewers would say that he looked like he felt guilty for hurting her. Then the woman cried and hugged him and said she was sorry, and he said he understood.

The other woman said, "At least I got free food and free tequila here. Plus, I learned new songs." She laughed. She had survived a serious illness and a car accident, and she was simply grateful every day to be "upright and not buried with worms."

"I'll teach my grandchildren the songs when I get home," she said. "Especially the one about slammin' down a cold beer while the bears watch with envy. It'll shock their parents."

Afterward, Ruthie said, in honor of Agatha Christie, the queen of mysteries, "And then there were twelve."

Ruthie was getting homesick. She missed Willow and Lucy. She missed her other thirty-one children and her grandchildren. She missed her Deschutes family out on the homestead. She missed Triple Mountain and the people. She missed her dogs—Atticus, who warmed her feet, and Mr. Rochester, who walked her—the cuddly lap cats, the curious pig, and the screaming white rabbit. She hoped Scarlett O'Hara wasn't screaming too much. It frightened the dogs so. Ruthie wrapped herself in her bedspread in her bedroom in the lodge and stared out the window at the mountains.

The stars sparkled on and off, the moon spun white, the trees whispered.

Ruthie couldn't see her, but a bald eagle flew right over her head. Her wingspan was eight feet long. The bald eagle was proud of her wings.

Ruthie thought of Tony and smiled. "Ooh la la," she said. "Ooh la la."

※

Back in Ruthie's town, Harold the hermit took his truck out to fish. He knew Ruthie was gone, and he missed her. She was like a sister to him, and he felt better when she was home. He had a gentle heart and a sensitive disposition. The world, with its noise and trouble, was too much for his mind to handle. So was his domineering family. That's why he'd moved to the log cabin he'd built at the edge of his family's property. He wanted to be alone.

The hermit wished Ruthie the best, though, and hoped that she was happy. Her husband, Dr. Russell, who'd always been kind to him, seeing him twice in his home and patiently persuading him to go to his clinic for his kidney stones, would want Ruthie to be happy, too.

He heard one of Ruthie's dogs, old Atticus, bark. He was sure the mostly deaf and blind Atticus, Mr. Rochester, the cats, and that very strange screaming rabbit missed her, too. He would freeze some fish for Ruthie and give them to her when she returned. Ruthie loved his Harold's Crock-Pot Fish Dish. There were twelve different spices in it, a separate sauce, and finely diced onions.

He glanced up at the sparkling stars as they seemed to flash on and off. They were exceptionally bright tonight. The moon looked like it was spinning through the sky. The trees whispered to him.

He saw a bald eagle right over his head.

He smiled.

※

"Hello, ladies! How is everyone today?" Jackson grinned at the women in the kitchen of the lodge the next morning. This was the most interesting season of *Marry Me* that he had ever hosted. As he'd told Henry last night, these women were funny, sarcastic, cynical, hopeful, intellectual, smart, and capable. The conversations were infinitely better with this group than the younger groups, who spent time complaining about other brides, lusting after a groom they barely knew, and then having explosive fights. The conversations on this season were deeper, more honest, mixed with wisdom and humor.

He knew some of the women, maybe most of them, had fallen hard and fast for Tony. That was not surprising. He was everyone's dream husband. Chivalrous. Calm. Measured. Plus, when Tony talked to the women, he stared right at them, his eyes not shifting left and right as most people's eyes did, searching for someone or something more interesting. Tony focused. He listened. When the woman stopped talking, he waited, as if to make sure there was nothing more she wanted to say. He thought about what she'd said, or a question she'd asked, and then he answered thoughtfully, honestly, kindly. He never focused on himself, didn't like to talk about himself. He always focused on the woman.

When Jackson asked the women how they were, they didn't answer because they had started talking about sex in the kitchen. They were so used to the cameras now, they hardly noticed them and didn't know that Jackson, handsome Jackson, devoted father of triplets, had spoken.

As the cameras rolled, the women told bawdy jokes about meeting lovers, some of them "secret" lovers, and chatted about the sexually daring things they'd done when they were younger— as in, sixty-five years old or younger—including sex in different outlandish and often public places, including a Ferris wheel, a movie theater, and the back of a Christmas tree lot overlooking a mountain. Jackson stood there, laughing, grinning, once again enjoying the women's conversation. They were so entertaining!

"How many men have you been with?" Maria asked the women. She wondered if she could get an idea for a painting out of this conversation. Maybe naked women playing on a river? Naked women dancing on top of a mountain? Naked women floating on a lake? There was freedom in being naked. She liked her ideas. Maybe she would do a series. A powerful naked-women series!

The answers on how many men the women had been with varied, from one to twenty-four.

"I've only been with five men," Carol Washington said. "The third one disappeared. He packed up all our camping gear, and poof! Gone. He's probably living like a cave dweller near a river and fishing. I've been with two men since then, each for about a year, then I got tired of them and their aches and pains and rigid ideas about what I should do for them. I packed them up and sent them out the door."

Some women clearly thought that five was a sad number. *Only five?* A few women shook their heads at this tragedy and looked at Carol—nearly a virgin in their estimation! —with pity. One woman reached across another and patted her knee. "There, there."

Others were envious of the number five. They'd been with the same man for decades. Two of the women had married high school sweethearts and had been with only one man.

Dallas drawled, "I did not appreciate the near-deathly stranglehold that we grew up with in terms of our sexuality from society, our families, and the church. We were supposed to be innocent little girls, eager to serve our husbands and earn that white wedding dress. It was one more way for men to control women. Thankfully, I did not bend to the patriarchy in that regard, and I have had a herd of devilish men in my bed, keeping me warm."

"I've been with two men," Ruthie said. "My first husband, who decided it would be best if he beat my body, and my second husband, who was a dedicated body-pleaser. As in, he pleased my body."

"Who-eee!" the other women said. Lucky Ruthie to have a body-pleaser, but only *two*? Why, it was another sexual tragedy!

"I told myself after I hit fifteen men, I could stop counting," Pamela said. "Last man I had was right before I left for this show. You know how I feel about alligators, right? For my date, I wore a dress with a faux alligator print and faux alligator heels, and I was revved up for a night of fun."

She made an alligator mouth with her hands and pretended to bite as the ladies howled.

"I'd say he was a five in bed," she continued. "No more. I'm sure he thought he was a ten. Most men think they're a ten."

The women agreed that it was so.

"There's an erroneous overconfidence in how men believe they perform in bed that women do not share," Dr. Benedetta said. "Men easily believe that their humdrum performance is exceptional simply because they are in possession of their miraculous penis, and it's inconceivable that a woman would not find it a throbbing pistol of pleasure."

"They're delusional," Velvet said. "If you tell a man he has the biggest penis you've ever seen, he will *actually believe it*. He will not realize that you are messing with him. It's a wonder their head—the one on top of their neck, not the other one—does not explode like a firework, full of undeserved ego and pride."

My goodness, the audience loved the honest conversations of the women on *Marry Me*. The men who were watching next to their wives and girlfriends, though, cringed. Were they good in bed? What about their size? Had women lied to them? Were they lying to them now? Would their head explode like a firework soon?

The female viewers were cackling—and hopeful. These "bridal" women, all around the age of seventy, had had full and rollicking sex lives that were still ongoing! Imagine that!

Shonda and Pearla wandered over to Jackson. "You seem to be unable to capture the room, my man," Shonda said.

"Yeah," Jackson said, laughing. "But this conversation is the best."

Sarah said something about leaving her husband in the cult and embarking upon a "lust run" after that in which she slept with multiple men during her first year of freedom. "Sex for me had to be endured with my cult husband. I would not move when he rolled on top of me like a pig and I'd pray that it would be over soon. I tried to pretend I was somewhere else. It hurt. I felt like I was suffocating. I always cried when he rolled back off. I didn't know that sex could be…sexy. Enjoyable. Some of the men were dull, nice but dull, but wow. A few were on fire. I liked the fire."

"I'm having a problem getting their attention," Jackson said to Shonda and Pearla. This had happened several times. "Ladies!" he said, but in a calm and polite voice.

Nothin'. They kept chatting.

"Ladies?" he said again, his voice pitched up, like a question.

Nothin'.

Maria finally noticed and said, "The man speaketh!"

"Oh, say ye, handsome man," Velvet said, following Maria's joke. "Utter your thoughts!"

He greeted them, told them he had "learned a lot" from their conversation, which he appreciated, then said, "We're going to have a vote."

"Vote for what? For whom?" the ladies asked.

"Ladies, this might be a hard activity, but we're going to put you in the first-ever Bride Voting Booth."

"What's that?" Maria asked.

"You're going to think about all the brides here, then you're going to go by yourself, to the den, and write down the name of the woman who you think Tony would be most happy with in a marriage. We will not be sharing the results of the votes with you at this time."

"What?" said Susie. "So, it's secret voting?"

"Yes."

"Will Tony know who gets the most votes?" Sarah asked.

"No, he will not. We thought it would offer insight for the viewers at home to see who you think Tony should marry."

"Can we vote for ourselves?" But they knew the answer.

"No. And we'll have cameras on you the whole time, so no trying to sneak a vote in." He wagged a finger and they laughed.

The women were, at first, a tad uneasy, then curious, then they looked around to figure out who they would vote for, and many of them knew their answer immediately. Who would Tony be most happy with?

Well, it wasn't that hard.

"Ruthie." Susie Whitlock, the cow-milking architect, said to the camera in the Bride Voting Booth.

There was actually no "booth." The dimly lit den was filled with comfortable, masculine furniture. A fire roared in the fireplace, though it was warm outside. There was a pink Bride Voting Box on a table in front of the cameras and a ballot.

Susie wrote Ruthie's name on the ballot and dropped it into the box. "Ruthie is my best friend here. I think we'll be friends when we leave, too. The other night, she showed everyone her great-grandmother's secret recipe for chili. It was absolutely scrumptious. I mean, we all got the farts. It was like we were made entirely of gas, so we had a loudest-fart contest, which was so funny. Velvet won. Ask Velvet about it."

"Ruthie," Carol Washington said, holding up her ballot. She drew a heart with Ruthie's name in it. "I want to marry Tony. He's a husband who will stay around and not disappear like mine did. We know that because he was married for so long to his late wife. But Ruthie? She's true, she's real, and she almost won the fart contest last night. Ask her about it. I should hate Ruthie, but I can't. Not because she almost won the fart contest, but because I think Tony likes her best."

"Ruthie," Pamela Topava said, staring right into the camera. "Look, Ruthie's one of the funnest people I've ever met. Is 'funnest' a word? I don't know. Ruthie would, though, because she's an English teacher. She has a huge heart. She has dozens of kids that she's helped to get their lives back on the right track. I think Tony needs a woman with a huge heart. I hope Tony chooses me. I like alligators, and I wouldn't mind if he took a little nibble out of me in the bedroom." She winked, then made the alligator mouth with her hands again and snapped them shut. "But I choose Ruthie."

"Ruthie," Dallas Grayson said. "Hell, if I were gay, honey, I'd marry that cowgirl myself, and we'd ride off into the sunset. Unfortunately, I am not gay and would like to ride Tony like a buckin' bronco. Hee-haw!"

"Ruthie," Maria Gonzales said. "I want to paint her. She said I could when we leave. She's going to come to my studio in New Mexico. I'm concerned I won't be able to capture her light, though. You know when people have that inner golden light? It shines from their faces, from their smiles. That's what she has. A light. And she asks you to join her in her light. Everyone is welcome to join." She sniffled. "She is a true friend to me, and I have not had a lot of true friends in my life."

"Ruthie," Dr. Benedetta Fields said. "I can read people, and I can read Tony. That man's a cowboy outside and a cowboy inside the bedroom. She's a lusty sort, too. She said she and her husband were a total match in the bedroom and had sex toys in their dresser drawers. I think, sexually, Ruthie and Tony are a match. But if I could, I'd still vote for myself first. Tony's the type who will always let the woman orgasm first because he's a gentleman. Remember, ladies, it's important that you take charge of your own orgasm. Don't let your man leave you lonely in bed."

"Ruthie," Velvet Hashbrune said. "I was showing her how to move around a pole the other night like a stripper, like my mama taught me. We used the skinny light pole outside the house. It was too thick, but we made it work. She got it right away. She's very limber. Now she has some of the skills to be an at-home stripper. She's got the figure for it, too. Her boobs are natural, by the way. No implants. She would have made a lot more money as a stripper than she did as a teacher. They don't pay teachers near enough…what? Did I win the fart contest? Yes, proudly, I did."

"Ruthie," Sarah Whitemore said. "If Ruthie and I had been in the cult together, we would have left as teenagers. I know it because Ruthie would have had the courage to do so. If Tony doesn't choose me, and I hope he does—I do cook and bake well, especially Vietnamese, Mexican, and Thai food—but if not, I hope he chooses Ruthie. I hope the three of us can all be friends. I would love that."

"Velvet," Ruthie said. "And not because she has a closetful of seductive stripper clothes and can rock and roll herself around a pole like an expert, which I'm sure Tony would love. I choose Velvet because of the life she's led, what she's overcome, her strength, witty humor, astute business acumen, and non-judgmental character. Plus, she won the fart contest. That was impressive, by the way. She and I will be friends forever, I know it. We've already agreed we're going to party our way through Europe on a river cruise when we escape *Marry Me*. We're going to wear bikinis and dance by the pool like we've only got one dance left in us!"

Four of the women were chosen to go on the next date. They had another marvelous time. They went boating and were pulled behind the boat on a giant inner tube. Some of them ingloriously popped out now and then, like popcorn, their bodies flying through the sky and plunging into the water.

Ruthie was surprised at how sad she felt when she wasn't chosen. The camera caught that flash of sadness. People at home said, "Ohhhh, Ruthie!" and felt bad for her. But then, in another flash, Ruthie put a smile on her face, her dimples deepening and told the ladies to have a heckuva time. The ones left behind headed out to the pool and talked about what they would tell their younger selves if they could reach back in time and offer advice.

"I would tell myself not to marry my first husband. Or my second."

"I would tell myself not to get married at all and to travel the world. For years."

"I would tell myself to go to medical school and ignore the men in my life who told me that 'women could not be doctors.'"

"I would tell myself to escape the cult, after I cracked my husband in the nuts."

"I would tell myself to be myself and not let my family and my husband tell me who and what I should be."

"I would tell myself to have more children."

"I would tell myself to treat my vagina like a best friend."

"I would tell myself not to drive to San Diego that day."

"I would tell myself to be a better mother."

"I would tell myself to stop drinking."

"I would tell myself to take the job in London."

"I would tell myself to run naked along a river at night."

"I would tell myself to quit being so scared and dare more."

"I would tell myself to join that group of women in Scotland who wear lingerie and bike through town at night."

"I would tell myself not to worry so much. In the history of this world, worry has never changed an outcome."

"I would tell myself that committing that teeny, tiny crime was not a smart idea."

Then they turned on sixties and seventies music and sat around and drank wine and tequila and passed a joint that Maria had brought and laughed hysterically.

Ruthie said, the shared joint in the air, "May you all have lives filled with wine and joints."

They held up their glasses and clinked them together. "Cheers."

Later, they held on to one another's waists and did a conga line around the pool, the music blaring, then they jumped off the diving board.

The audience at home howled. Many stood up and did the conga line with their families or friends or sorority sisters. The young ones hadn't seen the older ones in this light: My God! It was a miracle! You could still be alive and active and not a corpse in your seventies! Your bones still worked! You could still smoke a joint!

They all agreed that watching *Marry Me* offered so much hope for old age and such insightful advice about how to live.

19

Marry Me

Interview: Tony Beckett

Interviewed by: Tyler, the associate producer, who is going to ask some ridiculous questions. Bear with us.

Tyler: Hi, Tony.

Tony: Hi, Tyler.

Tyler: Can you name your top three brides in order and tell me why they're ranked like that?

Tony: No.

Tyler: Uh. Why not?

Tony: Because I will not rank women. They're not football teams. All the women here are beautiful inside and out. They've lived interesting lives and have handled adversity and problems and crises throughout their lives that have added to their resilience and sincerity. We've all survived a lot, and we're here having a fun time.

Tyler: But can you give us a hint at who you like best? Who is the most attractive? Who do you think is the hottest? Most likely to be Mrs. Beckett? From top to bottom.

Tony: I'm not going to talk about who I think is the hottest. That's disrespectful to reduce a woman to hot or not. I'm looking for personality and character and someone who thinks that I would be a match for her, that she would be happy living with me as my wife, and who loves me. Who is most likely to become Mrs. Beckett? If I do get married, my wife may or may not want to take my last name. She's welcome to, but it's not a requirement.

Tyler: When I was at Stanford, I took a sociology class, and there was a section on marriage and how couples should take written tests to see if they're compatible.

Tony: They should take written tests to see if they're compatible? Maybe they should try talking to each other?

Tyler: Uh.

Tony: Thank you for the interview. I'm going back to my home to read a book.

Tyler: One more question?

Tony: Have a good night, Tyler.

20

Two days later, there was an I Do ceremony. Ruthie wore a yellow dress with ruffles and a low neckline that she had bought with Willow and Lucy on a vacation to Vegas. They had bought yellow dresses, too, at the same store. Ruthie hoped they would know that she was sending them an "I love you" signal. She also put on a push-up bra to give the girls some extra oomph for Tony.

Before the ceremony, Ruthie and Tony had time to talk. He took her out to the patio, and they had a lovely discussion about their favorite TV shows when they were young. For Ruthie: *Bewitched*, *I Love Lucy*, *I Dream of Jeannie*, *The Waltons*—her favorite family member was Erin—and *Happy Days*. For Tony: *Gunsmoke*, *Bonanza*, *The Beverly Hillbillies*.

Movies? For Ruthie: *Funny Girl*, *Jaws*, *Fiddler on the Roof*, *The French Connection*.

For Tony: *2001: A Space Odyssey*, *Planet of the Apes*, *The Godfather*, *Monty Python and the Holy Grail*, *One Flew Over the Cuckoo's Nest*.

Bands and singers?

For Ruthie: Fleetwood Mac, The Pointer Sisters, ABBA, Dolly Parton, The Doobie Brothers, Van Halen, Styx, Kiss, Pat Benatar, Blondie, Carly Simon, Donna Summer.

For Tony: Led Zeppelin, Aerosmith, Sister Sledge, Aretha Franklin, The Eagles, The Rolling Stones, also The Pointer Sisters, The Beatles, Linda Ronstadt, Queen.

Which led them to Ruthie's job as an English teacher.

Tony asked, "How long were you a teacher, Ruthie?"

"Forty-five years. I loved it."

"Did you retire? Or quit?"

"I was forced out."

Tony gaped at her. "You were *forced out*?"

"Yes."

"What happened?"

She told him.

She was still steaming mad about it.

She tried not to wish bad things upon the women who'd brought her teaching career to an end, but it didn't work. So far, she had hoped they would contract chicken pox and gonorrhea, get hit by flying seagull poop in the mouth, bitten by wolves, and struck by lightning. She knew that was mean.

She couldn't help it.

Oh, and she hoped they would be plagued by flatulence at the most inopportune moments and their teeth would fall out.

When Ruthie was sixty-nine years old, a new principal named Dr. Selly Tabutt was hired at Triple Mountain High School. What an unfortunate last name! To have *butt* in one's name was rather embarrassing, but so fitting in this circumstance, as she was a butt. Selly Tabutt was the aforementioned woman who had the hips of an irritated buffalo, the face of a mean crane, and the temperament of a patronizing bat.

Selly was the former principal of a high school in the city, and she brought along her favorite sidekick suck-up—English teacher LeeLee Fish. LeeLee was twenty-four years old and, in her own mind, highly intellectual, admirably cerebral, and superior to others. She was, she proudly thought, an *educational philosopher*.

LeeLee had a special skill: She liked using educational and culture-war buzzwords. She believed the more she used them, the smarter she would appear. She was wrong. LeeLee told experienced teachers how they should teach, how they needed to "toss everything out that will not creatively self-power the child and bring emotional and intellectual mastery based self-leadership," and to "embrace an open-ended curriculum that is holistically student-driven."

"You mean students can study whatever they want?" Ruthie's friend, history teacher Adamo, asked during a staff meeting in September after LeeLee's Educational Insights and Diversified Intuition power point presentation. Adamo was trying not to laugh.

"Pretty much!" LeeLee chirped, flipping her tightly curled dirty blonde hair off her shoulders. "We want them to linguistically iterate! We want them to innovate and to boldly reform and reshape their experiential academic goals individually. We're pivoting into an academic growth mind-set."

What the hell is "linguistically iterate"? Ruthie asked herself.

"We're not going to teach math, history, science, and English anymore?" chemistry teacher Jose asked. Jose tried not to show his disdain. "We're going to allow giant holes in the curriculum? The students will not be learning about World War II, or grammar, or algebra, or read any traditional or modern-day classics if they don't choose to do so?"

"We want them to be rigorous self-guiders," LeeLee said, frowning at his question as if Jose were an idiot. "They will be in charge of their own holistic and broad-based educations and allowed to study what is most intriguing to them, as autonomous, independent thinkers!"

"What if they independently think that the only subject they want to learn this year is basket weaving?" Coraline, the art teacher, asked. Coraline, one could tell, was also trying not to show her intense dislike for this twenty-four-year-old self-imagined educational guru.

"Then we will support them in their progressive educational journeys to scholastic and artistic enlightenment!"

"There are Oregon state academic standards we need to meet," Ruthie said. "We are required to do so. Are you familiar with them?"

LeeLee was furious at the comment. She glared at Ruthie. "I know change will be particularly hard for you, Ruthie."

"Why?" Ruthie said. But everyone knew what LeeLee was implying, including Ruthie.

"You've been in education a looooonnng time," LeeLee said with a sad, pitying expression for this old woman.

The other teachers groaned.

"And you have not been in education long enough," Ruthie snapped.

The other teachers laughed and clapped.

LeeLee blushed. She then turned up the volume of her patronizing voice and scrunched up her nose. "We need to be mindful of how we treat each other, Ruthie. We need to allow and encourage everyone to own their own voice. You're not doing that today."

"I would like to use my voice to tell you that you need to call the state and let them know that you are adhering to a growth mind-set and are going to allow our independent-thinking teenagers to rigorously study whatever they wish, for their own academic enlightenment, including basket weaving, which they can practice all day every day. And, if the state approves it, I will mindfully throw out my plans to improve their reading and writing skills with all the encouragement I can muster."

LeeLee harrumphed. This was so irritating! She patted Ruthie's shoulder and said, her voice dripping with haughtiness for this ancient and stuck-in-her-ways woman, "We'll have a meeting later, the two of us, and I'll explain things to you."

"Get your hand off me," Ruthie said. "Or I will explain to you what I will do to you if you touch me again."

The other teachers smothered their laughter. LeeLee snapped her hand back.

"In addition," Ruthie continued, "you do not need to *explain* anything to me, and if you ever speak to me in that patronizing, nasal tone of voice again, implying that I am an old and confused woman, I will suggest that we discuss your personality with the school board. Have I pivoted in a way that you can understand holistically, or do you need to creatively self-power?"

LeeLee's large, powerful nose that could probably smell manure miles away scrunched up again in distaste, but at least she finally sat down and shut up.

That LeeLee wore strange bandanas, with sayings like Cat Power and Free the Bees, wrapped around her head and often curled her hair into two bear ears on top of her head further complicated matters.

Selly and LeeLee turned everything at the high school upside down, and when teachers, parents, and students complained, they said, with such a superior air, "Change is hard, especially for people who have been doing things the same way for decades. We knew this would be difficult, especially for certain people of more rigid and narrow mind-sets. But we must move forward, we must scaffold our successes, and we must grab hold of differentiated learning paradigms to prepare our students for their multitiered futures!"

It was said that so many people rolled their eyes at this during a parent meeting it was a wonder their eyes were not stuck, the ophthalmologist's office in town jammed with patients whose eyes were now in the back of their heads.

Selly had long, boring staff meetings because Selly liked the attention. Selly and LeeLee cut out all staff celebrations, saying they were "distracting from our measurable global and interior outcome goals."

They ended the traditions that had been part of the school for decades. For instance, Senior/Teacher Skip Day, when the teachers of the seniors skipped school with their students and went roller skating. They canceled Fishing Day, when the whole school went hiking and out to the fish hatcheries for a picnic. They immediately cut out the high school camping weekend, where everyone brought tents and slept out on the football field.

LeeLee said, "Students can get hurt roller skating, so we will no longer allow our students to participate. We're also not being respectful of children who don't know how to roller skate. It's not an inclusive activity for everyone."

Selly said, "Teachers skipping school is a poor example."

LeeLee said, "We are a pedagogic academic institution that embraces multiple cranial talents, not a campground." She didn't know that she had used the word *pedagogic* incorrectly. She felt smart saying it, though!

LeeLee taught one English class and four history classes. She wanted Ruthie out so she could teach only English classes. In addition, LeeLee couldn't possibly imagine in her tiny brain that a woman who was *so old* could be an effective teacher. LeeLee, insecure and unlikable, was also threatened by how popular Ruthie was. Ruthie started calling her "the Twit," but not to her face.

LeeLee and Selly were a gang of two. They made school miserable for all. In May, Ruthie was called into Selly's office for a conversation with her and LeeLee the Twit. Ruthie noticed that LeeLee was staring at her with both a satisfied smirk and a look of triumph as in, "I won!" She was wearing her hair in two braids on top of her head as if she were a six-year-old Pippi Longstocking, along with a glittery purple bandana that said, "I Own My Own Voice." She proudly said that she had designed it herself.

"Ruthie, we're going to take the English Department in a new and challenging and exciting direction next year, pushing our students to use deductive and inductive thinking," Selly said. She wiggled her giant, irritated-buffalo bottom on her chair. "I don't know if you're going to be fully on board with what we're doing."

"What are you doing?" Ruthie asked.

"We're changing what books the students will read and what they'll write." Selly tapped two pencils, one in each hand.

"We're not going to read or write in English class anymore?" Ruthie quipped. She didn't like these two, and she didn't pretend to. But she would, she told herself, be civil until she couldn't be civil anymore.

"We believe," LeeLee the Twit said, so smug, "that based on the reams of deep research we've read and extensively studied that we need a transformative change in the way that English is taught here at Triple Mountain. We want the students to embrace differentiated dimensions of learning and formative motivation. We want to do what's best for the students."

"What research did you use?" Ruthie said.

LeeLee blinked at her, then stumbled out, "Research from...uh...important institutions...and colleges. By professors in education and in English arts literature...and in teaching research and people research who do English teaching. College."

Ruthie's brow furrowed at her mumbo-jumbo word choices. "Which institutions? Which colleges? Which professors?"

LeeLee swallowed hard. "That's not important right now."

"Sure it is," Ruthie said. "You said that you're changing the curriculum based on information you read from institutions, colleges, and professors because you want to do what's best for the students. Which ones?"

"I don't think I need to be quizzed on this..."

"It's not a quiz. Let's not pretend it is."

LeeLee couldn't give her a name. She could, however, blush. Then she played with one of the bear's ears on her head. Her bandana slipped down over her face. She pulled it up.

Ruthie turned to Selly. "One name? One university? One professor?"

"Ruthie," Selly said, with another irritated-bottom wriggle, "what we're saying is that we will be using a different, value-based literary curriculum to systematically track and authenticate the students' progress. We want to build capacity in their literary knowledge base. Many of the books they're reading now in your class aren't appropriate for today's teenagers, who want to be in touch with their inner emotional lives. We want to bring them a robust set of books, fit for our modern world, which will serve them better on their academic journeys and self-exploration. This will involve unpacking our current standards and questioning what our best practices will be going into the future."

"You will need to trust and embrace this new,

transformational process that will support the students' multiple intelligences," LeeLee said.

"Let me understand this correctly," Ruthie said. "You're saying that Kurt Vonnegut, James McBride, Harper Lee, George Orwell, Charlotte, Emily, and Anne Brontë, Jane Austen, Charles Dickens, John Steinbeck, Zora Neale Hurston, Nathaniel Hawthorne, Toni Morrison, Octavia Butler, John Green, and Chimamanda Ngozi Adichie aren't relevant? What about *The Book Thief, The Diary of Anne Frank, Night, The Color of Water, Born a Crime, Othello* and *Romeo and Juliet, The Kite Runner, Solito, The Immortal Life of Henrietta Lacks, Wonder, Angela's Ashes, Educated, I Am Malala, Tuesdays with Morrie, Into Thin Air, The House on Mango Street,* and *The Underground Railroad*? You're saying these books are not *transformational* enough for our students?"

"We didn't say that," Selly said. "Not exactly. Not performatively."

"You did. You said that you want to bring the students books that will bring them value, which is implying that the books they're reading now, with me, are not of value. They're not building capacity—whatever that means."

"I…" Selly wiggled. She seemed very uncomfortable with her bottom. She had not expected such pushback. At her other school, the teachers had known not to express opinions, or she'd write them up and give them warnings. Of course, the union representatives had *always* been in her office complaining, and the staff had hated her. Before she left, she'd had her secretary buy a cake that the staff could come and enjoy when they said their goodbyes and thank-yous to her. No one came to say goodbye or thank you except LeeLee. LeeLee had worn a headband that said "Goodbye. Thank You." Even though LeeLee was coming with her.

"We're saying that we need to bring in relevant books," LeeLee said. "Most of the books and authors you mentioned I've never even heard of!"

Ruthie wanted to bang her head on the table, but she didn't

because she didn't want to appear insane. "Are you kidding me?"

"No," LeeLee said. She blushed again. Her bandana fell across her face again. She pushed it back up toward her bear ears. "We want the students to have the self-autonomy to choose and self-direct. I am a lot closer in age to the students than you are, so I think I have a better idea of what they would like." She sat up straight and raised her eyebrows at Ruthie as if to say, *Can you dispute the gigantic age difference here? Can you not see how out of touch you are?*

"I am not basing an English curriculum on what a student would like," Ruthie said. "They are not in charge. I am basing the curriculum on books that they should read because of their historical, literary, and/or social values. I am choosing books with characters that my students can learn from, analyze their motivations and perceptions, and see how and why they acted based on the time period they lived in, the culture, and their own flaws and talents. I want them to read books that will light their brains on fire and make them think."

"I want them to think, too!" LeeLee said, getting flustered.

"Do you?"

She sighed, so put out by Ruthie, this old woman. "People my age, and younger, want to read about what they're interested in, which, right now, is a lot of fantasy, vampires, werewolves, and graphic novels."

Ruthie felt her mouth fall open enough to catch a passing fly. "Is that a joke?"

LeeLee's face was red. Like a squished tomato. "No."

"You want me to have my students read books on vampires and werewolves? Fantasy? That's what they can read outside of my classroom. Not in it. And we're not going to read graphic novels, unless it's *Maus* by Art Spiegelman."

"Who? There's a book on a mouse?" asked LeeLee.

"Oh my God," Ruthie muttered.

"Don't be condescending to me!" LeeLee said. "I'm not going to put up with your bullying."

"You were bullied when I said, 'Oh my God?' Then, oh my

God, LeeLee, you should not be teaching. And don't try to silence me by using those claptrap buzzwords that you specifically have thrown around at other staff members this year to get them to shut up if they don't agree with you."

LeeLee blushed more. "I don't!"

"You do. You did. You told me I was bullying you. You did that so I would shut up. You use your buzzwords as weapons, to falsely accuse and to intimidate. Buzzwords don't work here, LeeLee. You don't appear smarter because you know lingo."

"Ruthie," Selly said. She was frazzled now and had a look of fright on her face. She had the temperament of a patronizing bat, and this wasn't going as she'd planned! "I'm sorry to say this, but you will not be teaching English next year unless you allow students to read the books that they want to read in your class."

"The students learn from the books I give them to read," said Ruthie. "They love them."

"If you do not agree," Selly plugged along, although her voice was tight and pitched now, as if she regretted this conversation, "we do have another position for you. We need someone who will monitor"—she coughed, she twitched her buttocks— "the computer lab."

Ruthie froze. She wanted to push them over in their chairs and watch their feet fly in the air. Instead, she stayed quiet for many long seconds, which made Selly and LeeLee the Twit nervous.

"I'm not going to monitor the computer lab. You both knew I would decline that offer." Ruthie's voice was measured and calm. "I have taught here for forty-five years. I have been a dedicated teacher, devoted to my students. I have long friendships with people here at school and in town. I want to ask you, Selly, and you, LeeLee, are you sure that you want to fire me? Are you very sure?"

"No, no!" Selly sat up straight as if she'd been electrocuted anally. She wagged a finger. "You are not being fired. You're being *transferred* to the computer lab, where your skill set is needed."

LeeLee smirked. "Transferred. Not fired. You'll be in a place that is a better fit for you at this time of your life."

"You've fired me. Don't try to twist this into something it isn't." Ruthie stood and smiled. The smile was friendly, cheerful, which made LeeLee the Twit and Selly internally shake. "I don't think your decision will be a popular decision here in Triple Mountain."

Selly's mean crane face suddenly looked stricken. She was pale now.

LeeLee's shoulders curved down, and she blinked several times, stunned. She was young and stupid, but she was beginning to think that maybe she had made a mistake. Neither one smiled back at Ruthie as she wished them a good day and left.

Ruthie was right. Selly and LeeLee's decision was not popular.

It was probably the most unpopular decision ever in that town.

Ruthie sent out an email that night to her students and their parents, the staff, the school board, the head of human resources, the superintendent, the editor of the local newspaper—who printed it—the entire Deschutes family, and her friends.

She would not allow Selly and LeeLee to spin this in a way that allowed them to escape responsibility or to imply that Ruthie was being let go because something was wrong with *her* or that she had done something wrong. No way. She would get the truth out. Ruthie straightened her shoulders. She was a Deschutes. She would not let two ridiculous women publicly stomp on her.

The dogs, cats, pig, and rabbit were all supportive as Ruthie wrote. They had rarely seen Ruthie this angry, so they were quiet and respectful. Scarlett O'Hara the rabbit didn't scream or scare the dogs. Atticus warmed her feet. Gatsby the pig didn't snort loudly.

Ruthie informed everyone that the new principal, Selly Tabutt (deliberately leaving out the title Dr.), did not want Ruthie to teach English next year, nor did LeeLee Fish, a new teacher at the school, who had come with the principal from the city, due to "curriculum disagreements."

She said that LeeLee would be the new English teacher next year and that students would be choosing their own books to read, with heavy encouragement from LeeLee to read books about vampires and werewolves, with the fantasy genre highly recommended.

I cannot follow this new English curriculum as I do not think that reading about vampires and werewolves is in the best interest of my students, Ruthie wrote. *I will be retiring at the end of the year. I want to tell ALL my students—every single one I've taught in my forty-five years here at Triple Mountain High School—that it has been a pleasure and an honor to be your English teacher.*

Remember, you should be reading one book a week, at least, as I taught you. Read in different genres. Read different authors, dead and alive. Don't forget to explore your creativity with writing, too. Writing will bring you peace and joy. And one more thing—I love you! You have given me the best years of my life, and I wish you and your family the very best always.

With all my love forever,
Mrs. O'Hara.

Instant chaos.
Unbridled outrage.
Red-hot fury.

LeeLee and Selly woke to their phones lighting up as if someone had put a sparkler inside and lit it. They arrived at school to students expressing to them, in ways only teenagers could do, their raw anger over Mrs. O'Hara leaving. LeeLee went to class, and her students refused to come in the door, telling her they didn't want her for their English teacher. She was a boring history teacher, they told her. She hardly knew anything, and she'd be worse as an English teacher! Mrs. O'Hara was their English teacher!

Selly went to her office and tried to barricade herself in, but her vice principal, her secretaries, unhappy staff members, the janitors, the librarian, and parents kept pushing their way in.

"Ruthie has not been fired," she stuttered time and time again. "She's going to monitor the computer lab."

Boom.

So many livid voices were raised Selly couldn't hear any words. As a math teacher announced, "That equation doesn't work, and you know it, Selly."

By nine a.m., all the students walked out of school to join with hundreds of other furious people from town, Deschutes family members among them, all protesting Ruthie's firing. They knew what had happened here.

They had brought signs, too. "Keep Mrs. O'Hara!" and "We Love You, Mrs. O'Hara!" And "James McBride. Julia Alvarez. Barbara Kingsolver. Charles Dickens. Mrs. O'Hara." Another sign had some bite: "I Don't Need a Vampire, I Need Mrs. O'Hara!" One sign included a howl: "Werewolves Belong in the Woods, Not in English Class!"

No one wanted Ruthie to leave. They wanted LeeLee and Selly to leave. *Immediately.* Their signs said that, too. "You're a Fish Out of Water, Ms. Fish!" and "One, Two, Three, Please Leave!" and "Selly, We Want to Sell You!"

Some of the students took over the school's office, including Selly Tabutt's personal office. She hid in a small room off the library with LeeLee. They locked the door.

The school secretary, Phyllis, who was quite close with Ruthie and had been for forty years and who couldn't stand pretentious Selly, or snotty LeeLee, gave the children cookies and told them they were welcome to stay all day, every day, until this "unbearable situation is resolved." She praised them for following their "civic duty" and "demonstrating to right a wrong."

It was a mess. Newspaper articles were written. People took sides. Well, LeeLee and Selly were one "side," and the town was on the other. No parent wanted their child, *in English class,* no less, to only read books about werewolves and vampires. They wanted their children to read the books that Ruthie gave them—as she had done when they were her students years ago.

Parents and grandparents complained to the school board and superintendent and said they wanted their child to have Ruthie for their English teacher, not "that weird, arrogant bandana girl." A petition to keep Ruthie was passed around online and garnered thousands of signatures in minutes.

LeeLee the Twit and Selly were the two most unpopular people in Triple Mountain, possibly ever in the history of the town, including the three sneaky Lenizen brothers who liked to start fires in the mid-1940s. One of their descendants was now a sneaky state politician, which surprised no one, as sneakiness and fire-starting ran in the family.

At a private emergency school board meeting to calm the calamity, LeeLee and Selly were asked to leave by the end of the year. There were nine people on the board. Two were Deschuteses. LeeLee the Twit and Selly left, humiliated and humbled, and at their next schools, they were not as bad. But Ruthie had gotten it into her head that she was going to retire. Russell had died at seventy-five years old. She was sixty-nine. Maybe it was time. Yes, it was time.

She would relax. She would read. She would be with her family.

Everyone begged her to stay at Triple Mountain High School. She said, "No, but I love you."

Ruthie's retirement party was a community potluck held in the gym. Businesses shut down so their employees, former students of Ruthie, could go. It was packed. The tables—people were encouraged to bring an extra if they had it—groaned with the most delicious food. People put time and effort into their offerings, which included recipes from Mexico, Korea, Japan, Ukraine, Thailand, Honduras, Greece, and Vietnam. It was for Mrs. O'Hara's retirement party after all!

A pig roasted outside the gym. Someone had made a full turkey dinner. The Cortezes, who owned the crepes shop in town, made hundreds of crepes. Five grills were set up for hamburgers and chicken. The Bao family brought in racks of ribs. The Martinez family brought their snow cone truck. Wine and beer were everywhere. The people who should have done something about this tiny liquor violation looked away and cracked open a can. All of Ruthie and Russell's children and grandchildren were in attendance, as were, of course, Lucy and Willow.

They laughed. They turned dance music on over the speakers, turned down the lights, and Ruthie showed everyone she had some mooooves! They hugged her, thanked her, told her they loved her. Speeches were made, tears fell, a long standing ovation brought the house down. Ruthie sobbed.

Ruthie Deschutes O'Hara was their legend. She was kind, but strict. She cared about her students and believed that *everyone* could learn. If you weren't giving your all, that was a problem for her, and she shaped you right up. She knew that reading and writing were the keys to a better, happier life, and you darn well better know it, too.

Selly and LeeLee both received formal invitations to be *in another city* during the retirement party. They were home packing anyhow, and they snuck out of town on the sly, their tails between their legs. Selly wriggled her bottom. LeeLee decided she didn't like buzzwords anymore.

Ruthie, for the rest of her life, would love and miss her students and the teachers at Triple Mountain High School.

"The way my teaching career ended made me cry. It was devastating," Ruthie told Tony, tears making her blue eyes bluer. "To think that two incompetent people could come in, new to our school, and get rid of me, a dedicated teacher, hurt. It still hurts. It makes me angry, too. LeeLee..." Ruthie paused. Should she say LeeLee's last name out loud, on the air? No, she wasn't that mean. "At the age of twenty-four, she decided that she knew better than

I did—it was the height of arrogance. She believed me to be one wobble away from a nursing home, my mind a mottled nest of confusion. Why? Because I was sixty-nine.

"Ageism is alive and well in this country, and we need to address it. It is unfair and it is un-American. Older people are kicked out of jobs because it is assumed they are not as competent because of their age. Woe to anyone over the age of fifty who loses their job. They may never work at anywhere near the level they were at before, all because of ageism and younger people's incorrect and harsh perceptions of their capabilities and talents."

Older adults watching the show stood up and cheered. LeeLee, now in a small town in Louisiana, hoped that no one would ask if she was *that* LeeLee. People found out anyhow. She was so embarrassed. Again.

"I get it, Ruthie," Tony said, such sympathy and understanding in his voice. "You loved teaching. You were pushed out. I am so sorry that happened to you. It shouldn't have. It was wrong."

"I loved reading and discussing books with the kids and then having them write. They wrote essays, fictional stories, short memoirs, nonfiction, poetry, plays, songs, everything. We wrote and read each day. I felt that I was helping young people. Educating them. I miss that."

He hugged her, and she hugged him back.

"Ruthie, your legacy will live on through your students."

Her students, living all over the country and the world, nodded. Tony was right. Ruthie lived on in them. She had taught them to love books and to love writing.

"Maybe, if you're lucky, I'll read you a sex scene out of a romance book one day," Ruthie said, laughing, swiping her tears away.

"Oh, I would like that," Tony agreed, his smile sexy, his blue eyes warm. He brushed his fingers over her tears. "We can act it out."

"Yes, do that!" The older adults declared with enthusiasm. That sounded like a fine time! They cheered again.

"Gross, Mrs. O'Hara," her students said. "Don't say that." But they laughed.

Tony bent his head and kissed her. It went on a long time. Whew!

"Get a room," Melda Zamborini, eighty years old in Omaha, Nebraska, said. "Those two are thunder and lightning."

Her wife laughed. "Let's go to bed, Melda. I'll read you a sex scene."

It was not surprising to the viewing audience that Ruthie made it through the I Do ceremony again that night, the golden spotlight beaming down over her head. She received her bouquet of pink roses and baby's breath after walking down the pink aisle.

Tony said, "Do you wish to continue our walk down the aisle?"

And she said, "Hell yes, Mr. Sexy."

He said, "Thank you." He winked at her.

She was the only one he winked at. The viewers noticed.

Four women went home in tears, including Carol with the disappearing husband who took all the camping gear. "At least this one didn't take the camping gear with him," she said to the camera. "It's too bad. I would have liked to get in a sleeping bag with Tony and snuggle on up to those muscles."

Another woman who was sent home said, "I hope he finds his wife. I do. No, that's not true. I don't." She teared up. She was a former hippie, a freethinker who rode a motorcycle and worked as an ICU nurse. "I hope he really misses me and knows he made a terrible mistake and calls me right up and invites me to his home in Oregon, and we get married and ride motorcycles together."

A third woman said, "I think I'm going to stalk Tony when the show's over. I did that once forty years ago when I found out my boyfriend took all the money out of my bank account. He thought he could escape me by moving to Oklahoma. He was wrong. I stalked him at home and work until he gave me my money back, plus money for my airline ticket. Every time he turned around, I was there, lurking like a scythe-wielding death eater. I even hid in his house and popped out at him at night—twice. Second time, he wet himself. We settled things amicably after that."

The fourth said, "Damn. I wanted to sleep with Tony. I think he has a powerful gun packed in those jeans."

Later that night, as Ruthie peered into the darkness, not knowing that two coyotes were on the prowl for dinner and an owl had found a new hooting partner, she thought, *and then there were eight.*

She decided to reread Agatha Christie's books when she got home.

―――

Jackson, sacked out on the floor of his triplet daughters' bedroom, was proud that *Marry Me* had turned into a huge hit. Every week, the show's ratings went up. It had lovable stars, especially Tony, Ruthie, Benedetta, Sarah, Dallas, Maria, and Velvet. It made for riveting TV that was entertaining but also deep, thoughtful, and interesting. It wasn't just about two seniors finding love, it was about life and getting older and the fun that was still to be had.

Even though he was exhausted, he chuckled. The worry about how the show would do, and how it would affect him and his family if it was pulled off the air, had left him.

Shonda and Pearla had both told him in the early hours of the morning after the I Do ceremony that their collective anxiety was improving because *Marry Me* was being talked about all over—in newspapers, on social media, and by other TV hosts. They decided to have champagne together.

"I don't feel like I'm having a life-ending heart attack every day anymore," Pearla said.

"I can now think about having a panic attack without having

one," Shonda said. "And I don't think that I'm losing my mind."

"My OCD isn't spinning my life into a tornado." Jackson raised a champagne glass. "It's backing off. Ladies, to *Marry Me* and not having symptoms of death, obsessions, and anxiety."

They clinked their glasses together in celebration of no more heart attacks and not losing one's mind.

***

Two days later, there was another date for two women. They would go to a cooking class in Whitefish, then a hike where they hoped they would not become a bear's lunch. Ruthie was not chosen for the date. That expression of sadness crossed Ruthie's face, and again she covered it up, but the cameras caught it. The audience at home caught it, too.

"What's wrong with that man?" they asked one another. "Why doesn't Tony ask Ruthie out? He seems to like her!"

The cameras also caught a tear before Ruthie said to the women, with infectious enthusiasm, "Who's up for a game of Truth or Dare?"

They were up for it! Why not? What did they have to lose?

21

Marry Me

Interview: Ruthie Deschutes O'Hara

Interviewed by: Tyler, the associate producer, who is still working on sensitivity and social cues and may never be successful at either because of his mental density issues.

Tyler: Hello, Ruthie. How are you?

Ruthie: I'm fine, Tyler.

Tyler: You haven't had a one-on-one date with Tony yet. Do you know why?

Ruthie: No. Do you?

Tyler: Uh, no. I'm not sure why. How does it feel?

Ruthie: How do you think it feels?

Tyler: Uh, bad?

Ruthie: Yes, it does. Tony is a remarkable man. I would love to have a date with him, but it's his choice, and he has not yet chosen me. I don't like having a man in charge of this dating thing. It seems very antifeminist to me, a bit reptilian, and quite cavemanlike, but it's what I agreed to when I signed up for *Marry Me*.

Tyler: Right. Because the groom chooses the bride he wants to go on a date with. Not the other way around.

Long pause.

Tyler: Do you have anything to say to that?

Ruthie: I didn't hear a question.

Tyler: Well, the groom, Tony... He chooses who he wants to take on the dates with him. It's all about who he wants to spend time with. Which bride.

Long pause.

Tyler: Uh. Do you want to say anything to that?

Ruthie: Again, Tyler, I didn't hear a question.

Tyler: Do you think he'll choose you soon?

Ruthie: Let's hope.

Tyler: When I was at Stanford, I took a sociology class on gender. The education I received was the best in the nation, not to brag, so I know a lot about men and women and traditional roles. Ha-ha.

Ruthie: I'm not sure you absorbed or understood the lessons at all. I'm going to go read a book now. Maybe you should, too.

Tyler: Okay. Bye, Ruthie.

22

The next night, Ruthie went to bed at the early hour of one in the morning after a long game of poker with the other ladies. They used M&M's for money. Some of the women ate their money. Ruthie won. She often won. She had a poker face to end all poker faces. Sometimes she faked happiness at the cards she received. Sometimes she faked frustration. Sometimes she faked a poker face.

Out on the Deschutes family homestead, they cheered her poker victory and poured the tequila.

"That's my cousin!"

"That's my sister!"

"That's my Aunt Ruthie!"

Aunt Tootsie shot a gun in the air to celebrate. Uncle Bashy set off firecrackers. Cousin Tato led everyone in the family song, extolling Errol and Lavender Deschutes, and their love story that started on a train, the family's gun and bow and arrow skills, Rattlesnake Lake, their "kick my ass" tequila, the secrets they kept, and their love and loyalty to one another forever and ever. Amen!

Almost all the Deschutes were there each time *Marry Me* aired. They set up huge TVs so they could watch *Marry Me* together. After the show they cranked up the music and danced. The Deschuteses were having the best time ever. They were so proud of their Ruthie.

Up in the pine trees, hidden in the meadows, at the edges of the lakes, and around the wetlands, the animals listened. Humans were so noisy. They sighed then got back to the business of being animals.

From the comfort of her four-poster bed in her room at the lodge, which Ruthie now had to herself as her roommates were gone, she stared up at the ceiling, hoping for wisdom or, at least, wry humor and an answer or two about love.

The lights were off, her window open to a light breeze, shadows shifting here and there. Some animals were out, prowling and hunting. Others were tucked in. A mountain lion slunk through the trees. A bear caught a salmon in her mouth and gave it to her cubs. An owl hooted. Another answered. They were new friends.

She thought that Tony probably liked owls. She liked Tony. She didn't want to, but she did. They had a lot in common. They were both family people. They were devoted to their children and grandchildren. They had both worked hard their whole lives.

They both liked playing the *New York Times* games, like Wordle and Connections and the crossword. They liked coffee and funny movies. They loved reading. During one conversation, they listed their favorite top twenty books, and they shared a few of the same ones: *Endurance* by Alfred Lansing; *Slaughterhouse-Five* by Kurt Vonnegut; *Titan: The Life of John D. Rockefeller, Sr.* by Ron Chernow; *Team of Rivals: The Political Genius of Abraham Lincoln* by Doris Kearns Goodwin.

They were different, too. Born to rebels, Ruthie was more free-spirited. Being in the Army and going to Vietnam had knocked any "free spirit" out of Tony. Ruthie laughed more, was an extrovert, and goofed off, not caring who saw what silly thing she was doing. Tony was quiet, an introvert, and was fun in a more restrained manner. Ruthie's humor could veer easily into raunchy. Tony's humor was subtle, dry, and piercing, which made what he said even funnier. Ruthie was blunt and bold. Tony had an iron strength and was thoughtful with his words, careful. Ruthie cooked like a she-devil, everything in one pot, no recipe ever the same. Tony was precise and organized, measuring all ingredients to exact amounts.

When the differences and similarities were all tossed together, it made things interesting, but not prone toward conflicts. Plus, they had a bubbling, combustible brew of passion and desire zinging between them. Yes, Ruthie admitted, she was physically attracted to Tony. She felt like a lusty teenager. She hadn't been physically drawn to any man in five years, since Russell passed away, but she found herself thinking about Tony at night, in bed, and what breath-catching adventures they could experience between the sheets together.

She felt guilty for thinking about Tony in this way, because she would always love her dear Russell, but she reminded herself, through a sheen of tears and a stab of pain, that she would see Russell again one day, but this was her life now, and she must live it.

Tony's face, weathered, strong, dignified, and serious—until he smiled, which turned him into a huggable, friendly bear—was so handsome. She could look at that face forever.

Yes, she might *miraculously* be falling in love with Tony. How could that be? How could this happen so quickly? Falling in love surprised her. It delighted her. It scared her. In love? What if he didn't love her back? That would hurt. Ah, yes. That would hurt.

She knew it would be her turn for a date soon, and she knew they would have the best time together.

But he hadn't chosen her yet, and she didn't understand why.

Yet she had been asked to stay at every I Do ceremony.

Ruthie groaned with exasperation at herself. She liked to be practical, so she made herself face the wicked truth: Tony hadn't chosen her for a date because he saw more future potential with the other women. He liked them more than he did her. He found the other women more interesting, more attractive, more captivating.

There was no other rational explanation. She put a hand on her heart, then patted it. She tried to will the pain away.

Ruthie was confused. A bit lost. She didn't like either emotion. She was seventy years old. Shouldn't she be done feeling like a rejected teenager? He seemed to like her, seemed to like laughing with her and talking to her. She thought they had something between them, but maybe they didn't. Tony was the type of man who made everyone around him feel special. That was probably it. She was misreading him. What a bubblehead she was. What a fool. What a silly lady.

"This is very unfortunate," Ruthie drawled out loud as tears poured out and an inner ache caught her breath and held it tight. "Because Tony is unique. A one-of-a-kind bear of a man."

Outside her window, a bald eagle flew by. Ruthie didn't see it, but the eagle peered through the window and saw her. Farther up the mountain, a band of mountain goats rested. Sometimes they people watched. They found people confusing. They sure cried a lot.

23

Marry Me

Interview: Velvet Hashbrune

Interviewed by: Tyler, the associate producer. The ladies have found him to be as dense as vanilla pudding. As thick as cheddar cheese. He could be sweet, too, but the pudding and the cheese often squished the sweet part out.

Tyler: Hello, Velvet. Everyone is going to want to know how you came by the name Velvet.

Velvet: My mother was a stripper.

Tyler: Uh. She was? She was a stripper? Like, she took off her clothes for money?

Velvet: Yes, I just said that. Strippers take off their clothes for money. Why would I say it if it wasn't true?

Tyler: I don't know.

Velvet: Her stage name was Velvet, so she gave it to me when I was born.

Tyler: I like the name.

Velvet: I do, too. I'm seventy-three years old, and I am not embarrassed to talk about the origins of my name. My mother did what she had to do to support my twin sisters and me at a time when women had few choices or opportunities.

Tyler: What are your sisters' names?

Velvet: Coco and Chantelle. Those were the stage names of my mom's best friends. My father died when we were young. He was on a horse, the horse spooked, and he fell off and was then trampled. My mother had only a high school degree. There was no money and no family to help us. She worked at a grocery store while we were in school, and at night, we had a babysitter come and stay with us, and my mother stripped. In half the time, she made twice stripping what she made at the grocery store, but she wanted a "respectable" job, and the grocery store paid for our health insurance. We had a very nice life because she loved us so much.

Tyler: Your mother worked a lot, didn't she?

Velvet: Oh yes. She worked so hard. Everything she did was for us. She didn't even have a boyfriend until my sisters and I all left for college. I majored in finance, Coco in business, and Chantelle in accounting. By the time we were in high school, though, she had quit stripping and had a very successful business sewing outfits for strippers. She was a talented seamstress. Her wait list was three months long, and she charged a fortune.

Tyler: What happened to the business?

Velvet: It's thriving. My sisters and I run it together. It's called Vixen's Charming Lingerie. It's a multimillion-dollar operation. We always have, and will, keep it in the family. We have six-feet-by-four-feet photos up all over our corporate office in Atlanta of our mother in her stripping outfits. We're very proud of her. She passed away last year, at one hundred years old. We miss her every day... oh dear. Hang on. Let me get my tears under control... You never stop missing a loving mother. Never.

Tyler: I'm sorry she died, but hey! My mom and grandma and my sisters all shop at Vixen's together. It's like an event for them. I remember seeing the lingerie my mother bought once. That was weird. But I went with them one time to Vixen's during spring break when I was at Stanford.

Velvet: Our lingerie and stripper outfits and panties make a woman feel like a sex goddess. There's nothing weird about it.

Tyler: I don't know if my mother feels like a sex goddess in her lingerie with my dad, but okay! But I doubt it. **(Makes a snickering noise.)**

Velvet: You're very young, and male, so you don't get it. Trust me, your mother feels like a sex goddess in our lingerie. That's why she continues to buy it. Your imagination is limited in this regard, as you are still only seeing your mother as a mother, instead of as an independent woman with intelligence, hopes, dreams, and a sex life, who is not here on Earth to simply be a mother and serve you.

Tyler: Uh. My mother doesn't serve me.

Velvet: Do you still live at home?

Tyler: I'm moving out soon. To my own place. Soon.

Velvet: Does your mother cook for you? Clean the house? Do your laundry? Listen to your problems?

Tyler: Yes. Absolutely. She's my mother. She likes to do my laundry and fold it and put it away. And she likes to clean and cook. I think. I'm sure she does. Yes.

Velvet: You're still not getting this. She serves you.

Tyler: Huh. Maybe. I don't think so.

Velvet: What do you do to serve her?

Tyler: What do you mean?

Velvet: What do you do for your mom to make her life easier?

Tyler: I don't know what you mean. Did you roll your eyes? You did. Okay. Uh.

Velvet: Maybe you should start cooking and cleaning the house and doing her laundry. Don't you think she's done it for you long enough?

Tyler: You think I should do my mom's laundry? **(He laughs.)** That'd be weird. Let's talk about something else. I'll look at the questions Pearla and Shonda gave me to ask. Have you been married before?

Velvet: Yes. Once. For two years. It was miserable. I got rid of him. I didn't kill him, although I would have if I could have gotten away with it. I think I'd be good at burying a body. I divorced him. I've had several long-term relationships but did not want to get married again.

Tyler: Do you have children?

Velvet: I was not able to have children. It broke my heart for many years, as I so wanted to be a mother, but I am an excellent aunt.

We do not get all the happiness we want in life, so I am grateful for my nieces and nephews and their children.

Tyler: It's true we don't get all the happiness we want in life. I didn't get into Harvard Business School. I know three people who did, and I have no idea why they got in over me. Anyhow. How do you like being on *Marry Me*?

Velvet: Oh, I'm having the best time. I got so tipsy with Ruthie the other night. Blame her, not me. She's got her family's tequila in boxes in the kitchen, and it is lethal. Drink that stuff and you feel like your insides have turned into the devil's wrath, but then this blissful feeling suffuses you like a rainbow, and all you want to do is dance naked by the side of the pool.

Tyler: Naked? That happened?

Velvet: Yes. After the cameras were gone. Skinny-dipping is so freeing. Have you done it? No? You should. You seem a little uptight to me. Are you blushing?

Tyler: Uh…uh. I'm not uptight. Maybe I am. Well, what do you think of Tony?

Velvet: I like Tony. He's a sex god. Like Zeus. I think he'd like to see me in some of Vixen's Charming Lingerie, too. I can still rock a thong and a bustier. When I yank the girls up high, men in their twenties will gawk at 'em like they've never seen a bosom before.

Tyler: Yes. I saw. I mean. No. I didn't look at your…your…Thank you, Velvet.

Velvet: Thank you.

24

Yet another stress-inducing I Do ceremony took place on Tuesday.

Tony and Ruthie took a short walk and sat on a bench overlooking Whitefish's lights, the cameras and a gang of crew members surrounding them, including Shonda and Pearla, who were rooting for Ruthie, but privately. Ruthie had no idea about the thundering impact she and her bold, brash, ball-busting banter (alliteration!) were making on the audience. The show didn't let them read the news. They didn't even have their phones. It was technological torture!

But Shonda and Pearla knew, and that's why their anxiety wasn't turning their brains into dizzying spirals of mush. Jackson was smiling much more now, too.

Tony and Ruthie laughed a lot. They talked about Oregon and how they loved living there, the places they had been and seen and loved. Then they got into some hard stuff, the deeper conversations they knew they had to have.

"How long were you in the military for?" Ruthie asked.

"Twenty-five years."

"And you fought in Vietnam."

A dark shadow crossed his face. "Yes. I did."

"I'm sorry."

"I'm sorry, too."

"Where were you stationed?"

"A few places. Mostly in Cu Chi. I was fighting in the jungles. Going down tunnels. Trying not to get blown up or, more importantly, trying not to let my men get blown up by explosives or booby traps."

"It sounds terrifying."

"War is terrifying for everyone."

"My husband, Russell, before we were together, was there."

"Where?"

"He was in Cu Chi, too. He worked as a doctor."

"I was in Cu Chi when I injured my leg when an IED exploded nearby. Your husband's name was Russell O'Hara?"

"Yes."

"I don't remember any of the doctors' names when I was initially treated. I was in bad shape and attempting not to make an early trip to heaven. I was in a lot of uncontrolled pain."

"I'm so sorry that happened to you, Tony. I truly am. Russell said it was a hellhole. It never left him."

"He's right. It was. We never should have been there. Old, entitled, wealthy men, who had never fought in a war, who were comfortably at home getting three square meals a day, sent tens of thousands of young men over an ocean to fight and die in a war we shouldn't have fought and didn't know how to win."

"Russell used to wake up at night from nightmares. He'd hear gunshots and bombs. He'd sit straight up in bed and stare as if he were right back in the jungles. I'd have to shake him awake."

"That happened to me for years. If I'm under a lot of stress, it can still happen, but I haven't had an episode for a while now."

As if the cameras weren't there, as if the crew were invisible, as if Shonda and Pearla had disappeared, Tony and Ruthie talked. Tony talked about Vietnam. Ruthie listened. She ended up hugging him for a long time. He hugged her, too, blinked several times, those dark blue eyes becoming a lighter blue, the emotional storm, the insidious grief for the men who never came home, clearly visible.

The viewers hardly breathed as they watched, especially the young ones. They didn't know much about Vietnam. Many of them later looked it up on their phones and were shocked. Books on Vietnam like *The Things They Carried* by Tim O'Brien, which Ruthie had read years ago, had an upswing in sales.

Tony kissed Ruthie. It was warm and sweet, a kiss of friendship, support, and comfort, which we all need. Passion is a carnal and sexual delight, but friendship carries the day.

Always.

"If they got a room and went to bed," Melda Zamborini from Omaha croaked out to her wife as she watched the kiss, "they'd feel better."

"I'd feel better if I had some pie," her wife said. "Pecan pie."

"I'll buy you pecan pie tomorrow. Let's go to bed."

With Tony and Jackson standing tall, both smiling at her, Ruthie made it through another I Do ceremony. That golden spotlight produced a sparkly cone over her head, and she received blue hydrangeas, this time with a blue ribbon, from Tony.

He said, "Ruthie, do you wish to continue our walk down the aisle?"

And Ruthie said, "You betcha, baby."

He grinned, winked at her, and said, "Right back at ya."

Dallas went home that night. Ruthie hugged her hard before she left. She loved Dallas.

Dallas said to the camera on her way out, "At least this didn't turn out as badly as my debutante season, honey. None of those old, privileged, white, toadlike men liked it when I told them how torturous it would be to be married to men like them. Bless my mama's heart, it's a wonder she ever went out into polite society again after that ruination."

"And then there were seven," Ruthie whispered. "Agatha Christie, your presence is still felt. Even on *Marry Me*."

Two days later, two women were invited out on a date with Tony. Ruthie was not chosen. Again. To be fair, those two women had not had a date for a while either.

It was a shame, because they were going into Glacier National Park to hike to Avalanche Lake, then they were going to Whitefish for dinner and dancing. Ruthie liked to hike and dance!

Ruthie was crushed but tried to hide it as quick as a wink. She was not a sulker! She was a Deschutes. When they were upset, they visited other family members or had shooting contests or raced their trucks on the homestead or jumped off the dock into Rattlesnake Lake to get the sadness out.

But Ruthie didn't have her gun, and she couldn't race her truck, and Rattlesnake Lake was too far away, so she bucked up and smiled through her pain. She missed her family.

"What's wrong, Ruthie?"

Shonda and Pearla asked Ruthie to come into the library that afternoon to sit in the "special throne," as Ruthie had dubbed it, for another interview. The "special throne" was a wooden chair, not a toilet. She was glad she wasn't being interviewed by Tyler the Child. He meant well, but my goodness, so young and naïve. Shonda and Pearla were much better at interviewing. Jackson was there, too, along with the usual gang of assistant producers, lighting technicians, camera people, etc.

"Nothing at all," Ruthie said, smiling broadly. But the camera caught it. The people at home caught it. They knew what was wrong. Ruthie had not been chosen for another date, much less a one-on-one date. This was an epic tragedy!

The other brides were surprised that Ruthie hadn't had a one-on-one date yet. In fact, Dr. Benedetta Fields said to Jackson, "Ruthie hasn't gone out with Tony alone yet. Is he having a medical issue with his brain and forgot to ask her?"

Jackson assured Benedetta there was no medical issue with Tony's brain.

"I'm sorry, Ruthie," Jackson said to her. His face was drawn. He was sorry. He knew this was hard for her. What was also hard was dealing with the triplets, who all had colds and were coughing and sneezing in his face when he held them. He could tell he was getting sick again from them. Plus, the other day they used their paints to paint the walls of their bedroom with giant flowers. It was a rental home.

"You seemed sad when you didn't get an invitation to go on the date," Shonda said.

"I'm on a reality TV show," Ruthie said. "This is not real life. If it was real life, I'd be talking to my very old dog and hoping my screaming rabbit, Scarlett O'Hara, didn't scare my cats. I do miss my pig, Gatsby. I would also be hoping to go out to lunch with my daughter, Willow, and my granddaughter, Lucy."

She really did want to go to lunch with them! She tried not to tear up, but she did. She missed Willow and Lucy so much. She bent her head and wiped away a tear. She was wearing a silk scarf today in a blended pink and red pattern around her head, the ends stylishly arranged over her shoulder. When she bought the scarf at a Saturday Market, she was with Willow and Lucy and bought them scarves, too. All three of them wore their scarves together. She hoped they would remember their happy times when they saw her scarf.

"Tony didn't choose me, and that's his right, and now I'm going out to the pool to do a cannonball, and then I'm going to find a shot of tequila." She looked straight at the camera. "And I suggest that you do that, too. Cannonballing and tequila take the sting out of life."

But that wasn't what Ruthie did. Ruthie went up to her room. It was quiet.

Two cameras in the hallway caught Ruthie brushing away the tears on her cheeks. Her face fell, the smile disappeared, and the viewers saw, clearly, her sheer pain.

They were upset for poor Ruthie!

What in the world was wrong with Tony?! Maybe he was having an *undiagnosed* brain issue, like Dr. Benedetta said. That was probably it. Why, they should get his head examined!

Benedetta and Sarah pounded on her door about fifteen minutes later.

"We're ready for the cannonballing, Ruthie!"

Ruthie stood, squared her shoulders, and yelled, "I'm coming, girls!"

A pool party and barbecue were arranged the next day for the brides and groom.

Tony said, "Would you like to talk, Ruthie? Take a walk?"

Oh yes, she definitely would. Tony was looking particularly fetching in his dark jeans and light blue T-shirt.

"Let's take one of these trails."

The trail led away from the lodge. Ruthie and Tony admired glimpses of the lake through pine and fir trees. They saw a great blue heron and stopped to watch it. The heron saw them, too, and monitored the humans carefully. Humans were unpredictable, and he did not want to put himself in an unpredictable situation.

Tony was curious about Ruthie's thirty-two children. He knew, from previous conversations, that she and her husband had taken thirty-one children in at various times to give them a better life or get them out of an abusive or neglectful situation, but he wanted to know more. "What are their names?"

"First, Willow," said Ruthie, smiling at the thought of her. "She's my biological daughter. When Willow was six, Russell and I invited a series of my high school students to live with us for different reasons. Basically, their home lives had collapsed. Sometimes they stayed a few months, sometimes a few years. Our second and third children were sisters, Halona and Chenoa. Then came Janya, followed by Carlos and his brother Diego; Maverick; Adelynn; Mary; Jaxton and Jaden, brother and sister; then Liam, Marty, and Joseph, two brothers and a cousin. Then we had what my husband called the 'girl run'—Alejandra; Cassie; Zoe; Kasa and Kali, who were sisters; Charlotte; Adison. And back to the boys—Logan, Anthony and Alex, Carter, and Wyatt. Next up, Shyla; Savannah and Scarlett, sisters; Dominic and Emilio, twin boys; and, finally, Jayla."

"I'll have to work on memorizing their names."

"Oh, I've mixed them up before for a second, but I never mix up who they were when they arrived in our home, who they became while living with us, and who they are today. I love all of them. They are the lights of my life. Our children are like a chandelier—each one is a shining crystal. They have particularly helped me so much these last five years. They visit me, call me, text me. I am surrounded by their love."

"You must have had a full house."

"Oh yes. We did. It was a four-bedroom home. One of those bedrooms was ours, and one was Willow's, so there were two extra bedrooms, but we also built a room over the garage, bright and light, so four children could sleep there at once if need be."

Tony was touched to his core as Ruthie told him a few of the children's stories—being abandoned, neglected, abused. How broken they were when they arrived at Ruthie and Russell's home. How Ruthie and Russell fed them, bought new clothes, provided a cheerful, warm, loving home. How they took them camping and hiking and out for ice cream. She did not say the names of the children whose stories she shared, as that would have been a terrible breach of their privacy.

"They came around," Ruthie said. "But they'd been hurt. They were angry, as they had every right to be. What had been done to them was unfair. I'm not going to pretend that they moved in and everything was perfect. It wasn't. There were emotional issues, behavioral issues, mental health issues. But now, almost all of them have safe, happy lives. The ones who don't are working on it, and I know they'll get there." Ruthie nodded. "I know it. I believe in them."

The children, now adults, who had lived with Ruthie and Russell, sat at home, or at the Deschutes family homestead, and watched the show and knew that the reason they hadn't ended up with their lives in the ditch, or themselves in a ditch—although one of their children actually slept in a ditch for a while because she was homeless—was because of Ruthie and Russell.

One, Charlotte, a heart surgeon, curled up with her husband and had herself a cleansing cry. She had been in Ruthie's English class. She loved learning about Octavia Butler and Anne Frank and Shakespeare. She was hiding from everyone then and tried to disappear, but Ruthie didn't let her disappear, and when Ruthie finally got her to tell the truth about what was going on at home with her mother's boyfriend, well, she found herself at Ruthie and Russell's house by that weekend. She was scared of Russell at first. He was a man, too. But she didn't need to be. He taught her how to fish, and he took her to work, and she found her calling. She wanted to heal people, heal their hearts, and that's what she did.

Anthony and Alex watched Ruthie on *Marry Me* together. They lived in one rambling house with their wives and seven children. Their wives were cousins. It was happy chaos in their home all the time, so much noise, but Anthony and Alex sat in silence and watched Ruthie intently. She and Russell had saved them. They were in her English class, and she noticed them. She listened to them. She made the right calls at the right time, when their situation was life-threateningly desperate, then said, "Come and live with us," and they did.

Anthony and Alex glanced at each other, then they both sniffled.

"Love you, Ruthie," Anthony whispered.

"Love you, Ruthie," Alex whispered.

They were not embarrassed to be crying in front of their children. They pointed Ruthie out to the kids and said, "There's Nana Ruthie!" and the kids went bananas.

"Nana Ruthie!" they screamed. "Nana Ruthie!" They jumped up and down. Two ran up and kissed Ruthie's face on the TV. "When can we go to her house again and see the doggies and the kitties and the piggy?"

Brothers Carlos and Diego watched *Marry Me* from their fancy homes in New York City and Paris, respectively. They came to live with Ruthie and Russell when they were literally abandoned by their mother at fourteen. They didn't know who their father was. Neither did their mother.

Their mother, who called herself Rainbow, had schizophrenia and told them they would be fine on their own. She put on a clown's wig, a pink princess dress, a puffy red coat, her yellow duck galoshes, and walked out with their red wagon, towing a cat named Plant. They sobbed as they watched her go. They both worked fast-food jobs in town to pay for their studio apartment and the bills.

They took Ruthie's English class and read *Night* by Elie Wiesel, *Flowers for Algernon* by Daniel Keyes, *The Outsiders* by S.E. Hinton, and *Jane Eyre* by Charlotte Brontë. She came to see them with Russell one evening in their studio apartment. That was when the invitation to live with them was offered. They said yes. They were starving. They were exhausted. They were emotionally crushed.

They took Ruthie's English class all four years of high school, like everyone else, but they also took computer and technology classes in which they had an "aptitude and acute intelligence," according to Russell, and their "technological talents should be explored." Each year, Ruthie and Russell sent them to a summer camp for three weeks, where they learned more about technology and computers. They also swam, sang camp songs, hiked, and had time to be kids.

Carlos and Diego went to college at Ruthie and Russell's insistence. They received full scholarships and grants, and Ruthie and Russell picked up the rest. They opened up their own technology company in their twenties, diving into social media. Soon, they were multimillionaires. They set up college scholarships in Ruthie's and Russell's names at her high school. The scholarships paid for four years of tuition and room and board for ten students every year.

When Ruthie said she loved all her children and how they were crystals together in a chandelier, Carlos and Diego both became so choked up they couldn't speak.

Ten of the children Ruthie and Russell brought into their home became nurses, doctors, physician assistants, or CNAs because Russell talked to them about his work. He took them with him to work during the summer and on weekends if they wished to go. He made arrangements for them to learn from other doctors and nurses, too. He spoke to them as adults and assured them that they could work in the medical field, too. They were shocked to hear this—shocked! They could be a doctor? A nurse? They were smart enough? Good enough? *Was Russell sure?*

They loved Russell. They respected him. They revered him. He was the father they did not have and longed for.

"There were a few children who struggled," Ruthie said to Tony. "That's to be expected after the difficult childhoods they had. They made mistakes. But I still have a relationship with all of them, even with the two who are in jail. I go and see them regularly. They'll be out next year. Neither one of them hurt anyone. Drugs brought on behavior that was not in their best interests, and they regret it. They reached for the drugs for relief from the pain their childhoods had caused them and to self-medicate mental health issues. If you knew their childhoods, you would understand. But I believe in second chances, and I believe in my beloved children, who I know will have successful lives now that they're sober." She looked right at the camera, which she had been told not to do many times. "You can do it! I love you!" She put up her fists in the victory stance and shook them, smiling broadly.

In separate prisons, Marty and Shyla were watching *Marry Me*. Ruthie had told them she was going on the show, as had their adopted brothers and sisters and Willow. All the kids kept in contact with one another, supported one another, encouraged by Russell and Ruthie to love one another. Marty and Shyla burst into tears.

"I love you, Ruthie," Shyla whispered, her body shaking. "I'll do it, I promise!"

"I'll do better, Ruthie," Marty cried, his head in his hands. "I promise. For you and for Russell. I still miss Russell so much. So much. Oh God. Russell. Help me."

They would do better.

In the future, Shyla would own a makeup company. It would go national. Her story of her broken childhood, her addiction, and struggles were part of the company's story, as were Russell and Ruthie and how their steadfast love saved her.

Marty would become a master welder who made sculptures that sold for thousands of dollars. He would weld a six-foot-tall heart for Ruthie and install it in her backyard amid yellow and white daisies. He planted the daisies so she would never forget how much all thirty-two of her children loved her.

Tony loved learning about Ruthie's children. Loved the idea of a huge family. He was a big man with a big heart.

Ruthie asked him about MaryBeth. He told her about how they met, their relationship, their love, how she had been killed. Tony wiped the tears from his face, and Ruthie wiped her tears, then his. Poor MaryBeth. She had clearly been a fabulous woman. They would have been friends, Ruthie was sure of it. What a tragedy. All the years MaryBeth had missed out on. The audience cried, too. What a loss! Poor MaryBeth! They were sure they would have liked her, too!

Ruthie was not threatened by MaryBeth, or how Tony had loved her, because she had known love, too. They were both seventy years old. They were embracing life and all the people they loved who had passed on to another adventure in the sky and those who were still with them. They were not twenty-five years old, when everything was new and shiny and uncomplicated. They were complicated. Their lives were complicated. They had memories and obligations and responsibilities to other people and animals.

And yet...

They were willing to jump into love again. *They wanted to jump.*

On the hike, marveling at one crystalline view after another, but watching out for bears, they laughed. A bear heard the laughter but went back to catching fish. A coyote, from her den, made no noise. Neither did her children. A red-breasted robin flew over them, curious.

They stopped hiking only when the crew asked them to. They'd gone far enough. They turned around and continued their conversation.

"They would have walked to Canada if we let them," Shonda said later, exhausted from all the hiking, but her nerves from her anxiety disorder still felt...settled. Better. Like the frazzled ends had melded together and softened when they were in the trees. She was a city lady, but maybe she should become a country lady, an outdoorsy lady.

"The camera folks were getting tired. Not easy to hike and film at the same time," Pearla said. "Good thing we didn't let them go to Canada." She, too, felt better. Being in nature helped. It was as if nature's serenity had seeped into her, along with a puff of wind, a little sunshine, and the glory of the mountain ranges.

"I think we have our bride," Shonda said, her chest heaving with exertion.

"Oh, for sure," Pearla said. "I hope they invite us to the wedding."

"Be nice and cross your fingers." Shonda bent over to catch her breath. "Ruthie owes us a dinner after that hike. I think I've got a blister."

Ruthie, on the hike, knew she had, without a doubt, fallen for Tony. "You old lovesick cow," she said out loud on the deck at the lodge when they were no longer together. "Let's try not to be pathetic about this."

People at home laughed.

That night, after Tony left, Ruthie made guacamole and homemade salsa in the kitchen at the lodge and brought out another bottle of Deschutes Family Tequila. The women had gotten used to drinking fire and then the warm, cuddly glow that came after that. They put on music and danced on the long, wood dining room table.

Later, Velvet proudly showed them pole dancing and stripping moves she'd learned from her mother. The brides were enthusiastic students, if only a tad stiff. The viewers loved it. What fun it was to be old! There was still life! Still laughter! Still silliness! The viewers were feeling more chill, groovier, about the whole aging thing. Yes, indeedy, they were.

And that Ruthie! Well, she was something special. What flexibility! What rhythm! She could dance and prance and strut! She swung around that imaginary pole and pretended to strip off her clothes with aplomb as if she'd been doing it for years. So impressive!

25

When Ruthie was twenty-four years old, she heard that Triple Mountain would soon be welcoming a new doctor in town. He would work at the new medical clinic. The old doctor, Herman Thompson, was retiring and moving to Florida. It was rumored that he had a girlfriend named Judith. She was seventy-five years old, too. Judith was his sister's best friend, and they'd known each other since fourth grade. Judith was widowed, too.

Ruthie was teaching English full time at the high school, and she was taking care of Willow, that dear, creative, happy, busy five-year-old. Willow had tons of blonde hair, like her mother, and her mother's cornflower blue eyes, two dimples, and a huge smile.

Thank God, all the Deschutes family members thought, Willow looked nothing like her snake-faced, weasel-butt father. They thought of him at the bottom of Bottomless Lake and hoped the bottom-dwelling fish had eaten him clean down to his lying bottom bones.

Ruthie and Willow had their own two-bedroom log cabin on Rattlesnake Lake. It was about nine hundred square feet, and it had belonged to Ruthie's great-uncle Bart. He had passed away at one hundred and one. He had built the log cabin himself, and it was an engineering miracle. The logs were precisely cut, the mortar tight, and no cold winter air dared flow in. He had a woodstove, new at only ten years old, that filled the entire cabin with heated coziness.

The family room and kitchen were one room. As a young man, Bart was modern in his thinking about how to live small, but well. Many large windows brought the light streaming in. Bart had liked light because he'd often gotten the "winter blues," so the windows had helped, as had a high, pitched ceiling.

Ruthie added blue and white plaid curtains that stretched to the floor on each window, except for in Willow's bedroom, which had pink velvet curtains. Willow's and Ruthie's bedrooms were down a short hallway, past a bathroom and a large closet for storing the canned and dried foods that Bart had prepared.

Ruthie's family helped her set up house—a blue couch, a flowered love seat, and a rocking chair arrived the morning she and Willow moved in. Two beds and a table and chairs were in place by afternoon. Ruthie liked to make a house look like a home, like her mother did. She took a little money out of her teaching salary and bought rugs and soft colorful pillows and made sure that she and Willow had fluffy comforters and heavy blankets on their beds.

Her plants, in blue, white, green, and red pots, lined the windowsills and hung from macrame in the corners. She added four lights with colorful shades on side tables and even one on the counter in the kitchen with a red shade. Framed photos of the Deschutes family hung on one wall, and Great-Uncle Bart's mother's quilt lay on the couch.

Ruthie and Willow pressed wildflowers in books, and when they were dry, they arranged them on mats and framed them for another wall. Right outside was Rattlesnake Lake, so the view was ever changing, with birds, ducks, deer, raccoons, coyotes, and an occasional wolf.

It was the perfect place to raise Willow, as it had been perfect for Ruthie. She was surrounded by family members' love and protection. Not everyone in their family lived around the lake — it was a gigantic family. Some had moved to cities for jobs, and a few were overseas. One worked for the CIA and was stationed in Russia. Some were serving in the military or away at college. But this was home base to everyone in the Deschutes family, and everyone returned for holidays, two weeks in summer, and, certainly, Rattlesnake Lake Jump Day.

Now and then, Ruthie would climb on a horse and go out to

Bottomless Lake. She would stare into it and breathe and remind herself that Wayne could not hurt her or Willow ever again. It calmed her down to be there, to tell herself that she would not be pummeled, or stalked, and that she would never lose Willow.

She was glad he was gone. She knew, down to every fiber of her being, that Wayne would have killed her. He'd been gunning for her, and the barn being lit on fire with the horses inside meant he had lost all control. No, Ruthie Deschutes knew that had he lived, she would not have. Willow might not have lived either.

She was a Deschutes. She had a hard, practical side to her. The Deschutes family protected their own. Her family had protected her and Willow.

As for her career, she loved her job teaching English at Triple Mountain. She wasn't much older than many of her students, but she brooked no disrespect. She and her students read fiction and nonfiction, memoirs and poetry, the classics, science fiction, autobiographies, and the latest literary blockbusters. Ruthie taught her students how to dig deep and read and dig deep and write.

She taught them how to think about stories and characters, ideas and imaginings, sensory details and descriptive words, correctly written sentences and grammar. "Analyze the text, the structure of the book, the dialogue, the voice and tone," she told them. "Apply what you read to your own life. What can you learn from this author? From this story?"

Her students, every single year, continued to win major state and national writing competitions. Later, some of her students would become famous writers, and all of them credited Ruthie.

It was a small high school, and she would often have the same kids for four years. Later, she taught their children, too, and woe to the child who was ever disrespectful to Mrs. O'Hara, as their parent would give them something to think about for the next month, and it wouldn't be pleasant.

Ruthie was strict. She pushed the kids. She told them the truth about their work and didn't coddle them. She was blunt. But she was, without question, the most popular teacher that Triple

Mountain had ever had for one overriding reason: All the students knew that she dearly loved and cared about them.

~~~

When Ruthie Deschutes met Dr. Russell O'Hara again, the man who had saved her life when she gave birth to Willow and almost hemorrhaged to death, it was because of a bow and arrow.

Her second cousin Billie Mae, twenty-six years old, had an arrow stuck in her shoulder. It was not Ruthie's fault. She had not shot the arrow off. It was her second cousin Hallowell's fault. Hallowell had not meant to shoot his sister with the arrow. He'd been trying to learn how to shoot a bow and arrow, and his aim had been cosmically bad. In fact, he'd pulled the arrow back on the bow, and somehow it had flipped in the air, twisted about, and landed in Billie Mae's shoulder.

Hallowell was so upset he started to cry, and when he saw all the blood, he passed out on the ground, facedown. Ruthie and Billie Mae, who was swearing at Hallowell for his "pig-snout stupidity," had to administer aid to Hallowell until he was revived and sitting upright. He was pale and white, like glue. Luckily, there was another second cousin nearby to help. Mandy, who was a manager at Deschutes Family Tequila, hauled Hallowell up into her truck to take him home to his mother and get him some rest and lemonade. Ruthie and Billie Mae climbed into Ruthie's pickup and headed to the clinic. Luckily, Willow wasn't there at the time, as she was with Ruthie's mother, making feminist gingerbread women.

Ruthie propped up Billie Mae as they entered the new clinic. Another cousin, Gigi, was the receptionist and came running. Gigi was going to school full time. Years later, she would end up being a nurse in charge of a surgical ward at a hospital in the city. Gigi helped Ruthie get Billie Mae, still swearing, into a room.

A few minutes later, in walked Dr. Russell O'Hara, calm and reassuring. His attention rested ever so briefly on Ruthie, then he said hello to everyone, but vaguely, as the arrow sticking out of

Billie Mae got his attention right quick. He attended to her, got the arrow out, cleaned the wound, and sewed her up.

While he worked, Ruthie stared at him, the night Dr. O'Hara saved her life coming back to her in sharp, ragged, fully formed, blood-soaked pictures. She remembered the searing pain and sheer panic and feeling the life draining out of her. She remembered seeing her dead relatives as the white ceiling turned to blue sky and opened up.

Dr. O'Hara would not remember her, she thought, but she remembered him. He was her hero because he had saved Willow and her.

But Ruthie was wrong.

When Billie Mae was sewed up tight, and she had stopped swearing up a storm, Russell turned his attention to Ruthie. He stared at her. She stared back. He didn't say anything. He told her later that he could not say that he remembered treating her because that would let Billie Mae know that they had met before, and that would have violated Ruthie's medical privacy.

In fact, as soon as Russell had seen Ruthie, he'd remembered her, but he had been distracted by that pesky arrow.

He had checked up on her every day while she was at the hospital, recovering from her injuries, the birth, and having flatlined on the table. She was easy to talk to. She had a golden light to her, a happy spirit that had been trampled and suffocated, but he could tell it was still there. She was intelligent, with a tricky, but kind, sense of humor, and they talked about books they had read and loved. She teased him, made him smile and laugh. She talked about her unique family, their antics and crazy traditions, and she asked him questions about himself so she could truly get to know him. He was smitten. His heartbeat fast around her. But there was nothing to be done. She was his patient. It would be inappropriate to ask her to dinner. Plus, he was ten years older. She was too young.

At that time, Russell hadn't been to Vietnam yet, although he would go shortly, where senseless tragedy and blood and chilling screams would surround him like a spiked vise. Post-Vietnam, he wanted to continue his medical career in a small, quiet, peaceful town. But it had been—what? —five or six years, give or take, since he'd seen Ruthie. He was relieved that she was healthy and well. He wondered what had happened to the violent husband.

"I know you, Dr. O'Hara," Ruthie said softly, her hands gripped tightly in her lap. "You were my doctor when I went into labor with my daughter, Willow, too early. I had… My husband…" She tried again. "My ex-husband had beaten me, and I hemorrhaged after the birth. I'm sure you don't remember me but thank you again for all you did for my daughter and for me."

"I remember you, Ruthie," Russell said, comfortable talking about it now, as she had been the one to bring up their history. "I have thought of you many times over the years." It was true. He had. Once smitten, you don't get over it. "How are you?"

"I'm well," she said. "My ex-husband, uh… He left me after that." She coughed. Billie Mae focused on her cowgirl boots. She would not reveal a Deschutes

family secret.

"I went back to school when my daughter was one. To the University of Oregon.

I'm an English teacher at the high school."

"Excellent," Russell said, his eyes soft, yet sharp because he loved reading. "Who are your favorite writers at the moment?"

There could not have been a more romantic question asked of Ruthie. Their love affair began. It would last over forty years, until death did they part.

"Charlotte Brontë, Emily Brontë, Kate Chopin, Toni Morrison, Maya Angelou, Zora Neale Hurston, Gwendolyn Brooks, Shakespeare, Steinbeck, CS Lewis. I find Ernest Hemingway boring, and I didn't like *Moby Dick* or *The Catcher in the Rye*. I suppose I'll still talk to you if you feel differently about those two books, but I will always question why."

He smiled at Ruthie Deschutes. "I feel the same way about *Moby Dick* and *The Catcher in the Rye*. However, I liked *The Old Man and the Sea* and *For Whom the Bell Tolls*." Dr. O'Hara took a deep breath and tried to be brave. Ruthie had been in and out of his head for years. Her smile never left him. *Ask her,* he told himself. *Do it. She is not your patient anymore.* "Perhaps we can talk about books over dinner? Are you...free?" His voice wobbled with embarrassment and nervousness. Russell was not a player. He was not smooth with the ladies. He was thirty-four and didn't even know how to flirt.

"Yes," Billie Mae said, her head snapping up, the arrow now in her hand, not in her arm. "Ruthie's free. She can go anytime. I'll take care of Willow."

Ruthie stared at Billie Mae, openmouthed, then back at Dr. Russell. She tilted her head up and made a decision. "She's right. I'm free."

"She's very free," Billie Mae insisted again, leaning forward. "Any evening, anytime. She's available, and she would like to go to dinner with you. When?"

Ruthie gaped, once again, at Billie Mae.

Ruthie was not free for long. Dr. Russell O'Hara had Ruthie at the altar on the Deschutes family land in six months, right in front of Rattlesnake Lake, on a clear blue day with a hundred birds chirping musically from the trees and almost two hundred members of the Deschutes clan, plus the O'Hara family and dozens of friends in attendance. The pigs were turnin' on the spits, the homemade wedding cakes towered (there had been a contest to see who could make the tallest cake), the tequila runnin' like a river.

The huge family band played late into the night, the uncles, aunts, and cousins who were musically inclined strummin' the fiddles, bangin' the drums, and ticklin' the guitar strings.

Billie Mae framed the arrow stuck in her arm and gave it to Ruthie and Russell as a wedding present so they would always remember it was she and Hallowell who put them and their love together. Hallowell could never look at the framed arrow. It made him pass out.

Ruthie and Russell raised Willow together. Willow loved Russell. They bought the yellow farmhouse so Dr. Russell could be closer to the clinic.

When Russell had terrible nightmares about Vietnam, Ruthie

hugged him close. When he struggled with flashbacks and post-traumatic stress, which sometimes brought on tears and a black depression, Ruthie was there for him. When she remembered what Wayne had done to her, Russell listened, and she blocked that period out of her life once again. When she was upset about a child whose home life was soul-destroying, they welcomed another child through their front door and filled their home with more love.

Russell and Ruthie had a Family Book Club with Willow and "their new children," where they discussed a new book each week, and they had their own private book club, too, reading the same book and discussing it in bed.

They were in love and in lust their entire marriage, the gymnastics in the bedroom always a thrill.

Ruthie Deschutes O'Hara would always miss Russell, every day, after he passed away. On the other hand, she would also be grateful, every day, for the time she had with him.

It was that gratefulness, and the memories, and their eternal love, that saved her and made her go on living even when he could no longer hold her hand while they watched *Marry Me* on TV.

A two on one date was announced by Jackson. Two women. One hot cowboy.

Ruthie was not invited.

The viewing audience, again, felt wretched for Ruthie. She blinked rapidly, then put her shoulders back and her chin up so she would not invoke pity. She was wearing a flowered blue sundress, another message to Willow and Lucy. Every Easter, they bought sundresses together in town at Kasa and Kali's Boutique, two of Ruthie's adopted daughters.

Pamela Topava, who'd had to escape a mean husband through a back window and who sometimes had alligators in her pool in Florida, was sent home at the I Do ceremony. Ruthie knew that she and Pamela would be friends outside of the show. Anyone who liked alligators like Pamela did would be fun to be around.

"And then there were six," Ruthie said.

The audience at home laughed.

"Agatha Christie," Ruthie said. "I think you and I would have been friends."

Ruthie; Sarah Whitemore, who had been in a cult; Velvet, who owned a lingerie business started by her mother, a stripper; Dr. Benedetta, the gynecologist; Susie, the architect who milked cows as a girl; and Maria, the painter from Mexico who wanted to paint Ruthie naked, were all who remained.

After the I Do ceremony, Ruthie and Tony managed to sneak a few minutes alone together with the camera people, Shonda, Pearla, crew members, and others, blah blah.

They chatted, easy and cheerful, as if they'd been chatting for years, had known each other back in the day, and had memories as wide as the starry Milky Way, as deep as the sea, from the tip of the snowy Rocky Mountains to the edge of the clouds, up the mighty Deschutes River and back again.

Tony kissed her.

Ruthie didn't blush, not exactly.

But her response—delighted, sweet, leaning back and laughing in his hug—was enough to make the people at home watching tear up and clap their hands.

Yay, Ruthie!

Romance was alive and well!

Love could be found at any age!

This was the best dating show *ever*.

Willow and Lucy sat on the couch together, watching *Marry Me*. Nancy Drew was snoring. She had such a loud snore. It was like listening to a drone.

"That was a wowza kiss, but what is going on?" Willow said with indignant impatience. "Why isn't Tony taking Mom on a date?" She took a huge handful of buttered popcorn from the bowl between them and shoved it into her mouth.

"She deserves it!" Lucy said, equally upset. She shoved a handful of popcorn into her mouth, too. "This is ridiculous! Nana Ruthie is the best one for him. Anyone can see that. They need more time alone together to talk. You can tell he likes her. I am so mad!" She accidentally sprayed bits of popcorn from her mouth. "So mad!"

"I am beside myself," Willow said. "Beside myself!"

The owl hooted. Clearly, even she was up in arms.

"She's wearing the blue flowered sundress she bought last year when we all went shopping," Willow said.

"I noticed," Lucy said. "I bought my red one."

"Mine was white."

They both couldn't swallow, lumps of tears in their throats. Lucy had been doing some hard thinking. Hard decision-making. Hard self-reflections.

"She keeps talking to us," Willow said.

"I know," Lucy said. "I'm a terrible granddaughter."

"I'm a terrible daughter," Willow said.

Willow and Lucy clinked their shot glasses together, tipped their heads back, and put the bottoms up. "To Mom," and, "To Nana Ruthie," they said, their voices choked.

"He must not have a brain," Willow said later. "Any other man would jump to take Mom out on a date!"

Lucy agreed he was clearly brainless. Maybe he had a hole in his head. It was the only explanation.

They couldn't wait to see her again. They missed her so.

26

Marry Me

Interview: Tony Beckett

Interviewed by: Tyler, the associate producer, who finds working all day so tedious and tiring.

Tyler: How's it going, Tony?

Tony: Everything is going well.

Tyler: You've had to send a lot of brides home.

Tony: Yes, that's part of the show, unfortunately.

Tyler: It must be hard.

Tony: It is. They are all amazing women.

Tyler: Who do you think is the sexiest?

Tony: You've already asked me that question. Let's not demean the women.

Tyler: Sorry. I forgot. It's been a long day. I'm exhausted. Totally worn out. Who do you think would be most physically compatible with you in the, you know, bedroom?

Tony: I'm not going to answer that question. Again, let's not demean the women.

Tyler: Brides.

Tony: What?

Tyler: Remember? You're supposed to call them brides.

Tony: Any more questions, Tyler?

Tyler: No, uh. Thank you.

Text thread between Tony, Shonda, and Pearla:

Tony: Shonda and Pearla, I'm not doing any more interviews with Tyler.

Shonda: Okay.

Pearla: Gotcha.

27

There was a one-on-one date two days later.

All the women got ready to congratulate Ruthie. Surely it would be her! The other ladies wanted to go, naturally, and there was some jealousy and wistfulness and maybe a tad of hopelessness because Ruthie would get Tony all to herself, all day, and that might spell doom for them, but they were older, and realistic, and it was Ruthie's turn.

Ruthie was hopeful. She stared straight into the camera, even though she'd been told not to, and said, "Crossing my fingers for good luck! I think I'll also cross my eyes!" She then crossed her eyes and walked toward the camera. The viewers at home heard the camerawoman and Shonda laughing. Shonda snorted, twice, then shrieked a little, which made it funnier.

Ruthie did not get the date. Jackson's face fell when he saw Ruthie's sad, but quickly covered, reaction. Ruthie deserved to go, Tony wanted to take her, but there were things going on behind the scenes that Jackson couldn't tell her.

Even Velvet, who was invited on the date, seemed surprised. She turned to Ruthie and said, truly regretful, "I'm so sorry, Ruthie. You deserved this date."

Ruthie's eyes flooded, then she smiled, lickety-split.

Velvet's eyes flooded, then she hugged Ruthie.

Maria and Benedetta were disappointed for Ruthie, though they wanted Tony for themselves. This was so perplexing. Tony seemed so intrigued by Ruthie, so smitten, but he apparently...wasn't. He was choosing other women who had already been on dates to, *again*, have another date with him.

"Stop that crying!" Ruthie said. "You go and enjoy yourself, Velvet. You've taught me a ton about seductive stripping and twirling around on a pole without throwing out my back. When Tom Selleck calls me for a date, I'll know exactly what to do to turn him on! I'll knock Tom's socks off, and I'll marry him, and you can be my maid of honor and do a striptease at the rehearsal dinner. Now, go!"

Velvet left to get ready for her date, flattered that Ruthie had chosen her to be maid of honor for her marriage to Tom Selleck. Velvet absolutely loved Tony. She so wanted to be with him forever. If only she and Ruthie could be sister wives! She wouldn't mind sharing a husband with Ruthie.

Ruthie snuck out of the lodge and onto the back deck late that night, after the crew had stumbled back to their hotel to crash. She brought a coat and a blanket, as even in summer Whitefish, Montana, could cool down quickly when the moon was gliding on through. She found a padded chaise lounge in a quiet corner in the shadows, dropped her head back and took deep breaths.

Up in the mountains, a cougar stalked his prey. He was starving. He'd hurt his paw on Tuesday and hadn't had anything to eat for two days. An elk settled down for the night after the limping cougar passed him by. The two friendly owls had a hooting contest. They did this every night. It was relaxing. White stars glowed extra bright, as though the Milky Way were trying to put on a show for Ruthie.

Ruthie missed her daughter and granddaughter desperately. She missed her other thirty-one children and their children. She missed her Deschutes family and her home and her pets. She still missed her teaching job, and she again cursed LeeLee the Twit and the uptight principal with the face of a mean crane.

She missed Russell. Tonight, it felt like her heart was crying.

She missed his kindness and friendship, his total acceptance and love of who she was as a person. She missed his humor and how he always listened to her. She missed hearing about his patients and what he'd done for them and their annual animal parade for the shelter and how they dressed up as cats and dogs.

Russell had been a good man. But he hadn't been perfect. He could be totally absent-minded. He had easily been riled up by laziness or poor attitudes. He had been known to upbraid patients who were not doing their best to save their own lives. There had been some ego there, too. He hadn't been a talented cook either, but he'd thought he was.

But who was perfect? No one. Ruthie herself knew she could be sharp-tongued. Too blunt. Efficient to the point of rudeness. Now and then, she'd be moody. Patience was not her best virtue. She could go on. She knew her faults.

Ruthie thought of Tony.

She was seriously attracted to him, the *love* word always on the tip of her tongue, as if waiting for the right moment to be uttered aloud. It became stronger every time she was with him. She felt guilty. What about Russell and their love? But she reminded herself for the hundredth time that Russell had been gone for five years. Anything could happen at her age.

If Tony wanted to be with her, she should take his hand and jump, shouldn't she? Wouldn't she want Russell to have someone else if she had climbed that golden staircase to the sky first?

Ruthie's face turned gloomy, and her mouth turned down as she pictured Russell with another woman.

No, she wouldn't want him to be with another woman.

Yes, of course, she would.

No.

Yes. She would want him to meet someone else. She would want him to be happy if she were dead, with that new, pesky woman. Well, somewhat happy. She would want him to miss her and always know that she was the best wife in the world.

And then when they were both joined together again in

heaven, she would want him to drop Wife Number Two as fast as he'd drop a rabid raccoon or boiling tar.

That was another one of her faults: She was a bit possessive over Russell.

But back to the present. In the blackness of the night, Ruthie blew out her breath. She wanted to hug Tony, be wrapped against that huge chest as she stared up at his wry smile. She wanted to kiss him and remove his shirt and pants. She wanted to talk to him and laugh.

When she looked into his eyes, she saw him, deeply saw him, and he saw her, too, she thought. It was the connection that you couldn't explain, passion flaring and a deep, inexplicable understanding of the other person that was reciprocated. It was a feeling of peace and relief, as you realized you had finally found your person. Someone who got you.

But maybe Tony didn't see her. Maybe there was no connection for him. No passion for her. No understanding between them. He wasn't asking her out on dates, and that was a problem. Maybe she was getting dementia, Ruthie thought. It was starting now. She should get her head examined. Was she delusional to think that there was something between them that Tony shared, too? Was she a crazy old bat?

She'd come on the show to reunite with Willow and Lucy. She had an ulterior motive. She wasn't here for the right reasons. This wasn't supposed to happen. Tony was not supposed to happen. Love was not supposed to happen.

She had wanted to ask Tony why he had not asked her out for another date, but she didn't want to come off as a whiny, withering, whimpering wizard of a woman. (*Another* alliteration!)

She heard a stick snapping and knew that an animal was sneaking by. She wondered what it was.

It was a raccoon, but he minded his own business, and Ruthie eventually went to bed, loneliness and a little fear, the fear of losing Tony, wrapping itself around her like a cold blanket.

There was a date the next day.

Two women, Jackson announced. And those two women were...Sarah Whitemore and Maria Gonzales. Jackson watched Ruthie's face and wanted to hug her. He, again, knew why she had not been invited out on a date, but he couldn't tell her.

Sarah and Maria had both been on dates with Tony before.

There was a shocked collective inhale of breath.

What about Ruthie?

The other women looked at her, and everyone caught the broken expression on her face, but Ruthie, wham and bam, shut it down tight—she wasn't a pouter—and she smiled, congratulating Sarah and Maria.

"Have fun!" she called when they stood to go.

Ruthie thought she'd cry. How damn embarrassing would that be? She'd disgrace herself. Plus, she didn't want to look like a bad sport or an object of pity—that would be the worst.

Sarah hugged Ruthie. Maria hugged Ruthie. Ruthie said, "Be naughty, not nice!"

After Sarah and Maria left, Benedetta and Velvet leaned into Ruthie and said, "I'm sorry, Ruthie."

"It's fine!" she said. "I'm fine. So, what's on tap today? Let's sneak out of this ruthless dungeon and go shopping in Whitefish!"

Shonda and Pearla said that sounded like fun, but they couldn't go. They needed to stay at the lodge for more filming.

The ladies snuck out anyhow. For heaven's sake. They didn't like following rules, and they didn't have to at their age. An Uber came to pick them up at the bottom of the drive. They had been hiding behind trees and bushes. They hurried to the car, cackling with glee, and climbed in.

28

Marry Me

Interview: Maria Gonzales

Interviewed by: Tyler, the associate producer, who is learning a lot about older women. He had no idea that any woman over the age of thirty-five could be interesting, even fascinating. He often feels like he's struggling intellectually around them, too, which shouldn't be happening. He went to Stanford, after all.

Tyler: Hi, Maria. Can you tell me about yourself?

Maria: Sure. My family escaped the cartels in Mexico when I was ten. My father was a police officer. He could not be bribed or corrupted. They tried to kill him, twice. In the middle of the night, we snuck out of the house. My mother, father, and me with my five siblings. I carried my two-year-old brother on my back. My father carried my sister, who was three. My mother carried my baby brother.

It was a long and dangerous trip. We went by car and by train, which we snuck onto. We walked endless miles. It was hot, we ran out of water and food, we got sick. My little brother almost died of pneumonia. My oldest sister fell and got a concussion. She didn't wake up for twenty-four hours. We were robbed twice. We were threatened. We were hurt.

We were detained in America and applied for citizenship. We were dead poor. My parents went to work in a chicken factory, and my older siblings and I went to school. The youngest ones stayed with my mom's sister. We saved all our money for a lawn mower and an old truck. When we had the lawn mower and an old truck, my father went into business for himself, mowing and edging lawns. We saved for a second lawn mower and edge trimmer. When we could buy both, and had enough clients, my mother joined him.

We got an apartment—two bedrooms—and we thought it was the greatest place ever. It was bright and safe, and the door locked. No one was trying to kill my father anymore. My parents told us that our job was to get high grades in school so we could go to college. We took care of each other when our parents were gone. They worked twelve-hour days. They were kind and gentle.

Good things happened in America to us, some bad, too, which I don't talk about anymore, except with my trauma therapist. Some people were welcoming. Other people made us feel that we were beneath them, that they were better than us as people, that our brown skin wasn't equal to their white, and we did not deserve respect. We were called names at school, like wetback and beaner and poor Mexican trash, and that hurt.

My parents' lawn mowing and landscaping company expanded. My mother instinctively knew how to design beautiful gardens. She could create an oasis from nothing. She drew plans with pathways, different garden rooms, retaining walls, fishponds, trellises, gazebos, arches, patios, and added trees, shrubs, and flower beds. She was a garden artist, and soon she was in demand. We all worked for the company on weekends and during summers. We earned our citizenship. We bought a small house in a nice neighborhood and a better truck. My siblings and I all graduated from college. I am an artist. We are proud of our history and proud to be American.

Tyler: Wow. That's an amazing story. My family has been through hard times, too. Our kitchen caught on fire in the Hamptons when I was younger.

Maria: I'm sorry that happened. That must have been scary and sad.

Tyler: It was! My parents and sister and I had to move to our beach house on Cape Cod while our contractor built us a brand-new kitchen with two ovens.

Maria: Oh. What a tragedy.

Tyler: Exactly.

29

Tony sent Maria home at the next I Do ceremony.

Tony felt so guilty. She'd shown him photos of her art, and it was flowing, original, colorful, and emotional. If he had met her at home, maybe things would have been different. She was wise, thoughtful, and had a backstory that spoke of hardship, cruelty, and deprivation, followed by courage, love, and resilience.

But she wasn't Ruthie. Tony wiped tears that were threatening to spill down his cheeks. The camera caught it. He hugged Maria goodbye, and she clung to him and cried on his shoulder.

She warbled out, "Look, Tony, you're a catch. I wish you nothing but the best, but if you want the best, it's Ruthie." She paused and sniffled. "But if you change your mind, please call me. I don't mind leaving tonight if it means I get to see you again. Adios."

He felt an overwhelming sense of shame and pain. How would it feel to be Maria? One woman being sent home after another. This show hurt people. He hurt people. He never wanted to hurt anyone. He didn't think he was much of a catch, but he sure didn't want to make anyone cry. What the hell had he been thinking even coming on this show? He harshly castigated himself for the twentieth time. He should have stayed on his land with his horses and old dogs.

But then he wouldn't have met Ruthie.

Would it be worth it for him if it worked out with Ruthie? Yes. For sure. But for the other women? Was it worth it for them? No.

Shonda and Pearla approached him. "So, the date you were

saving for Ruthie? The one with the helicopter? We are so sorry, but they're still having a mechanical issue."

"What? Still? What's wrong? Did the rotor fall off? We were supposed to be on this date days ago." His tone reflected his impatience and anger.

"I know. We're sorry. They're waiting for a part. It had to be shipped." This was all true. It was not a rigged event by the show. "We're going to have you take Susie and Benedetta out for a date on one of those red buses. You'll be taken on a tour on Going-to-the-Sun Road in Glacier National Park."

He looked down at his boots. He wondered if it was fair to go on with this show at all. How could it be? He had already chosen Ruthie.

"Tony?" Shonda asked. "Are you okay?"

"Yeah, I'm okay. I..." Tony said. "I've already chosen who I want."

"We know," Pearla said.

"You know?" Tony asked.

"It's pretty obvious," Shonda said, smiling.

Pearla smiled, too.

"Ruthie is everyone's favorite," Shonda said. "We had a vote with the crew a week into the show on who we thought you would choose."

"And?" Tony said.

"Ruthie had eighty percent of the votes."

"That is not surprising," he muttered.

"But the problem," Pearla said, "is that the show isn't over. Can you do this date with Benedetta and Susie tomorrow? Then you can go on the date with Ruthie in the helicopter. We'll send you the next day. There won't be any wait between dates, as there usually is. It's all day long, into the evening. We'll make it up to you two."

"This is not fair to Benedetta and Susie," Tony said. "I'm leading them on. We should end this." Tony had not kissed anyone on the show except Ruthie. He hadn't wanted to, and he felt it would be betraying Ruthie. How would she feel if she later saw an episode where he was kissing another woman? That would not be fair or right. She might feel betrayed.

Shonda and Pearla had encouraged him from the start to kiss the other women—all of them, if he would! —and he'd told them in no uncertain terms that he would kiss a woman if he damn well felt like it and if he felt she would be receptive.

"I understand how you feel about Benedetta and Susie," Shonda said. "But the women signed up for it. They knew what they were getting into. It'll be fun. It's you three alone on the red bus. The views are gorgeous. We've got lunch ready. It's delicious. The ladies will have a super time. It'll be an amazing memory, and they'll get more screen time."

"Their grandchildren will see them and be proud of them," Pearla said. "They've made it almost to the end. That's something special. Let them have their day. We'll even buy them Glacier National Park sweatshirts and hats to wear. It gets cold at the top. They can stay another few nights at the lodge, too, until the next I Do ceremony."

Tony sighed, looked up and away, those blue eyes so romantic, so steady when you caught his attention. Shonda and Pearla were half in love with him even though he was too old for them. Probably. Maybe not. Probably not.

"Okay," Tony said. "But then that's it. I'm done. I'll take Ruthie on the helicopter date, and if it's still having a mechanical issue, then I'm telling Ruthie, and the other women, the truth, and we end this."

"Agreed," Shonda and Pearla said.

Tony nodded and headed off.

"When I'm around him, my anxiety simmers right on down," Shonda said, her voice dreamy. "I feel…electrified. But mellow, like I'm on a cloud. I'm beginning to think I could date an older man."

"He's like human Xanax," Pearla said, her voice almost a whisper. "He makes you calm down, feel deliciously woozy inside, and then you start to believe that the world is going to be tilted in the right direction as long as he stays by your side."

"He's like a galaxy," Shonda said. "He makes me see stars."

They both laughed so hard they bent over and crossed their legs.

The next morning, Tony came to the lodge with Jackson. Usually, it was only Jackson, and he announced the date and who was going on it, but it was different today.

Tony was wearing jeans, boots, and a black T-shirt. Inwardly, all the ladies admitted to wanting to drag that man upstairs to bed and fling him on it.

Ruthie's heart thumped like Scarlett O'Hara's back foot when she was teasing the cats. It had to be her for the date, didn't it? She felt like a teenager. Giddy. Happy. Tony was like cake. Delicious. Yummy.

It was a cool summer day, so Ruthie had on her jeans with a swirling diamond design on the back pockets. She had found them when she was shopping with Willow and Lucy. They were a little tight, but she was proud of her seventy-year-old butt. She was wearing her bright white tennis shoes and a T-shirt that said "Tequila Brings Out the Wild Woman in Me." Her four gold hoops with the hearts at the bottom were in her ear lobes—given to her by Willow and Lucy.

"Hello, everyone," Tony said.

"Hello, ladies," Jackson said, right beside Tony. Jackson was tired. The triplets had clogged the toilet with Tinkertoys. It had flooded the whole bathroom. He'd heard them giggling and talking about their new "swimming pool" and instantly had known they'd caused trouble. The day before, they'd dressed up in their vampire Halloween outfits with their fake white vampire teeth and escaped out the back door of their rented house to the street. They'd started skipping to the ice cream parlor in town. No money with them, as expected. Ice cream, to them, was free. They were supposed to have been napping. Henry had been beside himself.

Tony looked tired, too. Worn out, Ruthie thought. He needed a nap. With her.

"We're almost done with this journey," Tony said. "It's been…" He paused. "It has turned into something I never imagined."

The women agreed.

"Today, we're going to take a red bus up Going-to-the-Sun Road, and we're going hiking. We've got a picnic lunch…"

Oh, that sounds like fun! Ruthie thought. She would love today!

"I've been told that I can take two women," Tony said.

Two? Ruthie thought. *Well! That will still work.* She liked the women here. They would have a fabulous time.

"Benedetta." Tony's voice choked.

Ruthie grinned at Benedetta, sitting right next to her, and Benedetta beamed back. They had the same sense of humor—often dipping into raunchy, pretty much what you would expect from a gynecologist—so this matchup was perfect!

"Susie," Tony said

Susie. Not *Ruthie.*

The roar of pain started in Ruthie's chest. It was like a piece of glass cut through her skin and into her heart, then shattered. She felt herself sway on the couch, her shoulder leaning heavily against Benedetta's. Benedetta wrapped an arm around her, quickly analyzing Ruthie with concern. She was a doctor, after all. The pain radiated from her chest down to her stomach. Her stomach responded by contracting.

Ruthie caught Tony's gaze. She didn't know how to interpret his expression. It was solid. Not revealing much…but deep inside, did she see regret? Sadness?

She smiled at him, but she felt her mouth tremble. She wouldn't let him know that she felt like she'd been kicked in the face with a cowboy boot, but she did.

Everything was a blur as Benedetta, after giving Ruthie a one arm hug on the couch, and Susie stood to go on their date.

"See you soon, Ruthie," Tony said, his voice...rough, rumbling. He looked like he wanted to say something else, but he didn't.

Ruthie's neck felt tight, like someone was strangling her. She smiled at him again as best she could but didn't say anything, because she couldn't get any words out of her constricted throat. Her smile teetered this way and that, and she imagined she looked like a gargoyle with stomach flu.

"I'm sorry, Ruthie," Jackson said after the women and Tony left. He sat on the couch next to her and patted her shoulder. He felt bad for Ruthie, but she would be thrilled to go on the helicopter ride tomorrow. They had been assured that the helicopter would be ready to go. It was, by far and away, the best date. They would be landing up in the mountains by a crystalline lake, the view panoramic. "I'm really sorry."

"That's okay!" Ruthie said, but she struggled to pull herself together, and her mouth wasn't working right. It wouldn't smile. She knew what this meant, though. She would not be chosen at the I Do ceremony to stay. That was quite clear. All of the women had had previous dates. Tony was taking them out again because he wanted more time with them. She had misread him. She had seen what she had wanted to see, not reality. Yep. She'd blame it on her dementia.

She thought she might have a heart attack.

"Are you okay?" Velvet asked, rushing over. "Ruthie?"

"Take a breath," Sarah said. "Please."

"Oh yes. I'm fine." But this was it, Ruthie thought. She was done.

"Your hand is on your chest," Shonda said, her face scrunched with worry as she knelt in front of her. She put her hand over Ruthie's. "Are you okay, Ruthie?"

"Yes, I'm fine!" She smiled again. The camera caught the sheen of tears. "I think I'll go lie down for a minute."

They nodded. They understood. And they'd gotten enough film—that was important. Next week, the viewers would see this emotion-laden scene.

Ruthie climbed the stairs with only a little wobble here and there. She lay down to make sure her heart wasn't giving out, then stood and packed.

There was a camera in Ruthie's room, but no one was watching it right now. The cameras all went off at night, but it was fair game to film the brides until then—the brides knew that. Shonda and Pearla didn't know what was happening, or you could bet they would have been up there in a flash, begging her to stop.

Ruthie booked a taxi to the airport. She wasn't allowed her own phone so she asked for the phone of a young producer walking by in her best English teacher voice. He broke the rules, naughty young man, and handed his phone to her. "You're my grandma's favorite contestant," he told her eagerly.

Ruthie's heart ached. It shouldn't. It was ridiculous. She was on a reality TV show. This wasn't real life. She had lived real life for seventy years. Ruthie had never thought she would fall in love and marry again. It had seemed preposterous to her.

But she had fallen in love with Tony. It was shocking to her, and the pain was nearly paralyzing. She'd found her person in Tony, but he had not found his person in her.

She longed for her kids, especially Willow, and her home and pets. Maybe Willow and Lucy would talk to her when she was home. She hoped they would. She bent her head and cried. Tony wanted someone else. She understood. She liked the women here, too. She cried again.

⁂

Later, when the crew saw that Ruthie had been bent over on her bed, crying in her bedroom, shoulders shaking, even the toughest ones there became emotional. She was seventy years old! She was widowed! She had wanted to find love! This would probably be her only chance! Her heart was shredded. They knew it. They could see it. This wasn't right.

When the viewers saw the clip, they cried, too. Almost all of them had had their heart broken, too. They understood. They empathized. A forty-six-year-old father in Omaha whose wife had left him; a seventy-two-year-old farmer in Arkansas who had lost his husband; and a twenty-two-year-old college student whose girlfriend had broken up with him all sobbed.

Life could shred you apart when the one you loved did not love you.

30

Marry Me

Interview: Ruthie Deschutes O'Hara

Interviewed by: Shonda and Pearla, co-directors.

Shonda: What are you doing, Ruthie? Please sit down. Can we get an interview?

Ruthie: I will sit for five minutes at the most. I've decided to go home.

Shonda: What? No. Please don't. Ruthie. Oh. My. God. Don't. We want you to stay. Why do you want to leave? We love having you here. Please. Let me take your suitcases back upstairs for you.

Ruthie: I have had the best time here, but it's time I went home. I need to see my kids, my grandkids, my family, and my dogs, cats, rabbit, and pig.

Pearla: Ruthie, are you leaving because you haven't had a date with Tony?

Ruthie: Excuse me. Give me a moment.

Pearla: Oh dear. Can someone get her a tissue?

Ruthie: I miss home. And I think I've done what I wanted to do here.

Shonda: What did you want to do here?

Ruthie: To be honest, the reason I signed up for the show was because my daughter and my granddaughter and I used to watch *Marry Me* together, and I wanted them to see me on the show. I knew they would think it was a fantastic idea, and it would be fun for them. It would give us something to talk about, to laugh about. I thought it would be a blast for me, too. I never thought I would...I would...

Shonda: Yes?

Ruthie: I never thought that I would actually, necessarily, *like* the groom. Oh, I thought he might be kind and relatively smart. Although, the grooms in the other *Marry Me* shows were often plagued by a lack of intelligence, and a few were barely verbal, almost prehistoric in their understanding of life, and they weren't readers, I could tell, so I did have my doubts about your ability to attract intellectual, emotionally deep, and unselfish men.

Pearla: You didn't think many of the previous grooms were smart?

Ruthie: Please. I doubt any of them had ever read Hawthorne or Khaled Hosseini or Geraldine Brooks or Octavia Butler

Pearla: But you think Tony is smart?

Ruthie: Tony is brilliant.

Pearla: So, you like Tony?

Ruthie: How could you not like Tony? He can talk about anything under the sun, including books. His life, and all that he has accomplished, is impressive, especially his service to this country and his tour in Vietnam and how he built his business. I respect him. I like that he cares about his land and adores his sons and their families. He was an excellent husband to MaryBeth, loyal and true. He takes gentle care of his animals. One of his horses is twenty-four years old and is treated like a queen. One of his dogs is twenty-one. You have to love a man who loves his old pets. He's funny. He even laughs at my jokes. He's serious, and he can enjoy life. He likes and cares about people. He has an open mind and compassion for others. He has depth, he's led a self-examined life, and he's introspective. Most men like being introspective about as much as they would like to walk a rat on a leash to work.

Shonda: Then why leave?

Ruthie: Because it's time.

Pearla: Please don't quit.

Ruthie: Young lady! I am not quitting!

Pearla: Oh! Yes, ma'am. No, ma'am.

Ruthie: I have never quit anything in my life. I am a Deschutes and an O'Hara. We do not quit. I am leaving a situation that has become unbearably painful to me, where the outcome will only cause more pain. I am a sensible and practical woman and see no need to continue. I miss my life in Oregon and the people I love. There is no reason to delay my return.

Pearla: Yes, ma'am. No, ma'am. I'm sorry. That was a poor choice of words on my part, ma'am.

Shonda: I don't think that Tony wants you to go.

Ruthie: I am quite sure he will understand, as he, too, is practical and sensible. In fact, why put him through saying goodbye to me? Let's spare each other the drama and that silly pink carpet and the golden light above my head that makes me look like an old banana. Lord, he and I are old enough to know we don't need more emotional goodbyes in our lives. We've each endured that enough. I need a new book to read, some cats in my lap, a dog on my feet, and I'll start to feel better. Shonda, you and Pearla and the rest of the crew here are some of my favorite people, and I've had a tremendous experience, but I'm going home. Gatsby misses me.

Shonda: Who is Gatsby?

Ruthie: My pig.

Shonda: Please don't go. Can you wait until Tony gets back? Let him know? See how he reacts?

Ruthie: I left all of you a box of Deschutes Family Tequila. It's in my room. I wish you the very best. Come and visit me in Oregon! Now give me a hug.

31

After she received her phone back, Ruthie agreed to cancel the taxi, so she was in a van with Shonda, Pearla, Jackson, and two other crew members, cameras pointed at her face. They couldn't possibly miss the opportunity to tug tumultuous emotions out of their viewers and fling 'em around. Ruthie sat in the back seat. She didn't say a word and only one – *one* – tear left her eye which was somehow more poignant than if she were sobbing, the loss too wretched for more tears.

The producers later added sad music. Ruthie cried, and most of America cried with her. She was seventy years old! When would she find love again? This was shockingly unfair. Her first husband beat her. She couldn't have more kids because she almost died from the attack. She'd lost her second husband, a doctor. She was an English teacher for forty-five years and taught kids to love books, and she took in thirty-one "new" children! She deserved love and romance before she died!

What was happening? This wasn't the happy ending everyone wanted! They wanted to see Ruthie in a wedding dress! They wanted to see the sexy cowboy in a tuxedo! They wanted to know that when they were seventy, they could find love again, too, and be delirious with joy and hope. They wanted to die having sex or die in love or die, at least, in the arms of their beloved.

When Shonda tried to talk to her, Ruthie reached out, held Shonda's hand, and that was it. Shonda fell silent. All was quiet.

The viewers cried again. "Oh, poor Ruthie!"

At home, Ruthie's dogs, cats, pig, and rabbit were getting a lot of attention from the four children. *Too much* attention. The little girls wanted to dress the dogs up with pink ribbons and flowered hats. Atticus was exhausted. He didn't like wearing pink ribbons. He thought they emasculated him. He didn't like flowered hats. He was proud of his manhood. He simply wanted to warm up Ruthie's feet, which was his job, and get some peace, for heaven's sake. Hadn't he earned some peace at his age?

One of the toddler boys rode Mr. Rochester like a horse. Mr. Rochester put up with it sometimes—he had a tender side—but other times he hid under the bed. His back wasn't the same as it used to be. The toddler constantly yelled things like, "Giddyap, horsey!" and, "Ride 'em, cowboy!" and it hurt his ears.

The kids put Scarlett O'Hara, who was mortified, in a purple baby stroller with their other dolls. She was not a doll! She was a dignified rabbit! Scarlett O'Hara stealthily hop-hop-hopped away and hid as soon as she could and made sure she didn't scream and call attention to herself. Gatsby was chased, his tail pulled by the four-year-old until he squealed. Sigh.

The cats' dignity had also been compromised. The kids would grab Fitzwilliam, Darcy, Elizabeth Bennet, and Lydia Bennet under their arms for a hug. They felt as if they were being stretched like rubber bands while being swung like pendulums. The kids were so hard on the cats' fragile nerves, they spent most of their days outside, chasing mice for therapy and hiding in trees, though two were deathly afraid of heights. Elizabeth Bennet found an old tequila bottle with no cap and licked what she could out of it. She felt better.

The animals missed Ruthie. The Deschutes family out on the homestead missed Ruthie. She was their matriarch. Their loving leader. Her thirty-two children missed her, especially Willow and Lucy, who cried often about their broken relationship. Willow and Lucy regretted the whole silly thing and were miserable.

The townspeople missed Ruthie, too. She was their favorite teacher, though she was pushed out by those two awful women, nicknamed Principal Big Bottom and Bandana Bimbo. The hermit, Harold, missed her, too. He always knew his friend was there if he felt like talking or needed help. They'd known each other for endless decades, and he would feel better when she was home.

Ruthie missed them, too.

On the plane, she told herself to figure out exactly how she was feeling. She had learned long ago that taking some time and sorting through her emotions, labeling them, helped her to sort herself out, and the one word she came up with was *grief*.

Tony hadn't died. She hoped he had a long life.

But she knew she loved him, and he was gone. Out of her life.

Losing someone you loved when they left you didn't produce the same kind of overwhelming grief that you felt when someone you loved died.

But it was still grief—insidious, knock-you-to-your-knees, steal-your-breath-away, sharp-edged grief.

You'd thought your life would be with this person. It would not be. You'd thought you would dream together, plan together. You would not. You'd thought you would have children and grandchildren and travel the world. There would be no children or travel. You'd thought you would have a partner to laugh with at midnight and someone to hold your hand when life turned into a twister. There would be no laughing at midnight, and this person would not be holding your hand during a twister.

That was crushing. The person wasn't dead, but they were gone, and they took your happy, hopeful dreams with them.

On the plane, alone at last, Ruthie leaned her head back and let the steaming hot tears flow again.

You see, Ruthie had already known grief.

Grief came to her on the day of the Pet Parade. Ruthie and

Russell had organized it every year for decades. Participating required a ten-dollar entry fee. Many people donated far more, including the hermit and the hermit's family, personal friends, doctors and nurses, the staff at Russell's clinic, Deschutes family members, Deschutes Family Tequila, and their informally adopted children, who loved animals, too.

All the money went to the local animal shelter. It was a no-kill shelter. The shelter itself was a model for how all shelters should be—open, clean, safe, huge cages, lots of toys and blankets, and both indoor and outdoor play areas with play structures for both dogs and cats. Their employees, including full-time veterinarians, were well paid and well qualified. They took in animals from the area and accepted animals from other states and countries. Many of the animals were in horrifying medical and emotional shape when they arrived. The clinic's goal was to heal them back to robust health and find the perfect home for their rescues. They ran the rescue like a doggy daycare complete with snacks, nap time, and playtime, with volunteers coming in every day to "show some love."

"Meow! Bark! Let's Save Some Animals!" was the parade's slogan. Ruthie dressed up like a white cat. Russell was a black cat. Their costumes were furry and came with faux claws and cat hats. For the parade, which everyone participated in, you could dress up as an animal if you wanted to, or you could come on your bike with your cat in a basket, or you could walk your dog on a leash, or you could ride a unicycle and juggle, as one man did every year, wearing a frog hat.

Russell was seventy-five years old, Ruthie sixty-five. He had seemed slower, tired lately, but wasn't that normal for a seventy-five-year-old doctor who still saw patients all day long? But how could he quit? He was Dr. Russell to their whole town. Everyone loved him. More than that, they *needed* him. They trusted him. Healing people was his life.

After the cat and dog parade and the town potluck picnic that always followed, Ruthie and Russell took a little tumble into bed.

Russell popped a pill so, as he said, "Everything stands up, strong and tall." They wore their cat hats during their gymnastics for fun, then took a short nap to recover from that bit of pleasure and a shower to get rid of the cat fur. Ruthie made a nice salad, wearing only a pink, flowered, lacy apron, her naked bottom out, which made Russell laugh.

Then Russell collapsed, right there in the kitchen of their farmhouse. Ruthie thought Russell had collapsed from laughter, even though she often cooked and baked seminaked. Russell said her baked Alaska always tasted better when she made it naked.

But Russell didn't get up. He rasped out to her, "Something's wrong, baby. Call 911."

Their dogs and cats and the rabbit and pig all knew that something was wrong. The dogs barked, the cats circled, the pig snorted, and the rabbit (not screaming Scarlett O'Hara, but her mother) nervously hopped back and forth, but Ruthie saw none of that. She bent over Russell and knew, because she was smart and a doctor's wife, that Russell was in trouble. She called 911. She kissed him, his forehead, his cheeks, his mouth, told him she loved him, loved him, she loved him so much, and her tears spilled on his cheeks.

He said, "I love you, Ruthie." Then he chuckled and rasped out, in a whisper, "You're my favorite cat."

But he was in pain and pale. His breathing was too fast, his pulse racing, and he was lying on the floor.

She unlocked the front door and ran to her room. She yanked off the apron and pulled on jeans, a bra, and a blue T-shirt that said "The Brontë Sisters Are My Heroines." She was not gone more than thirty seconds, the animals becoming more and more agitated, meowing and barking and whining.

Ruthie bent down to her love again, the love of her life, the man who had literally saved her own life, and hugged him.

Russell said, "Baby, don't cry. You know I can't stand it when you cry."

Her tears fell on his face, then she ran and whipped open the front door when the paramedics, fire department, and police arrived. "Hang in there, Russell, sweetheart. They're coming. Please, baby. Hold on, honey."

Police cars, a fire engine, and two ambulances descended on their yellow farmhouse. Ruthie later heard they'd whipped through town, sirens blaring, at top speed. Those people knew Dr. Russell. If he hadn't treated them, he had treated their families, their grandmas and uncles and aunts and moms. They knew Ruthie, too. She had been their teacher.

They were competent, fast, and they tucked Dr. Russell and Ruthie into the ambulance in seconds before she knew what was happening, the roar of her panic, the pounding of her heart all she could hear. Two police cars escorted them at high speed to the hospital, where a crowd of medical professionals anxiously waited.

Later, one of the doctors at the hospital, Halona Day, who had lived with Russell and Ruthie with her sister, Chenoa, for three years because their violent parents were in jail, told Ruthie and Russell the news, so gently, after many scans and tests.

"I'm sorry," Dr. Day said. She stopped to collect herself. She told herself not to cry. It didn't work. She loved Russell and Ruthie. When they "adopted" her and Chenoa, they saved them. Their childhood had been abusive, filled with neglect. Russell and Ruthie filled their lives with love and care. Russell had taken Halona and Chenoa to work with him because, he declared, "I know down to my soul that you two girls will be excellent, caring physicians." Chenoa was an emergency room doctor in Portland.

Dr. Day told them it was cancer. She showed them the results of the scans and tests.

"I think I have about six months, give or take," Russell said, composed and dignified, in doctor mode as he analyzed his own tests.

"Yes, about that," Dr. Day said, choking up. "I am so very, very sorry."

"Me, too," Russell said. "Well done, Halona. I know I've said this before, but you're an excellent, caring doctor. I knew you would be, just like Chenoa."

She burst into tears as Ruthie reached for Russell and hugged him tight, her entire world collapsing.

A week after Russell was released from the hospital, he and Ruthie took a family walk around their property, a regular occurrence. As the sun went down, the yellow rays spreading across the flower-filled meadow, then behind the blue mountains in a marvelous display of vibrant colors, puffy clouds, and a magical golden sparkle, they shared a kiss.

Atticus, whose knees were bothering him, climbed into the red wagon on top of his blanket as Russell pulled him along. The cats—Fitzwilliam, Darcy, Elizabeth Bennet, and Lydia Bennet, who had all been traumatized by Russell's collapse—circled around, immensely relieved that Russell was back, even though he looked pale. Gatsby the pig, snorting as he conversed with Russell, wouldn't leave his side. Mr. Rochester was so happy to be walking Ruthie again that he smiled and hung his tongue out, extra-long.

Screaming Scarlett O'Hara's mother hopped about but became distracted by yellow daisies so missed part of the family walk. When she realized what happened, she screamed and frightened Atticus and Mr. Rochester, who both jumped and whined, envisioning the devil rabbit chasing them. The screaming was a family trait, one could say, from one Scarlett O'Hara to the next.

"Ruthie, my love, we must, as they say, make the best of the time we have left."

She nodded and squeezed his hand.

"I think it's time we went a little wild and crazy," Russell drawled.

Ruthie laughed through her tears and said, "Bring it on, baby."

They went wild and crazy! Russell and Ruthie embarked on a ten-day river cruise in Europe together. They enjoyed it so much they went wild and crazy again and got off one boat when the cruise ended and climbed onto another one. They walked on cobblestone streets and stayed in the cities until after midnight, drinking too much wine and eating fancy dinners. They cheered on street performers and danced in town squares when bands were playing. They went to shows and concerts in towns and on the ships and sang along. They ate whatever they wanted and made new, fun friends on board who were older and also going wild and crazy, living with passion. They sat on their balcony and watched the cities move past, and while holding hands, they reminisced about the best times of their lives.

For their third cruise, Willow, her husband, Michael, and Lucy came with them for two weeks in Norway, and they had a ball.

Alaska called, and they went on yet another cruise and watched whales and sat in red rafts in the ocean and watched a kaleidoscope of stars at night. Next was a month on the Oregon coast, watching the waves from an enormous house with floor-to-ceiling windows. They invited their thirty-two children, and they were all in and out, bringing their laughter and love. The children hid their tears because they did not want to upset Ruthie or Russell, the people who had literally held out their hands to help and, in so doing, had saved their lives.

Every night, there was a sunset that Ruthie and Russell waited with great interest to see. What would happen tonight? What combination of colors would they admire? The sun glittered off the waves, like white diamonds, but as it sank, the colors would expand. Magenta. Gold. Dark blue. Red. Orange. Yellow. If you looked away for thirty seconds, the sunset would be a different painting when you looked back. So often, the sun's rays would streak through the puffy clouds and create a white, glowing tunnel down to the waves. It seemed that there was an opening to heaven, right there, a stairway above the water.

Russell knew he would be climbing those steps soon. He felt it. But he had enjoyed these last months with his dearest Ruthie, with Willow, Michael, and Lucy, with their thirty-one other children and their grandchildren. He felt so grateful for his life that he was brought to tears every day. He had had loving parents and siblings. He had become a doctor. He had survived Vietnam, as so many young, fearless men had not. He had Ruthie—oh, he was such a lucky man. Sometimes he watched her sleep, marveling at how fortunate he was.

He didn't want to die, but why fuss? Why spend these last months angry or depressed? That wouldn't change anything. He cried sometimes, though. He would miss Ruthie and his children and his job, but he told himself to quickly buck up, he could cry in heaven.

He told everyone he loved them, including his family, Ruthie's family, their children and grandchildren, his neighbors, his friends in town, and the staff at the clinic with whom he had worked for decades. He went to visit Harold the hermit, who cried and cried. He called old colleagues and old friends and old Army buddies and told them what they meant to him and that he loved them. He said his goodbyes and his thank-yous. The old colleagues and old friends and Army buddies were overwhelmed and cried with him.

Russell O'Hara was deeply, emotionally grateful for his life and everyone in it.

It took six months for the disease to win, exactly as Russell had thought. He refused treatment. The treatment would have made him miserable, and he knew it would buy him, at most, three months, but it would not be three months of time worth living.

Russell died in bed at their yellow farmhouse, Ruthie wrapped around him, right at the end of a sunset that blazed across the sky like fire and a rainbow mixed together. Fitzwilliam, Darcy, Elizabeth Bennet, and Lydia Bennet were on the bed with them. Atticus was warming Ruthie's feet, as was his job. Mr. Rochester had his paws on the mattress, his worried face inches from Russell's. Gatsby was in the corner, snorting with distress, and Scarlett O'Hara's mother, scared, was under the bed, shaking, trying not to scream.

An angel with a small golden halo came through the clouds and took Russell's soul. She reached out a hand, and Russell, shocked at first—my goodness, angels really did have expansive white wings! —grabbed her hand and felt himself start to rise off the bed. He didn't feel sick anymore, or weak, or exhausted. He felt...*young again*! Healthy and full of energy and excited. He knew he had officially died a seventy-five-year-old man. He felt like he was twenty-five! He embraced this new adventure.

Mr. Rochester barked, staring worriedly straight up at Russell as he moved in the air across the room. Atticus whined and he, too, stared at the risen Russell in confusion. The cats shifted and meowed in distress, the angel's wings ruffling their fur. Gatsby, poor thing, ran straight for him, snorting, though Russell was five feet off the floor. Scarlett O'Hara's mother scrambled from underneath the bed and hopped up and down, trying to reach him.

"The animals always know," the angel said, smiling. She loved animals.

Russell looked back down at his sweet Ruthie, crying on his chest in bed, which was no longer rising and falling, and he instinctively let out a wail of grief and tried to return to her, to comfort and to hold, but the angel, ever so gently, said, "No, Russell. I'm sorry. It's time," and pulled him away.

Russell and the angel began his journey.

They sailed through the roof, then flew together over the yellow farmhouse and the deer in his backyard and a coyote prancing through the meadow. They startled a bald eagle, who angled away. They paused over his medical clinic, where he saw a montage of all the people he had helped, as if the angel had made him a movie. His mouth hung open, and he finally understood the true impact he had had on his patients' lives.

She held his hand as they arched over the town of Triple Mountain and over to the Deschutes homestead where he saw all his in-laws who had embraced him as family and become true friends. He saw everyone jumping into Rattlesnake Lake together, Ruthie in a red polka dot swimsuit, he in blue shorts.

They spun over the rivers he had fished and the mountains he had climbed and the valleys he'd hiked. They flew over his childhood home, where he saw himself as a kid with his late parents and brothers and sisters, which brought a huge smile to his face. When they flew over his old high school, he saw himself with his old friends, and he laughed, and then she flew him over Vietnam, where he could see himself decades ago, operating, saving lives. In one scene, he saw himself encouraging a soldier who had suffered a grievous leg injury to fight, to wake up, to never give up.

The angel flew him over the big house they'd recently rented at the beach so he could see all his children and grandchildren, happy, playing games, running on the beach, laughing. His tears flooded his cheeks. What a remarkable family he and Ruthie had.

Next, they were over the sand and the frothing ocean waves filled with whales and leaping dolphins and luminescent fish. The angel carried him up through the bright opening in the clouds to his new stomping ground, filled with family and friends who had made this journey before him. He would soon be welcomed with shouts of excitement and long hugs. They stopped on the golden staircase, and the angel settled her white wings and let him look back.

It was the day of his funeral, and he saw his beautiful Ruthie. He cried. He would miss her so. He saw Willow, Michael, and Lucy and their other beloved children and grandchildren. He saw the Deschutes family, his surviving family members, his friends, and the staff from the clinic. Even Harold the hermit was there, though he hated being around other people, so his presence choked Russell up even more.

The service was held at the local high school where Ruthie taught. The gym was cavernous, and it was filled with people—the floor, the bleachers, standing room only.

"This is your legacy," the angel told him, her voice admiring, caring.

He was stunned at all the people who had come to see him off.

"Your legacy is filled with love," she said. "Your love will last. The spirit of your love will stay forever."

Ruthie gave the eulogy. She talked about how he'd saved her life when her first husband had almost killed her and Willow. Many people hadn't known this part of Ruthie's story, and they were touched. She talked about Russell's service to the country and how he loved being a doctor and helping his patients. She talked about his role as a father and grandfather to Willow and Lucy and how he loved, eternally loved, Michael, all thirty-two of their children, their spouses, and their grandchildren, his family, the Deschutes family, his loyal friends, and everyone in town.

"Grief," Ruthie said softly, boldly, "is a part of life. We experience joy, and we experience grief. One must accept both sides. We are human, and grief is part of our journey, the hardest part. But I believe that we will see the people we love again. When I flatlined after giving birth, and Russell literally brought me back to life, I saw relatives I loved who had passed. They were there, loving me, holding me, encouraging me." She paused and gathered herself as her voice cracked. "When we see our loved ones again, it will be in a different time and a different place, but we will say goodbye to this life and hello to a new life. The people we miss so much now, the people we adore, they will be there, waiting for us, welcoming us."

The wrenching sobs were heard across the gym.

"We will see the people we have loved and lost," she said again, her voice breaking, but echoing, in that gym. "We will see Russell. We will all be together. And this time..." She let the tears flow down her face. Why hide them? "This time, we will be together forever."

She paused as they all cried for Russell, as they cried for the people who had already gone to the new place, the ones they loved and missed so much they ached.

"I will leave you with one more thought," Ruthie said. "When someone needs a helping hand, hold your hand out, like Russell did. You have one life to live. Let that be a life of service and kindness to others. Live like Russell lived. Live with love."

The angel gracefully put her white wing across Russell's shoulders as they shook with emotion.

"Now, everyone," Ruthie said, tilting her chin up and smiling, "let's believe that Russell is here with us now, and let's stand and give him the standing ovation that he deserves."

Everyone rose clapping, crying, grieving for Russell. They gave him the standing ovation he deserved, and it went on for a long time.

Russell was overcome with emotion. "I am so grateful for my life," he told the angel, his voice breaking.

"We are grateful for what you did with your life, Russell," the angel said. Her wings fluttered. Russell didn't know yet, but he was going to be an angel, too, and gently take people up to heaven. The angels had voted, and the result was a resounding yes.

Russell would miss Ruthie so. Every minute of every day. When he was ready, they turned to go, but the angel let him glance back one more time to see his sweetheart. He would watch over her in the years to come. The angel had told him he could do so.

He put a hand to his lips and blew a kiss to Ruthie. She tilted her head up as one of his favorite songs, "Back in Black" by AC/DC, played, the music rocking off the walls of the gym as everyone smiled. Everyone knew that Dr. O'Hara had loved AC/DC! The words were on a huge screen, and everyone sang along.

Ruthie felt the kiss, felt his love, he knew it. Suddenly, a smile hovered on her lips and her face lit up because she felt him nearby. That was the relationship they had always had. They were two people, but one, bound eternally by love.

The white clouds above the golden staircase opened up, and Russell was home. His family and friends rushed toward him, crying with happiness, enveloping him, holding him, loving him. They had been waiting! "Welcome, Russell! We missed you! We love you!"

The angel patted his back and smiled at him before she

attended to another loved one down on Earth. "Well done, Russell. Well done."

"Thank you," he said, the tears slipping down his now-young cheeks. "Thank you."

Grief didn't let up for Ruthie for the first year. It almost killed her. Ruthie wanted to die. She could barely breathe. She cried all the time, even at unexpected times, like when the grocery store ran out of strawberries. Russell loved strawberries.

Ruthie's daughter and granddaughter, her thirty-one other children and their families, and her friends all tried to ease her grief. The Deschutes family kept her busy with birthday parties and anniversaries and jumps in Rattlesnake Lake and horseback riding and four-wheeling and target practice.

"No one can ever be too skilled at shooting," her brother Turner said to her. "Come on now, Ruthie. You're an excellent shot. Let's see it."

When she didn't attend family functions, they understood when she said, "Grief has gotten to me today, and I cannot come over."

After a year, she started to see lights here and there, sparkling, small, but they were there, poking through the blackness. Even the cats, dogs, rabbit, and pig started to see the lights. They missed Russell, too, and that whole scene with the woman with the white wings and a gold ring over her head and Russell disappearing through the roof had been baffling and scary.

Ruthie's whole world was not all a lonely black tar pit anymore. She did not spiral as much, lost and alone, feeling hopeless and lonely. She started to want to live and not to die, and grief loosened its grip.

Grief would be back again, days and weeks, in and out of months...but as the years went on, grief came less, and it wasn't so destructive, so leveling. Grief didn't bring her to the ground as much as it had before, the sobs not so racking, as if her bones would break.

Ruthie went on.

She taught English to her high school students. She had students who needed to learn about the poets Emily Dickinson, Gwendolyn Brooks, Walt Whitman, and Natasha Trethewey and how to write their own poetry. She had classics and modern literature to share with them, and they all needed to learn how to write better and use proper grammar and sentence structure.

She coordinated the annual Pet Parade. She took care of kids who needed help. She drank tequila, but not too much. She smoked an occasional cigar. She started to laugh again. She lived.

She had to.

She had a daughter and a granddaughter.

She had thirty-one other children who needed her, though they were almost all adults now.

Ruthie had helped with the family business her whole life, though her primary job was teaching, and she started doing a little more work for them to fill the time. Deschutes Family Tequila was extremely successful, run by Ruthie's brother Stanley and her twin cousins, Hilda and Shaley, who were sixty-eight years old. They sold Scotch and whiskey now, too, and merchandise that said "Deschutes Family Tequila." Ruthie would often think up funny sayings for the T-shirts, like "Any Night Is Tequila Night" and "Straight Shot, Anyone?" and "No One Gets Between Me and My Tequila." The merchandise made a fortune.

Deschutes Family Tequila gave money away each year to the humane society, the town library, the schools, summer programs for kids, and struggling families. The company provided the seed money for a huge park near town complete with two lakes, a swimming pool and slides, playgrounds, picnic tables, and walking trails. It bought land in Triple Mountain and donated it so that it could never be developed beyond biking and walking trails. Ruthie was one of ten family members on the committee that gave away the money. This took up her time, too.

When she longed for Russell, she put her chin up and her shoulders back as best she could, and when she couldn't, she would stay home and cry. But she was Ruthie Deschutes O'Hara. She would not give up. She had fought her way out of that black, incessant grief, back to a life worth living.

She would love her family and friends, ever more, all day long, as Russell would have wanted, though she missed him so.

32

"*She* what?" Tony said, his voice tight and strained. He had let Susie go after their date to Glacier National Park. He was reeling from guilt. She was an outstanding person, and they liked talking about construction and design, and she liked detective and police shows like he did, but Susie wasn't Ruthie.

Tony was distraught that Ruthie was gone. "Ruthie left? When? Why?"

"Ruthie said it was time for her to go," Shonda told him, Pearla next to her.

"Did she say why?" He ran a frustrated hand through his hair.

"No," Shonda said, but there was a pause. "Maybe."

"She...hinted." Pearla looked down, then up. "Yes."

"What's going on?" Tony demanded. He sounded like the military man he was.

"Ruthie thought she was going home during the next I Do ceremony."

"Why would she think that?"

"Because you haven't chosen her for a one-on-one date, Tony. She thought it was hopeless, that you didn't want her, especially since some of the women have now been on two dates with you."

"I was saving the helicopter date for her, as you know. I knew she'd love it. It was going to be an all-day-and-into-the-evening date. She would have loved the views, the horseback riding, the picnic. I was going to tell her to bring a book so we could read together. Oh God." Tony swore. Those words had to be bleeped out for TV. "Where is she?"

"She's at the airport. She got there super early. She didn't want to stay here anymore. Her flight leaves in an hour."

"I need to borrow a car. Now. Right now."

Shonda and Pearla gaped at him.

"Keys?" Tony said.

In the history of time, eight people had never gotten into a van so fast. Thankfully, they all thought, Tyler was nowhere to be found, so they didn't have to bring him and his degree from Stanford. One person, a production assistant, climbed in without shoes. It had been a warm day, and in her hurry, she'd forgotten to put them on.

Tony took the keys from the driver. The driver was left at the lodge. Shonda, Pearla, Jackson, Valentina and Ricki with cameras, the shoeless assistant, and a lighting technician piled in, the door barely shutting as they took off. They climbed over one another, panting, tumbled into seats, disentangled their legs, and squished in their gear. Valentina was in front, the lens pointed straight at Tony as he drove.

Shonda asked the questions. "Where are we going, Tony?"

"You know where we're going. We're going to the airport."

"Why?"

Tony said, "Look, I know you need film for the show, but let's drop the questions you already know the answers to."

"What do you like about Ruthie?" Shonda asked.

"She likes books, old dogs, and horses."

"What else do you like about her?"

"Everything."

Tony left the keys on the dashboard when he jumped out of the van at Glacier Park International Airport. Construction was ongoing with concrete barriers, porta-potties, fences, orange netting, and machinery, but he darted around it. He was tall and in shape and moved like a man forty years younger.

The shoeless assistant was tasked with moving the van to a parking spot. She was not pleased. She was going to miss out on all the excitement! The airport scene, with one lovesick lover chasing after another, was featured in so many romance movies, and now it was happening in real life, and she had to *move the van*. Not fair!

Tony didn't wait. He sprinted through the airport's doors. He knew Ruthie would already be through Security. He headed to a ticket agent. The flight Ruthie was on was full. He said, "When's the next flight?"

She told him it was in two hours to San Francisco. "We have one ticket left."

"San Francisco it is, then. Thank you." He bought the ticket and raced to Security. He needed to talk to Ruthie, to persuade her to stay. He did not wait for the camera crew or Shonda or Pearla. The team rushed to the ticket counter, balancing their gear, sweating hard, huffing and puffing. A ticket agent beckoned over the frazzled group of people with no luggage. She was immediately suspicious. No luggage and heavy cameras.

Shonda leaned in. "We're the crew for the dating show *Marry Me*—"

"*Marry Me!*" the ticket agent interrupted, her face lighting up. "I love that show."

"Can you get us through Security without buying tickets so we can film? We have a runaway bride, and the groom is trying to talk to her," Shonda asked, knowing the question was ridiculous.

"Get you through Security with no tickets?" She laughed. "No. Are you kidding me? Hell no. Totally against all rules and regulations. But you have a runaway bride?" The ticket agent was thrilled. She clapped her hands. Her name was Alishba. She and her mother, aunts, and sisters all watched *Marry Me* together. They loved Ruthie.

"Is it Ruthie?" she asked, her voice pitching up. "Is she the runaway bride?"

"Yes, yes!" Shonda said, delighted. "It's Ruthie."

Alishba giggled. "She's our favorite. We had T-shirts made

that say 'Jane Austen Is My Guidance Counselor,' just like Ruthie. But I still can't get you through without tickets."

"Okay. Give me seven tickets to your next destination."

"We have no tickets left on the next flight going out to Seattle or to San Francisco. What's your time frame?"

They didn't have one. They weren't going to be on the flight. All they needed were tickets to get through Security. "Whenever."

"Huh," said the ticket agent. "There are seven tickets to Los Angeles at ten o'clock tonight."

"We'll take them!" Shonda said. She handed over the studio's credit card.

The team hurried off to Security, hobbled by their gear. There was virtually no wait. Jackson was recognized by a few people, and he smiled and waved. Running through the airport made him realize how out of shape he'd gotten. He used to be able to run across a football field like a flash of light. Now he was sweating so hard he felt like he was leaking. Even his butt felt too big. He heard his grandma's voice scolding, "You're too big for your britches." She hadn't meant it literally, but he felt it.

They all whipped off their shoes and threw them onto the moving belts. Their cameras and other paraphernalia were screened. They put their arms up and stepped into the scanner. Two of them had to endure full-body frisks. All done.

As they were shoving their feet into their shoes and whipping belts through one loop on their pants, to be adjusted later, they checked what gate Ruthie would be at as she waited for her flight to Seattle, then on to Redmond, Oregon. They didn't understand that Glacier Park International Airport was tiny. They wouldn't need to know the gate. One plane went in and out at a time.

They sprinted up the stairs, gasping for breath. They ignored the dead animals on the wall—the moose, bighorn sheep, and the buck with an impressive rack. They ignored the stuffed bear that advised them to "Buy Bear Spray." They ignored the cool, new outdoor eating area with the view of the Rockies.

They knew they would barely make it. Hopefully, Tony had

already stopped Ruthie from getting on her flight and was talking to her now.

"Hurry!" Shonda semishrieked. "Hurry! We can't miss this!"

"Run, everyone!" Pearla ordered, tripping up the steps. "Run!"

"I'm coming!" Jackson said, his chest heaving. "I'm right behind you."

Alas, they were too late. Just like in the romance movies.

The doors to Ruthie's flight had closed.

Ruthie was headed back to Oregon.

Tony turned away, dejected, worn out, his hand pushing back his thick hair. Shonda and Pearla approached, but he waved them away, saying, "Not now," then turned and walked back through the airport, his broad shoulders sloping down, head up.

They filmed his retreat. Sexy, brokenhearted Marlboro Man–type walks off—alone—as new love leaves him. Oh, the tears that shall be shed!

Jackson leaned over, hands on his knees, so he could catch his breath.

This was embarrassing.

When he returned to the lodge in Whitefish, Tony sat down with Benedetta, Velvet, and Sarah on the deck in front of the mountains, dusk beginning, opening the curtains to the upcoming sunset and the surprise in the sky. Some animals were bedding down for the night. Others were stretching, on the hunt for dinner. Two fox kits wrestled. Two bear cubs raced each other to the river.

Tony told the ladies the truth, gently, surrounded by the crew and their cameras and lights and other paraphernalia. The production assistant who had to park the van was wearing her shoes, but she was still a bit sulky. Jackson, Shonda, and Pearla stood back. They liked Tony a ton, but, selfishly, they knew this was going to be the best *Marry Me* ever. *Ever.*

"I can't tell you how much I have enjoyed meeting all of you, spending time with you," he said sincerely, genuinely. "Your stories about your pasts, who you are today, what you've been through, your hopes for the future, have all combined to make you the incredible women you are. I respect all of you so much. I like all of you..." He trailed off, his heart tired, this whole *Marry Me* journey difficult and demoralizing, except for the time he'd spent with Ruthie.

"But we're not Ruthie," Velvet said. "And you want Ruthie."

Tony blinked at her, stunned.

Benedetta, Velvet, and Sarah were crushed, but they had all known. They'd known for weeks.

"How did..." Tony stumbled. "How did you know?"

"It's the way you look at her," Velvet told him. "Don't be dense. We can see."

"How do I look at her?" Tony asked.

"With love." Velvet patted his knee. "I don't blame you. She's my favorite, too. She's my best friend here. Can I come to the wedding? I love weddings, and I would love to see you and Ruthie tie the knot. I'll make Ruthie an amazing stripper bridal outfit that she can wear on your honeymoon. You'll like it better than she does, I guarantee it."

Tony laughed, then smiled. His smile was sad because he didn't want to hurt the ladies, but he was feeling a glimmer of happiness thinking of marrying Ruthie.

"As a doctor, Tony," Benedetta said, "I shouldn't believe in love at first sight. There is no science to back it up. I like science. But from first sight, you only wanted Ruthie. Falling in love is..." She paused. "Indescribable. Why one person and not the other? Is it chemical? Biological? Is there some sort of attraction current? A deep recognition? I don't know. But I'm convinced when you've met your soul mate, you know it, and I think that's the case here."

A soul mate. He had found that with MaryBeth. Had he found it again? He answered himself. Yes. He had found another soul mate. Who knew there could be two? He blinked, then stared off into the distance. The sun was headed down, the sky streaked with white, purple, and orange, the mountaintops glowing.

Up in the foothills, the cougar wandered, looking for dinner. His foot felt better. Three deer, a mama and her babies, settled in for the night, soft and warm. The red and yellow western tanager flew to a high branch to enjoy the stars. A black-headed grosbeak hid its red breast amidst the leaves one tree over, and a song sparrow rested its voice, looking forward to singing tomorrow.

"Are you going to her?" Sarah asked.

"Yes."

"You're sure, aren't you?" Sarah said, grinning at him. "This is so romantic."

"I have rarely been so sure of anything in my life," Tony said.

"Love is grand, isn't it?" Sarah had not found love in the cult, but she hoped she would find love soon.

He smiled, finally. "Yes. It is."

There was no need for an I Do ceremony. He felt that rush of guilt again. He apologized to them, completely and sincerely. They told him all was well and gave that big ol' cowboy a big hug.

He exhaled, and his face relaxed. A smile lingered, and hope—yes, *hope*—filled his soul.

Jackson hugged him, too. "Good luck, man. You deserve her and she deserves you." He cleared his throat. "How do you feel about babysitting triplets? I really think they'd like to visit you and Ruthie…"

Tony, Shonda, Pearla, Jackson, Valentina, Ricki, the formerly shoeless sulky assistant, and a gang of camera people and crew, etc., landed the next day at the airport in Redmond, Oregon, from Glacier Park International via Seattle, and headed out to Ruthie's small mountain town. They rented three SUVs for themselves and their gear. They told Tyler he had done a fabulous job and could go home. He'd said that worked for him because he was meeting some friends soon from Stanford.

Tony drove straight to Ruthie's yellow farmhouse in the country, the day merry and bright, the mountains a postcard.

"It's beautiful out here," Shonda murmured. "My nerves feel soothed."

"I can't believe it," Pearla said. "I loved Montana, but I think I love Oregon more. I'm a city girl, but maybe I could change. Yep. Maybe."

"You won't be buried in snow very often, or for long, in Oregon," Tony said.

"This would be a cool place to raise the triplets," Jackson said. "They escaped again yesterday and walked to town wearing their dragon Halloween outfits." He sighed and rubbed his face. No one had told him and Henry how hard raising kids was going to be, especially if they were fearless five-year-old girls.

Triple Mountain, Ruthie's small town, was picture-perfect, they agreed. Three main streets ran parallel to one another. Pine and fir trees lined up, their branches waving a cheery hello, the scent soothing. They noticed the long park with the lakes and playgrounds. A school was at one end of town, a medical clinic at the other end, and in between there were breweries, bookstores, cafés, coffeeshops, two bakeries, the library, fire and police departments, a church, another church, art galleries, clothing stores, and a pot shop. People were everywhere, folk music dancing through the air.

They drove through, took a left at the fork, continued on for a few miles, saw two deer, took a right at another fork, saw a buck and an eagle, then stopped in the driveway of Ruthie's farmhouse with the light blue door.

Tony climbed out of the SUV into a sweet silence, other than birds chirping. The house was charming. He wasn't a man who threw around words like *charming*. In fact, he didn't think he'd ever used that word, but the house deserved the term. He liked the light-yellow paint. He liked how the house was nestled in the trees, but not too many, so the sun shone through. Two willow trees fluttered on either end of the house, and cherry trees lined the drive. He knew they would be as pretty in spring, blooming with pink flowers, as Ruthie had told him. The porch was wide and white, and white flowers bloomed on a vine.

"Hang on, Tony," Pearla said. "We need to get the cameras up and ready."

Everyone piled out of the SUVs as fast as possible, a twirling tornado of people trying to get organized. This time, the assistant managed to remember to have her shoes on. She was not going to get left behind again.

Tony waited patiently. He was almost done. There would be only one more scene, he hoped, and then he would never allow himself to be filmed for a TV show again. Ever.

Jackson clapped him on the back. "For what it's worth, you made the right decision, my man. Ruthie was my favorite from the start."

Tony nodded. "Thank you. Let's see if she's interested in me."

"You're nervous, aren't you?"

"Scared to death." He didn't look scared. His face was serious, but calm. Inside, Tony Beckett was shaking.

"Huh. You served for twenty-five years in the Army. You fought in Vietnam for two years. You own land and live in the boonies. You've gotten through many tough times in your life, but now you're scared to death."

"Yes. Let's turn this around, Jackson. Let's say you were afraid you were going to lose Henry. How would you feel?"

Jackson shuddered. "That's easy. Scared to death."

"And there ya go," Tony said.

"Don't scare me like that Tony," Jackson whispered, leaning in. "That wasn't very nice. Now I'm going to drop the triplets off at your front door without any warning at all, and Henry and I are going to the beach for a month."

"We're ready!" Shonda said. "Let's go."

Tony strode toward the house and knocked.

A man opened the door. Behind him was a woman and four small children who were jumping, hopping, or singing. There were two dogs, two cats, a small snuffling pig, and…a rabbit. *Ah,* Tony thought. *That's Scarlett O'Hara, who frightens the other pets with her screaming, just like her mother did.* It was in the rabbit's DNA. The rabbit tried to hop hop hop out the door, but one of the kids grabbed her and put her in a purple stroller.

"Hello," the man said, smiling, regarding the cameras with amusement.

The woman said, "You all must be looking for Ruthie."

"Yes," Tony said. "We are."

One of the dogs lay down slowly, as if he ached. He seemed old. That must be Atticus. He was wearing a white bonnet. He seemed embarrassed. The black cat meowed. Was that Elizabeth Bennet?

"The Welcome Home, Ruthie party is starting right now," the woman said. "We're a little late because we had to pack up all our stuff and clean the house since Ruthie's back. We're headed over now. You can follow us. Ruthie let us stay here so the kids could run around in the country when she was gone. She's so nice. The kids had a super time with all the animals. I think the animals liked the company."

Tony glanced down at the other dog. Mr. Rochester. He seemed worn out. He was wearing a pink fluffy bow. The pig squealed indignantly when a kid pulled his tail. One of the kids picked up a cat underneath its front legs and swung it back and forth like a pendulum. The cat scrambled to escape.

"The Welcome Home, Ruthie party?" Tony said.

"Yes!" a little boy said, jumping up and down. "Nana Ruthie is home! Nana Ruthie is home! And we're going to swim in Rattlesnake Lake to make sure we don't get bit by rattlesnakes this year, and we're going to have hot dogs and cake, and I'm going to drink tequila!"

"Oh no. No, no, no," the man said. "No tequila. That's only for the older people."

The little boy stopped jumping, crossed his arms over his chest, and glared. "I want tequila!" He stamped a foot.

"Absolutely not."
"Yes! I'm drinking tequila!"
"Nope." His father spoke sternly to the boy.
The boy glowered again. "Then how about a puppy?"
"Do you want to follow us over?" the woman asked, wagging a reprimanding finger at her son.
They did.

The animals all sighed with relief when the family left. Peace would soon be upon them.

33

Ruthie could not believe what she was seeing.

She blinked. Perhaps she was hallucinating. Maybe she was actually asleep and dreaming. Was it the tequila? But she'd had only two shots. Her limit. Usually.

Standing in front of Rattlesnake Lake in a red flowered sundress, surrounded by friends and family who had put together a party to welcome her home from *Marry Me*, she watched as three SUVs entered the family homestead. Tony got out of one. He stood and stared at her while the crew, including Shonda, Pearla, and Jackson, scurried around to get set up.

Two shots of tequila shouldn't have made her conjure up the image of Tony. That had never happened before. She shook her head. By golly, he was still there.

"Helen," she said to one of her two best childhood friends, "do you see a tall, sexy cowboy in jeans coming our way, or am I delusional? Is my dementia acting up?"

"Not delusional, sugar. No dementia. And yes, I see a manly man coming our way."

"No signs of delusion yet," Alice said, the second of her two best childhood friends. "But that man has hips I could ride like a buckin' bull."

"He's a blend of Robert Redford, Paul Newman, Jimmy Smits, Denzel Washington, and Tom Selleck," Ruthie said, her voice near a whisper.

"I see it," Helen and Alice said together.

Two of her brothers, Stanley and Turner, came to stand next

to her. They were built like tanks, grizzled around the face, and they had been worried, like many people in the Deschutes family, about the sad, defeated expression on Ruthie's face when she returned yesterday from *Marry Me*.

"Big sister," Stanley said, "is this the groom?"

Ruthie teared up.

"Oh, my heart," Turner said. "You're crying, aren't you, Ruthie? I'll get the tractor out and run him off our land. I thought you said he was a peach of a man, but he didn't choose you?"

"I did." Her words trembled. "He is a peach."

"Lord in heaven, I do not like to see you unhappy, Ruthie," Aunt Melda said, who was ninety-two years old and holding a beer in her hand and wearing a sword on her hip. She liked the sword. It was from one of her trips to Japan. She'd figured she could wear whatever she wanted starting when she was the ripe old age of thirty-five and had been doing so ever since. She was a legend at Deschutes Family Tequila, as she had overseen the Accounting Department for fifty years and had won national awards for dueling.

"I'm not unhappy, Melda," Ruthie said. "That's not why I'm crying."

"Ah," Aunt Melda said. "Tears of joy and lust. Would you look at that manly man? No wonder you're crying tears of joy and lust. I'd be crying like that, too, if I could get a man like that in my bed to warm me up. I'd even take off the sword for him."

"Nana Ruthie!" Vincent's twelve-year-old granddaughter, Camellia, said, upset because Ruthie was upset. She held her hand. "What's wrong? Do you need cake? I can get you a piece of cake. Or do you want a shot of tequila? I'll get you a shot!" She ran off. She was a Deschutes, after all.

"Ruthie," Tony said, arriving in front of her, his blue eyes warm, but worried. He towered over her, and she tilted her head up. "It's good to see you."

Ruthie tried to talk, but she couldn't. She smiled a shaky smile, then turned to smile at Jackson, Shonda, Pearla, Valentina, Ricki, and the other crew members. "Hello, everyone."

They greeted her warmly.

She turned back to Tony and tried to smile, but it was weak, her dimples hardly out.

"I wanted to see you," he said, his voice so gentle, "and talk about why you left Montana."

"I thought...it was best...for everyone..." Ruthie stopped talking as her voice wavered and wobbled.

Tony stepped closer, as if he wanted to hug her but wasn't sure if he should. "Yes?"

"I thought that I should leave."

"Why?"

"Because, well, it's silly." By now, the Deschutes family members were all crowded around. There were dozens of them. No one thought to give them privacy. Their family wasn't private. Everything was out in the open. Everything was discussed. People had hurried in from Rattlesnake Lake, paddling their boats and inner tubes to the shore, then running over to the family action. Others had spilled out of their homes and tumbled out of the family clubhouse as word had spread that, "Ruthie's man has come to get her!"

"I thought, Tony, because you hadn't asked me out on a date, and other women had had two dates, that I would be going home next."

"So, you left."

She nodded. "I didn't think it was necessary to stay. Why put both of us through that awkward end? Why prolong things?" She hadn't thought she could take the stab in the heart when she didn't get that silly wedding bouquet, but she didn't say that. "Plus, I was homesick."

The Deschutes family nodded. That happened to all of them. Why, they belonged here together on the homestead!

"I understand," Tony said. "In your position, I think I would have done the same. I wish you hadn't, though."

"You do?" Hope filled her, sweet like honey.

"Yes. There was a date for us planned. A helicopter ride. A picnic on top of a mountain. I knew you would love it. The helicopter had mechanical difficulties for days, so it was put off. I was saving that date for you."

"Ah. I would have enjoyed that."

"Ruthie," Tony said, his eyes tired, hurt, but hopeful. "It's you."

"Me?" Ruthie's eyes were tired and hurt, too, but now a spark of hope started to glow.

"Yes."

"What about the other ladies?"

"They went home. It's always been you, Ruthie, since the first night." His voice was low and rumbly. "I didn't even want to go on with the show after two weeks. I didn't think it would be fair to the other ladies, but I had signed a contract. I had agreed to do it, so I did. I wanted to keep my word."

The Deschutes family was quiet, whisper like quiet. This was completely, utterly not like them. But they'd be quiet for their Ruthie so she could get this romance thingy straightened out.

"Ruthie," Tony said, then glanced about, a bit surprised that there were so many people around. They were in bathing suits and shorts and T-shirts that said "Drink Tequila and You'll Feel Better" or "Deschutes Family Tequila: Take a Shot" and cowboy boots and flip-flops. They were eagerly listening in, pressed up close to the couple.

"Ruthie, I have never met anyone like you."

"We haven't either," a number of people said, but other family members told them to, "Shush up."

"You're fearless. I admire you. I respect you. You live life at one hundred percent. You like adventures. You're so..." He paused. "Effervescent. I love that we can talk about books and movies and history together, and that you're an excellent poker player. I love your laugh and the way you make me think, and that the other women in the house think of you as their best friend. I love that you dedicated your life to teaching and to taking care of kids. You're the funniest person I've ever met, you're so smart, and you've lived a life of caring, giving, and love."

"She's always had a lot of love to give," her brother Turner said. "That's the truth."

"Nana Ruthie is full of love!" said the little boy Tony had met at the farmhouse. He was still mad that he couldn't have tequila. He held Nana Ruthie's hand. "She's full of it!"

"Plus, you are beautiful," Tony said, muffling his laughter after the boy's comment.

Some people clapped. Others said, with conviction, "Yes, she is."

Ruthie beamed. Her tears streamed.

"I missed you," she whispered.

"I missed you, too." He took a deep breath. "Ruthie, the show told me from the very start that if I found someone that I was in love with I would need to say to her at the end, 'Will you marry me?'"

She nodded, laughed, the skirt of her red sundress fluttering in the breeze. "That seems a little quick, don't you think? To decide you want to marry someone so soon, especially when one is on a reality show?"

Tony grinned. He was a handsome devil, she thought. He was going to be marvelous in the sack.

"I agree. I think it's way too soon for normal people to get engaged," he said. "It's too fast. We've been on a reality show. We have not lived in real life together. But, Ruthie, we are not normal, our situation is not normal, and I am positive about you, about us. I know that we can have a happy life together. I have no doubts in my mind at all. It would be an honor, it would be a privilege, to be your husband." He got down on one knee, right there in front of her family and friends, who clapped and gasped. "Ruthie Deschutes O'Hara, will you marry me?"

Ruthie, it was said later, looked happier than she had in years. Five years, to be precise. Her smile lit up her whole gorgeous face. She laughed, she cried, and then she finally said, "Yes. Oh yes, Tony. I will. I do."

Tony laughed, too, warm and low, hugged her close, picked

her up, twirled her around, exactly like in the movies, and they kissed. The boy who wanted tequila had to duck so he wouldn't get hit by Ruthie's feet. The Deschutes family, some in bathing suits, some shirtless, others wearing T-shirts that said, "Drink My Tequila" or "Bottoms Up with the Deschuteses," cheered.

A week later, everyone watching at home went crazy. The show ended with Ruthie's feet in the air, crossed at the ankles, her red flowered sundress spreading out like a garden, Tony looking broad-shouldered and handsome, their faces beaming.

Those Deschuteses were tough, but they cried. This was the most romantic thing they'd ever seen! Their dear Ruthie! Married again! They were thrilled! She deserved someone to love her! They couldn't *wait* for the wedding. No one had a wedding like the Deschutes family.

They passed out shot glasses, and everyone clinked their glasses together, including Jackson, Shonda, Pearla, and the *Marry Me* squad.

"Cheers!" they all shouted. "To Ruthie and Tony!"

"Bottoms up!" Ruthie said.

The boy who was upset about not getting tequila later snuck a shot glass and tasted the tequila. He spit it out and yelled, "What is this? Pee? Mom, I think I drank pee!"

The "Welcome Home, Ruthie" party was a smashing success. Tony, at ease with people, met her family. They embraced him, welcomed him. Ruthie's four brothers, Stanley, Turner, Warner, and Vincent, did spend some serious time with Tony, asking him questions, making sure he would be respectful and kind to their Ruthie, she deserved it. He gained their approval.

Tony and Ruthie went out in a rowboat together on Rattlesnake Lake. Jackson, Shonda, and Pearla rowed out in another. The other crew members headed out onto the lake in rafts. They did some filming and a lot of partying.

The Deschutes family had inner tube and rowboat relay races. They swam to the dock in the middle of the lake and cannonballed off it. (All kids and those who couldn't swim must wear life jackets! No exceptions!! Especially you, Great-Aunt April!)

They played volleyball and horseshoes. They made s'mores at night. They sang songs the family had been singing for years, including the Deschutes family song. The guitars and the fiddles were brought out. One of the grandsons played his cello. He was smart and obsessed with his cello. He would play in the New York Philharmonic one day. Two young cousins played their flutes. One of them would become a music composer who wrote a score for a major movie that ripped your heart out. Jimmy brought out his drum set and showed everyone what he could do. He was twelve years old, but within ten years he would be traveling the world with a popular band. Years down the road, Jimmy Deschutes would be known as one of the greatest drummers of all time.

A barn owl and a great horned owl hooted, joining in the musical fun. They didn't appreciate the drums, but they liked the fiddles, cello, guitars, and the flutes. The deer, elk, cougars, and the bears stayed away, but they watched from the trees, the mountains, and hills. This family was loud. But they didn't appear dangerous. Still, they were human. Who knew what they would do next?

Harold the hermit ambled over and hunched down in the shadows. He watched but didn't want to join in. Harley had come over and invited him. He had been told he was welcome to their parties anytime, by Ruthie and other members of the family with whom he'd gone to school, but he became nervous in groups of people.

Harold the hermit was glad Ruthie was back. She was kind, and he liked seeing the lights in her home at night. Then he knew he wasn't completely alone. He was happy that she'd found a man to marry. She deserved it. He saw a coyote sit down about ten feet from him, curious about the festivities. The hermit had always been close to wildlife. He didn't think they saw him as human anymore.

Ruthie and Tony left the party at about one in the morning, exhausted, happy, grateful.

They held hands as Ruthie drove them home in her truck through quiet streets and back out into the country. Above them, the Big Dipper was making a grand, shiny appearance, as was Sirius and Orion's Belt.

They stopped to marvel at the miracle of it all.

Life.

What a miracle.

"I've said it once, I'll say it again," Melda Zamborini, the eighty-year-old in Omaha, Nebraska, said to her wife after watching *Marry Me*. "I'm glad they're finally getting a room. They were meant to be together."

"Like you and me," her wife said, and they held hands. "Forever."

"This is your husband?" Tony picked up a photo of Russell in Ruthie's living room later that night, his stare intense. Russell was in his military uniform in Vietnam.

The animals were beside themselves with relief. Ruthie was back! They thought they'd been abandoned to a human pack of wolves who poked and prodded and had no sense of polite decorum or respect for an animal's fundamental right to live without hell-raising chaos, chasing or being forced to play dress-up or be ridden like a horse.

The grateful dogs and cats were swirling around their feet,

after receiving hugs from Ruthie and introductions to Tony. Scarlett O'Hara hopped about with jubilation on top of a table. She almost screamed—she was so ecstatic. Gatsby the pig leaned against his best friend Ruthie's leg. Atticus settled on Ruthie's feet—it was his job to warm them up, after all, and he would perform his duty. Mr. Rochester couldn't wait to walk Ruthie on her leash. They would have a grand time! Fitzwilliam, so emotional, meowed like a song, and Darcy sang harmony. Praise the heavens! Their picturesque life had been restored!

Ruthie and Tony stood together, shoulder to shoulder. No cameras. No one else. Just them. Finally.

"Yes. That's Russell. After Vietnam, he said he wanted a quiet life in the country. That's how we met for the second time, here in Triple Mountain. We didn't end up having much of a quiet life, though," Ruthie said ruefully. "In fact, it was loud, but it was the right kind of loud."

"This...this...is the doctor," Tony said, his words catching, his voice like sandpaper.

"Pardon?"

"This is the doctor who saved my life, Ruthie." He took a deep breath as if to steady himself. "Russell saved my life in Vietnam. He was the one who operated on my leg, who kept telling me to fight, who yelled at me to stay with him, who did everything he could to keep me from bleeding out and dying."

"Oh my God," Ruthie breathed. Russell had saved her...and Russell had saved Tony. "It's...it's..."

"A miracle," Tony said. "I can't believe it." He set the photo down and picked up another one, a closeup of Russell's face when he was in his thirties, his arm around Ruthie. "I honestly can't believe it. I've never forgotten his face. Not only when I was brought in, half dead, but in the days that followed. Russell kept checking on me, made sure I lived, made sure I *wanted* to live, made sure I didn't lose half my leg and that I didn't get an infection or have complications that could have killed me. He made sure that I didn't give up in that hellhole. He saw me in the morning, at night.

I don't even know if he went home. His goal was to save as many people as he could and…" Tony could hardly speak. He stopped. Composed himself. "I owe him my life."

"I owe him mine, too," Ruthie said, leaning hard against Tony, overcome with emotion, with awe, and with gratitude.

How could this possibly be? What were the chances that Russell, later married to Ruthie, would save the life of Tony in the jungles of Vietnam, who would also marry Ruthie decades later? Was Russell saving Tony meant to be? Had it all been fate?

"I'm so glad he saved you."

Tony put down the photo. "I'm glad he saved you, too." He hugged her close. "Look, Ruthie. I love you. I know Russell will always be a part of your life. He's been a part of mine forever. I've never forgotten him." He dropped a kiss on her lips, and they stood like that, connecting, loving, passion building. "I will take good care of you, Ruthie. I promise."

"And I will take good care of you, Mr. Handsome," she said and stood on tiptoe for another long and lusty kiss.

They did not sleep in Russell and Ruthie's bed. That would not have been comfortable for either. They slept in the guest room, as Ruthie had the night before so her son and his wife could have the master bedroom. It was a nice guest room. It was pink, as the last girl there had liked pink, and had a queen-sized bed.

He kissed her. They were naked and warm and cozy. Ruthie had been right. The sex was utterly fantastic. They were lucky indeed.

"That was pretty fun," Ruthie drawled.

Russell laughed and pulled her on top of him again.

"A second tumble already?" she asked.

"Can you keep up?" Tony grinned.

"You bet, cowboy."

The rift between Willow, Lucy, and Ruthie was over, the hurt feelings gone.

Ruthie had not meant to offend Lucy by buying her fiancé off for $10,000, but Jared had reminded her of Wayne. She couldn't let Lucy get married to someone like that. The signs were there—the bruises and excuses, the control and manipulation, the greed and the narcissism. Lucy was crushed when she found out Jared took the money, but then that anger turned on Ruthie, as Ruthie knew it would.

It was invasive and domineering of Ruthie to buy Jared off, Lucy said. She should have let Lucy make her own decision. It was, in its own way, controlling. Ruthie recognized all of this. She knew it going into the deal. Lucy was right. Ruthie apologized, but the thought of her beloved granddaughter being attacked again, of being petrified of a raging man, had been more than she could handle.

After Jared the monstrous fiancé was bought off, he spent the money at a casino and then got back together with Lucy, who had been emotionally ruined by his insidious control. He lied and told Lucy he took the money because he was "insulted" by Ruthie and had saved it to use for their honeymoon. Ruthie knew he'd spent it all at the casino, because her cousin's daughter managed the casino where he'd lost all the money, plus more.

After Ruthie shared her story of her first husband on TV, Lucy finally got herself together and decided she was done with Jared. What had she been thinking? Why had she stayed with him when he was so awful to her? Why had she been attracted to him in the first place? She knew she had to figure herself out, but more immediately she had to gather up her courage to break up with him and have a backup plan for safety.

Lucy feared Jared and his temper, but her Deschutes family protected her, as they always protected one another, and her great-uncles Vincent, Warner, Stanley, and Turner told Jared if they saw him near Lucy again, they would "make him disappear."

Stanley snapped his fingers and said, "Like that," and Turner pretended he was reloading a gun. As they were both armed with hunting rifles at the time, and they were in camo, their threat made quite a bang. As in bang-bang. But this time, this dangerous man did not end up at the bottom of Bottomless Lake with the fish eating his bottom. He did take off though and didn't bother Lucy again.

"I am so sorry, Lucy," Ruthie told her granddaughter again, hugging her close.

Willow hugged both of them.

They had had their reunion at Ruthie's farmhouse the night she'd gotten home from *Marry Me,* along with Michael, Willow's dear and loyal husband, who was so relieved that peace had been restored and that his daughter, Lucy, was safe. He hated Jared, had begged Lucy to dump him, and thought buying him off had been a splendid, enlightened idea, as he had told Willow and Lucy many times.

"It's okay, Nana Ruthie," Lucy said. "I blew it. I'm so sorry for not listening to you about Jared and for not talking to you and getting mad. I was a mess. Jared got in my head when he love-bombed me, and all the sudden, I didn't know who I was, I got lost, and I was crying all the time like I'd had some sort of nervous breakdown and clinging to him, and he kept saying he was sorry, and I was messed up and exhausted and scared, and I couldn't think anymore. I love you so much, and I feel terrible and guilty. I am a dumb slug."

"You are not a dumb slug," Ruthie said. "You are a dazzling Deschutes, and I love you. I will never interfere again. I promise," Ruthie said.

She meant it, mostly.

Sort of.

Perhaps.

Marry Me for seniors was an enormous success. It was the highest rated *Marry Me* season ever. It captured millions of viewers. Magazines, newspapers, and morning and evening TV shows covered it. Influencers on social media discussed it endlessly.

Ruthie and Tony had agreed, in their contracts, to participate in an ending show, hosted by Jackson, to wrap things up and to tell everyone where they were in their relationship. They fulfilled their obligation and did nothing more. The network begged them for further interviews, videos, updates. What about a tiny update? One teeny, tiny camera crew?

They said no.

"We're done," Tony said.

"We're done," Ruthie said.

They left for the Oregon coast. They hid out in a little cottage above the sea for two weeks until the excitement died down. Their bed was bouncy and fluffy. They married at Rattlesnake Lake. Ruthie's cousin Harley married them under a white arch covered in yellow, pink, and red roses. Everyone was sworn to secrecy because Ruthie and Tony didn't want the press at the wedding. It wasn't hard for the Deschutes family to keep a secret. They had done it for generations about all kinds of things, legal and illegal. They never betrayed the family's secrets.

All of Ruthie's kids and their families were invited, but luckily they managed to keep the final guest list to around two hundred and fifty, including Tony's boys, his extended family, and best friends, like Carl, Rosa, Connie, and Zane from back home. Ruthie also invited the brides (not Audrey) from *Marry Me*, Shonda, Pearla, Jackson and Henry and the naughty triplets, Valentina, and other crew members they were close to. They were so happy to be invited but swore they wouldn't tell. Tyler's invitation somehow got lost in the mail.

There were to be "absolutely no gifts," Ruthie and Tony's invitations said. The photo on the invitation was of Tony and Ruthie. He was bent over, Ruthie straddling his back, their arms outstretched, both grinning. Atticus was lying on the ground, tired of all these shenanigans, and Gatsby the pig was under Tony's legs, facing backward, only his bottom and tail in the photo. Elizabeth Bennet stared straight up at Ruthie. Remarkably, the photographer caught Scarlett O'Hara in midjump, long ears straight up.

For the wedding dinner, they hired a family-owned restaurant in town to bring in the barbecue—ribs, chicken, and steak. The tables groaned with salads, macaroni and cheese, and hot bread. The Deschutes family provided a river of alcohol. Ruthie knew the perfect DJ, the son of one of the first children she and Russell had adopted, and he had everyone groovin' and shakin' it down on the wooden dance floor that was always hauled out of storage for celebrations. The wedding cake was four layers high. Made by Bommarito's Bakery, it was chocolate with thick, swirling pink icing and real flowers spiraling down from the top like a flower waterfall. On the top was a little sign that said, "Marry Me!"

Willow and Lucy were her bridesmaids. Tony's sons were his best men.

Ruthie's ring sparkled like the galaxy, flashing off the multitude of lights strung overhead like the ceiling of a tent.

An excellent time was held by all at the wedding.

The animals and birds did not like the booming get-down dancing music, the conga line, the karaoke, the fireworks, or the whooping and cheering.

They were glad when the wedding party racket was over at three o'clock in the morning, as they were ready to burrow in and sleep.

Before Ruthie and Tony went to bed that night, Ruthie lit candles, then slipped on a slinky, sexy burgundy number from her favorite lingerie shop, Lace, Satin, and Baubles. It pushed up her impressive rack.

Tony said, "I'm definitely not tired anymore."

"You better not be, cowboy," Ruthie told him.

They took a tumble into bed.

Love is a gift.
Love is precious.
Love is eternal.

34

Fifteen years later

"I love you, Ruthie."

"I love you, too, Tony." She held him tight, in bed, the white comforter warm and snuggly. Tony's eyes were shut, his face strained, weary, as the sun shone through the windows. Though he was hurting now, he had aged well. She had aged well. They were eighty-five years old. They knew they had been fortunate to have the time they did.

"Fifteen years together, right?" His voice was raspy, as if it hurt to release the words.

"Fifteen years, honey. I had ulterior motives when I went on *Marry Me*, but I'm so glad I did."

"I'm glad you did, too." He inhaled, his chest rising. He moaned when he exhaled. "We've had the best time, haven't we, Ruthie?"

"I have loved every minute with you, Tony. I feel so lucky to have met you, to have had these years with you."

"Give me a kiss, Ruthie."

She turned, lifted herself up, and kissed him gently, softly. He opened his blue eyes after the kiss, their faces inches apart. They had wrinkles. Her hair was white, as was his. But when they stared into each other's eyes, blue to blue, they saw only the soul of the other person, their essence, their character, and all the memories and laughter they had shared together.

They had sold her yellow farmhouse after they got married.

They had sold his property. They needed a new place to live to start their new life. They resettled on the Deschutes River, in a home on ten acres where they made brand-new memories together. The home was bright with floor-to-ceiling windows and a two-story fireplace. The river ran through their backyard, its journey sometimes slow, other times crashing and tumbling. It provided the musical notes to their lives.

Two guesthouses and a large room over the barn were perfect for their families and friends. They invited Harold the hermit to visit anytime and he took them up on it now and then.

Tony and Ruthie had introduced their children to one another. Suddenly, Tony's two sons had thirty-two stepsiblings. They had a weeklong reunion altogether in the summer, along with other Deschutes family members. Tents were pitched, camper trailers driven in. They had so much fun. That was among Ruthie and Tony's goals—to have fun, to enjoy life.

Ruthie did not adopt any more children, but she and Tony donated money and time to help kids in need. They both joked they were busier in retirement than when they'd been working. They still raised money for animals during the annual Pet Parade. Tony dressed up as a rabbit, in honor of Scarlett O'Hara. Ruthie dressed up as a pink cat.

Tony groaned in bed again.

"Are you okay?" Ruthie studied him, ready to help. She knew, though, that he wasn't okay.

"I hurt. I ache all over." He sighed, clenched his teeth. "My bones feel like they're cracking."

"Do you need a heating pad?" She knew how he hurt.

"No. Not now. I need to stay still and not move."

Tony closed his eyes. Ruthie felt her heart twist. She loved him so. She put her head on his chest and listened to his heartbeat. His hands moved, lightly, up and down her back, then they stopped.

Ruthie didn't move, didn't want to disturb him. Moving him would only cause more problems.

They were so grateful to have had these fifteen years together.

Fifteen. She had found love twice in her life. She was suddenly emotional, tearful.

Tony groaned again. "This is bad. I didn't realize it would be this bad."

"Do you want some water?" she asked him, her voice a loving whisper.

"No, honey. I'm okay. I can't drink anything right now."

Ruthie settled down again, hugging her husband. They had had so many adventures together. Tony had arranged for a helicopter ride, picnic, and horseback riding to make up for the date she didn't get on *Marry Me*. They'd had new experiences. New conversations. They had traveled the world. They had skydived. They had danced and sung and even roller skated. As always, they had never stopped talking about books and history and music.

"Are you hungry?" she asked him, blinking back her tears. She loved him so.

"Not yet. I don't think I can eat. I feel weak."

Ruthie wished he was hungry. She wished he wanted to eat. He needed to eat for strength. She laid her head back on his chest. She had found comfort right here with him. Love. Sex! Passion. She sighed. He groaned again. She patted his arm, wanting to comfort him, to show him she was here, *always* here for him, until death did they part.

Tony sighed. "I think I'm going to need medicine."

"Okay, I'll get it, honey." She made to get up, but a pounding on the door made Ruthie jump.

"Hey, you two!" Velvet's voice rang through the door. "What's going on in there?"

"Get up!" Benedetta hollered. "What? You're staying in bed all day?"

Tony laughed, then said, "Ouch. That hurt."

Ruthie laughed, too, their laughter jumbled together between their chests.

Velvet's and Benedetta's husbands made some noises, too, about "laziness," and "old people," and, "not wimping out."

"Up and at 'em!" Benedetta said.

"The wine tour starts in an hour," Velvet boomed. "The bus will meet us right at the dock. We're going for breakfast now. Are you coming or not? They're serving mimosas."

"Bring your thermos, Ruthie," Benedetta called out. "We're all going to pour mimosas in the thermoses for later."

"And don't forget your windbreakers! They said these French vineyards can get chilly," Velvet said.

"We're coming!" Tony called, then swore and grabbed for his ribs.

"There's no way I'd forget my thermos, Benedetta! Do you think I've lost my mind?" Ruthie yelled back, and Tony winced as he took the full brunt of the yell in his ear.

"You haven't lost your mind yet, Ruthie!"

"See you downstairs," Velvet said. "I need coffee when I'm up at the crack of dawn like this. This is bad for my hormones."

It was nine a.m. Not quite the crack of dawn, unless you'd been up salsa dancing until midnight, as the six of them had been last night.

They were on a river cruise through Europe. It was a ten-day trip. They'd been traveling together for fifteen years and were used to one another's antics, practical jokes, and uninhibited, enthusiastic dance skills.

"Ready, Tony?" Ruthie planted a smacker of a kiss on Tony's lips, then rolled off. "I'm going to have too much wine today, then I'm going to dance in the disco tonight."

Tony shook his head. "I am not dancing until midnight again tonight, baby. Didn't you hear me? My bones are breaking. My muscles are shriveling. My whole body wants to stay in bed and hide."

"You're a fine salsa dancer, Tony. I knew our lessons would pay off someday. I liked seeing your hips swirling."

"I think I sprained my hips. They'll never work again. I'm a stiff skeleton."

"Well, Mr. Stiff Skeleton, you'll be fine once you get a mimosa in you. Now let's go! I am not going to miss this." A tour of a French vineyard sounded about perfect, Ruthie thought. Wine and cheese. Yes, to yum.

Tony got out of bed, slowly, inch by inch, complete with complaints. "Did you hear my bones screaming? They just screamed."

Ruthie smacked him on the buttocks. "I love ya, Tony, but grab your screaming bones and let's go, cowboy. We've got another day to live."

About the Author

Cathy Lamb lives in Oregon with her husband. They were set up on their first date by a tough undercover vice cop with a romantic side.

They have three grown children who are beautiful and adored. Their names are Rebel Dancing Daughter, Adventurous Singing Daughter, and Darling Laughing Son. They also have two naughty cats who have shredded the furniture.

Cathy spends a lot of time talking on the phone with her brother, Jimmy, and sisters, Karen and Cindy. She pretends that she is "doing housework," while talking. She is not. She is sitting on the couch eating chocolate chip cookies.

Cathy is writing another book. It will be out soon. Probably. Maybe. She doesn't really know when.

She wishes you well and thanks you (truly!) for reading her books.

You can find her on Substack, Facebook, or her website.

Made in United States
Troutdale, OR
09/21/2024